Dirty Work: An Anthology

Tara Wyatt et al.

Published by Smashwords, 2016.

This is a work of fiction. Similarities to real people, places, or events are entirely coincidental.

DIRTY WORK: AN ANTHOLOGY

First edition. August 16, 2016.

Copyright © 2016 Tara Wyatt et al..

Written by Tara Wyatt et al..

ACKNOWLEDGEMENTS

There may be three names on the cover of this anthology, but turning a handful of story ideas into a book takes more than a few dedicated people. It takes people like our cover designer, Nicki Pau Preto of Bold Book Design, who was patient and gracious despite our requests for feats of Photoshop strength. It takes people like our developmental editor, Rhonda Stapleton, who helped make our characters real and our settings come alive. It takes people like Arran McNicol, who helped us polish these stories *and* whose copy edits inspired multiple conversations about the proper use of "come" versus "cum." And last but never least, it takes readers. Book people are the very best people, and we're so grateful for the opportunity to put stories in your hands.

Uprooted

by Amanda Heger

Chapter One

She *had* to get out of here. As soon as possible. Sooner, even.

Every second Natalie spent in Elm Creek poked another hole in her lungs, suffocating her slowly from the inside. But on the outside, she had keep the switch flipped. Had to be smiley but not too smiley—her granddad had just died—bubbly but not ditzy, strong but not bitchy. The weedy expectations had only grown thicker in the decade since she'd left.

"You can't just, you know, do your magic legal stuff and handle it?" she asked.

Alex shook her head and took another sip of iced tea. "Not how it works, Natalie. It's complicated. It takes time. There's paperwork."

"What kind of wizard lawyer are you?"

"One who's doing you a favor." Alex barely looked up from the stacks of paperwork in front of her. Wizardry or no, Alex was ridiculously smart. And she'd been best friends with Natalie's older sister for something like twenty years now.

So basically, she was better than a wizard.

"You know I really appreciate it, right?" Natalie asked. She ran a hand along the railing of the deck. The late morning sun was just beginning to warm her skin, and in an hour or two it would be out in full force. If she were back home in St. Louis, she'd take a book to Forest Park or lace up her tennis shoes and go for a trail run along the river. Instead, she'd be stuck in Elm Creek, North Carolina, packing up the dusty knickknacks no one else in her family had claimed.

"I know you do." Alex finally looked up and a piece of her blond pixie cut fell across her forehead, but that stray piece of hair didn't mask the sincerity in her eyes. "And speaking of favors, this a big one you're doing for Lindsey."

Natalie blew out a breath. She could read between those gargantuan lines. Everyone knew Natalie avoided Elm Creek like it had the plague, the Zika virus, and Montezuma's revenge. But here she was, handling the sale of her late grandfather's house.

Despite everything.

"Well, it's not like Lindsey could come out here, while on bed rest, and spend all day packing up my grandfather's vintage salt and pepper shakers." Natalie shrugged it off like it was nothing. But it was something. A big something. Her older sister was on the verge of losing her not-yet-born daughter, so the stress of handling all this was out of the question. Lindsey was also on the verge of losing her job due to the whole bed-rest situation, so ignoring their inheritance—Granddad's old house on five acres of prime Elm Creek real estate—was also out of the question.

"I think you're getting soft in your old age." Alex handed over the file folder. "I'll see what I can do to rush it. The sooner you can get all the stuff cleared out, the better."

"Great, thanks." Natalie stood from her patio chair and wrapped her arms around Alex. "You're my favorite not-sister."

"Which is why you should stay for brunch. I mean it."

"I can't."

"You can," Alex said.

"You just told me to get all the stuff cleared out of the house ASAP."

Alex ignored her flimsy excuse. "They'll be happy to see you. Really."

Natalie couldn't believe anyone in Elm Creek would be happy to see her. Not after the way everything had gone to shit when she was seventeen. Not after the way she'd crushed lives and run away from the sleepy small town she used to love. Leaving everyone else to clean up her mess. "Alex, I can't explain. I just—"

"You don't have to explain. That was a long time ago, and people here still love you. Even if you don't believe it."

She definitely did not believe it, but she gave Alex a faint smile. "Maybe next time."

"Hello? Anybody home?" The voice came first, followed by a tall brunette holding a bottle of champagne in one hand and a jug of orange juice in the other.

"Sunday Funday!" Another woman appeared with curls that hung to the very deep neckline of her flowered shirt.

They were both vaguely familiar. Grown-up versions of people she used to see around the halls of the high school. Girls in her sister's class who'd left for college before everything had happened. But they'd lived in Elm Creek, so they knew. And today—every day, if she was being honest—Natalie couldn't deal with the shame.

"You guys remember Lindsey's sister Natalie, right?" Alex said.

"Sorry to hear about your grandpa." Curls pulled four champagne flutes from the padded bag on her shoulder. Followed by a container of some kind of dip. And a set of napkins. And then crackers. The woman was like Mary Poppins but with brunch supplies.

"Thanks," Natalie said. "He was sick for a long time. I'm glad he's not suffering anymore." She'd repeated those sentences so many times in the weeks since he'd died that she practically heard them in her sleep.

"How's your sister? Still on bed rest?"

Natalie nodded. "Doing better, though." She took a step toward the stairs.

"Oh. We should FaceTime with her while you're here, Natalie." The brunette—Natalie wished like hell she could remember their names—started filling glasses with bubbling mimosas. "Just orange juice for you?"

Natalie hugged the folder to her chest and shook her head. "I'm actually on my way out. Thanks again, Alex."

"You can't go yet," the brunette said. "You haven't even seen the best part of Sunday Funday."

"Natalie." Curls lowered her voice and adjusted her top. Now, not only was she Mary Poppins, she was Mary Poppins with a fabulous amount of cleavage. "You want to stay for this. Trust me. Give us five minutes, and if you aren't convinced, we won't keep you."

"Convinced of what?"

"You'll see. In five, four, three..." Her voice faded further as all three women's eyes widened at something behind Natalie.

Unless there was a leprechaun with thirteen pots of gold behind her, Natalie wasn't going to stay. But she turned anyway and instantaneously realized what the fuss was all about. "Wow," she whispered.

Alex stepped up beside her, and all four of them stood in a row, looking out over the lawn. Looking out over the shirtless, definitely-not-a-leprechaun, definitely muscular man with his back to them. He pulled a lawn mower down from a beat-up old truck, and even from fifty yards away, Natalie could see his muscles work.

"Told you," Alex said. "Cuts his parents' grass every Sunday, all summer. No shirt."

"At this point, I'm pretty sure he does it just to mess with us." The brunette took a sip of her drink.

"Definitely," Alex said. "You know he could get one of his underlings to cut the grass. He owns the company now."

"Don't care why he does it. As long as he keeps doing it," Curls said. She turned to Natalie. "Just wait until he turns—"

"Hey, ladies." Adonis Back turned and pulled off his baseball cap.

That simple movement was all it took for Natalie's heart to stutter to a stop. She'd watched this guy pull off his baseball hat hundreds of times. As a teenager—just before he'd lean in to kiss her—and sometimes as an adult, in her more explicit "daydreams."

She ducked her head and turned toward Alex. It couldn't be. Could it? "Is that—"

"Natalie Green?" the guy asked.

Fuck.

Creature of habit. That was how Chris described himself.

Every day, he got up, went to the Hennessy Lawn Care office, and took care of business. And every Sunday, he brought a mower to his parents' house—where for the last year he'd lived too, in their over-the-garage apartment—and cut the lawn. He loved pulling the cord on one of his freshly tuned mowers. He loved the hum of the engine filling his ears and crowding out everything else. No worries. No Elm Creek gossip. Just him, some fresh air, and the smell of newly cut grass. This was his church.

Sunday was the one day each week where he got to be a guy cutting grass. He didn't have to be the business owner or a salesman or that guy with a chip on his shoulder. Of course, he had to be a guy cutting grass in front of Alex's "brunch" crew every week, but he'd gotten used to it. Even grown to like it, if he was honest. Being ogled by three attractive women wasn't the worst way to spend an afternoon.

But being ogled by Natalie Green...

This was a different animal altogether. An animal that made him feel ten years younger and a lot less confident. This animal had rabies, and Chris wasn't sure if he needed to play dead or get the hell out of Dodge.

"Hi," she said. Like she wasn't quite sure who he was. Like he hadn't spent half that summer worshipping her naked body.

"You guys know each other?" Alex asked.

"Yeah," he said.

"Sort of." Natalie looked away as she ran a hand over her straight, dark hair. Her face had grown sharper, lost some of that teenage roundness. It made that dimple—the one that sat high on her right cheek—stand out even more.

That dimple had gotten him into the whole mess in the first place.

"I didn't realize you guys ever lived here at the same time." Alex cleared her throat, and Chris knew he should turn away. Lose himself in the lawn work and try to forget this ever happened.

Not that he'd once managed to forget that summer.

"We moved here right before Natalie left." He pulled on the brim of the ball cap, waiting to see if she would offer anything.

Nothing.

Chris had heard her grandfather had passed away. The Elm Creek gossipmongers had that news spread through half the town before the poor man had even died. According to them, Old Man Green had died four times before he finally kicked the bait bucket. Of course, according to them, there was a salt circle around the city limits that kept Natalie Green from ever setting foot inside.

"I should go. Thanks again, Alex," Natalie said. "Chris." She nodded at him before starting down the steps.

He'd heard it, there in the way her voice softened a bit when she said his name. She remembered.

Of course she fucking remembered. A person didn't forget a summer like that.

He'd found her sitting against the dry creek bed, alone, throwing rocks into the woods. Throwing didn't begin to describe it, though, not really. She'd vibrated with furious energy after the accident, and it was more like watching a miniature, less green Hulk chucking rocks to keep from destroying everything in her path.

Two weeks later, she'd taken his virginity along that same creek bed.

And he'd been a goner.

"Natalie, wait." He jogged toward her car, catching her a second before she opened the door. But now, out of the microscope of the other women, he had no idea what to say. "Hi."

"Hey." She looked up at him then, and for the first time he saw how beautiful she'd really become. She looked less angry than he'd remembered, but sadder. Less bold, more cautious.

"I'm sorry about your grandpa," he finally managed.

"Thanks. He'd been sick a long time—"

"Still. He was a cool guy. Sorry to see him go."

"I didn't realize you knew him." She fiddled with a tiny gold heart on the end of her necklace.

"This is Elm Creek. Of course we knew each other."

That brought a small smile out of her, and Chris found himself trying to pull out another. "Who do you think gave him that dog of his?"

"You? You gave him Cormack?" Natalie furrowed her brow, but it worked. Her lips turned up at the edges, just a fraction of an inch. Someone who didn't know her would have missed it.

He didn't.

"Found him wandering at an old job outside of town. Was going to drop him off at the Humane Society or something, but first I had to stop by your grandpa's house and cut the grass. One look at the dog, and Benjamin Green was in love." Chris grinned and leaned against the car, her grandfather's old woodie station wagon. The thing looked like it had more years on it than the dinosaurs. "How is Cormack, anyway?"

"Awful."

"Awful? What's wrong with him?" Maybe this was like one of those Lifetime movies his sister always tried to get him to watch, where the dog died of heartbreak from missing his owner.

"Let's see." Natalie began ticking off her fingers. "He hates me. He refuses to eat anything but people food. And he thinks he's a goat."

"A goat?"

"Stands on every piece of furniture and just stares at the wall." She shook her head.

"You got him, then?"

She sighed. "For now. When Grandpa moved in with my sister and started hospice, I took the dog. But my landlord freaked, and now I have to find him a new place before I go back."

"Sorry."

Natalie shrugged as if her shoulders were made of cement. "Me too. Well..." She gestured toward her door. "Good to see you." She didn't sound convinced.

"Wait." He needed answers. A lot of them. He'd been holding all his questions in for ten years. Why had she left like that? Disappeared as if he'd been nothing—as if they'd been nothing. Had she ever thought about him—about the two of them—in those intervening years? Did she still have the nightmares? "Do you need someone to cut the grass tomorrow?"

"What?"

Goddamn, why was he such a bumbling idiot? He pointed to his truck with the words HENNESSY LAWN CARE: SINCE 1979 running along the side. "I bought my parents' business last year. Last summer, we cut your grandpa's grass every Tuesday. If you're staying there—"

"No, not staying. Selling. Getting ready to sell. That's why I'm here. Alex is helping."

He knew she wasn't staying. This was Natalie fucking Green, after all. But that twinge of disappointment in his gut wouldn't shut up. "Selling means you'll need good curb appeal."

She opened her mouth—her perfect Cupid's-bow mouth—then closed it again. "Okay."

"Okay?"

"Yeah. Send one of your guys or whatever. That would help a lot, actually. Maybe sometime in the evening?" She opened her car door and tucked her legs inside.

Chris tried—and failed—not to stare at them. "Sure." But when the door slammed shut and her engine turned over, he was already mentally rearranging his schedule to be the one at her house tomorrow.

Chapter Two

The dog had three modes: moping, barking, and climbing on top of furniture. But not normal furniture, like the couch or Granddad's old bed. Natalie would walk into the dining room and find Cormack stretched out across the dining room table. Or the coffee table in the den. Or the old desk in Granddad's room. Basically, if there was a flat, raised surface, the slightly overweight chocolate lab could get to, he tried to lie there.

"Come on, boy. Don't you want to eat?" She shook his food bowl, and the clink of kibble on metal filled the otherwise empty house. For a half second, Cormack raised his head, then went back to laying it forlornly on the dining room floor.

Natalie sighed. Her grandfather had loved this dog so damn much. Every time she'd talked to him in past year, Granddad had gone on and on about Cormack's latest adventures. Even in those last few weeks, when Granddad had been so sick he'd moved to St. Louis to stay with Lindsey and her husband, the dog had been his biggest concern. And now the dog, along with the house and everything in it, was her responsibility.

Which meant she had to find a place for Cormack—in addition to the piles of Granddad's stuff—before she could put the house on the market. And that place couldn't be with her. Her landlord had made that more than abundantly clear.

Cormack laid his head on her foot. "I know, bud. I'm sorry. I miss him too, you know." She rubbed the dog's velveteen ears and took in the dozens of boxes stacked along the living room wall.

Granddad's house wasn't large, but it was full. About to boil over, actually. Sometime in the last ten years, he'd taken up garage sale-ing, convinced one day he'd strike it rich on *Antiques*

Roadshow. Instead, he'd ended up with colon cancer and an attic full of other people's Christmas decorations.

Ba-da-da-dum-da-da-dum-dun-duuuun.

Ba-da-da-dum-da-da-dum-dun-duuuun.

And a doorbell that played "Dueling Banjos."

"Just a second!" Natalie glanced in the dusty hallway mirror. Ponytail askew, ratty workout clothes—so ratty she didn't even wear them to the gym. But she'd brushed her teeth that morning. That was something, right? Besides, it wasn't like she needed to be presentable to pack up Granddad's 101 Weirdest Potholders collection.

Cormack panted and circled at her feet. It was more movement than she'd seen him make since she'd been at the house. *Poor thing is going to be really disappointed when Granddad doesn't walk through that door.*

"Get back, boy. It's only someone here to cut the grass." She sent the dog into the kitchen before she opened the door. "Hi, I'm—"

Screwed. Completely and utterly, one hundred and ten percent screwed. Because right there, standing on Granddad's doorstep—right where he stood when she hightailed it out of Elm Creek the first time—was Christopher Hennessy. Again. Twice in three days she'd been forced to confront the love of her high school life.

Every time she saw the guy, he was more attractive. How was that even possible? That summer, he'd been at least a nine on her teenage Richter scale. But now? Tan biceps, perpetually boyish grin, and abs that could stop traffic. Literally.

Not that she'd waited in her car, pretending to play on her phone for a few extra minutes while he'd worked—shirtless—on Sunday. Not at all.

"I'm a mess," she finally managed.

Almost imperceptibly, his gaze flicked down her body. "It's a good kind of mess. You look great, Natalie. I should have said that the other day."

She smoothed her hair and tugged on the end of her holey tank top before crossing her arms to cover the coffee stain. "Thanks. You want to come in, or...?"

Chris stepped into the house and a blur of fur and paws came charging toward them. The dog spun and woofed and pranced right up into Chris's personal space. A completely different animal than the melancholy mountain goat he'd been two minutes before.

"Hey, guy." Chris crouched down and gave Cormack a scratch on his chest. In return the dog laid a sloppy, wet kiss right on Chris's forearm.

His exceptionally gorgeous forearm.

"Come on, Cormack. Get back." Natalie hooked a finger around the dog's plaid collar.

"It's okay. Haven't seen this guy in a while." Chris gave the dog a final pat and stood, nearly leveling her with a smile. It was a version of that same shy, sweet smile he used to give her as a teenager. Now with the confidence of a man.

Natalie shifted her weight from one foot to the other and back again. This wasn't how she'd pictured their reunion. Not that she'd pictured it at all.

Okay, fine. Maybe she'd pictured it after every bad breakup in the last ten years. And maybe on those days when she'd catch a whiff of freshly cut grass and remember what it was like—the excitement and exploration that came with her first love. And maybe, just once or twice, she'd stalked his social media after a few too many beers. But the reunion definitely didn't involve standing in her grandfather's doorway, in a tattered pair of running tights, talking about a dog.

"You okay?" His forehead crinkled.

"Yeah. Sorry. A lot going on." She waved to the stacks of boxes and papers scattered in the living room behind her. She needed to get out of here, out of this house *and* this conversation as fast as humanly possible. "What's up?"

He looked at her like she'd asked him if Santa Claus was real. "You wanted someone to cut your grass?"

"Right. Yeah. Sorry. I guess I expected a teenager or something." Her heart refused to slow down. Or beat evenly. Or do anything other than lose its ever-loving mind.

"I had some time in my afternoon. Figured I'd swing by and make sure it got done right. Looks like it's been a while."

You have no idea.

Fabulous. He'd been in the house all of a minute, and she was already thinking about sex. Apparently, the old cliché was right: some things never changed. Especially if that "thing" involved the guy who taught you about orgasms.

"Wow. That's really nice of you. Thanks. Do I pay you before, or...?"

Chris's gaze darted to the stack of boxes behind her, the piles of paperwork strewn on the floor. "Let's say this one is on me."

"Are you sure?"

He grinned at her and tugged his baseball cap a little lower. "Sometimes it pays to know the owner of Elm Creek's one and only lawn care company."

"Chris." This was a horrible idea. She already owed him things—long-worn apologies and explanations—she could never make good on. She didn't need to add this to the pile. "How much is it?"

His expression turned suddenly serious. "It looks like you've got a lot going on. Let me help you with this."

"But—"

"Are you really going to insist on paying?"

She nodded. Cormack rolled over and put all four feet in the air.

Chris squatted and patted the dog's ample gut. "Fine."

"How much?" Natalie let out a long exhale. "Is a check okay?"

"Nope." He locked his gaze on hers.

"Cash, then? I may need to go to the ATM."

"Nope."

"What do you want, Chris? A cashier's check?" A nervous laugh trickled out of her.

"Dinner. Me, you, an extra-large pepperoni. Preferably from Landry's." He jerked his head toward the direction of downtown.

Speaking of horrible ideas.

"Deal?" Chris stuck out his hand.

"I don't have a table. Sold it on Craigslist yesterday."

"I'm sure we can figure it out."

Fuck. He really was gorgeous when he smiled.

She was like a one-note band when he was around. And that one note was a steady *sex, sex, sex.* Maybe sometimes paired with a couple of quick beats to the curve of those biceps. Three notes then. A chord. But still, she had things to do. And the sooner she did them, the sooner she could get out of Elm Creek. Eating pizza on the living room floor with Chris Hennessy was not on that list of must-do items.

"Deal," she said.

The lawn had been out of control. The thick, overgrown grass would have taken Natalie a century to mow with that little push mower in her grandfather's shed out back. But after an hour on top of the Cub Cadet, Chris had forced the thick coat of Kentucky Blue into something manageable. He put the mower into park in the back of the truck, and his eardrums hummed with silence as he turned the key.

All he had left to do was go back inside. Inside, where he'd have to sit beside Natalie Green and pretend he wasn't wondering about the birthmark she'd had. The one on her left butt cheek, just below those two perfect dimples on her lower back.

Chris hadn't shown up intending to haggle for a little bit of her company. And now, as he looked down at his grass-stained jeans and wiped his sweaty forehead with the hem of his shirt, he was struck by how stupidly impulsive that move had been. Not only was he about to have dinner with the girl who'd crushed him ten years ago, he was going to do it while covered in pieces of her lawn.

And probably while thinking about that birthmark.

At least he had a clean Hennessy Lawn Care shirt in the truck. A stray he'd seen hiding on the tiny backseat. He'd just strip off this one real quick and—

"Hey. I, uh…"

He whipped around—shirtless—to find Natalie staring. Hard.

And, fuck him, after that first rush of feeling startled, he loved it. Loved the way her gaze raked over his stomach. Loved the way her chest rose and fell a little faster than normal. Loved that he— just standing here, sweaty and shirtless—had such an effect on her.

Of course, an hour earlier, she'd opened the door wearing those tight pants, looking all sexy and sleepy with her messy hair, and he'd been the one staring a little too hard for human decency.

"What's up?" He leaned against the truck, clean shirt in hand.

"Oh, right. I, um, wanted to say the pizza's here. Came a few minutes ago while you were out back."

"My eyes are up here, Green." He couldn't resist teasing her. Couldn't resist seeing the hint of pink creep up her cheeks. That alone was worth the price of admission.

And then she laughed.

God, it was good to hear that laugh. Ten-years-ago Natalie never laughed. Not like that anyway, all open and free. Ten-years-ago Natalie had been limited to wry laughter that came with a heaping side of fear and anger.

"What?" She pulled at the sleeves of her sweater. Sometime, while he'd been out here getting dirty, she'd cleaned up.

He shook his head. "Just good to see you happy."

"Thanks." She closed her eyes for half a second, like she was steeling herself for something important. Then the moment was gone.

The sound of cicadas filled the space between them.

"Pizza?" he asked, pulling on the fresh shirt.

"Pizza."

He followed the spicy scent of pepperoni inside. In the living room, Natalie had constructed a table out of moving boxes and covered the whole thing with a green tablecloth straight out of 1979.

"Sorry. It was the best I could do."

He flopped down on the ground at one end of the boxes. "It's perfect."

For the first few minutes, the air felt thick with silence and unasked questions. In that silence, Chris wondered if sitting down with Natalie Green would only end in getting up with his heart broken.

"So..." she said.

"So." He took a bite of pizza, buying time and trying to remember what they used to talk about as they wandered along the creek a decade ago. "What have you been up to for the last ten years? Did you ever start that bad greeting card store?"

She rolled her eyes. "Surprisingly, they tell me there's not a market for 'I'm Only Buying You This Father's Day Card Out of Societal Obligation' cards."

"I don't believe that. What about the 'Mommy's Not Really Gone on a Business Trip' card? That was a winner."

"One day."

One day. The memories bubbled up then. Natalie's "one day" list—the old, creased sheet of paper she'd kept in her back pocket—full of all the things she'd do one day.

"So what then, if you're not in the morbid greeting card business?"

"Psychology." She offered her pizza crust to Cormack, who lay patiently between them. "I'm working on my Ph.D."

"Do I have to call you doctor now?" he asked.

She grinned. "Not yet."

"Not yet?"

"I still have to write my dissertation. Then you'll have to call me doctor."

"Noted." He grabbed a pepperoni off her plate and fed it to the dog. "And you're really selling this place?" Old Man Green's house had seen better days, but Chris knew the land had to be worth a few hundred thousand. Maybe more.

"Yeah. Have to sort through everything and get it cleaned out first. But Granddad was—"

He looked around at the stacks and stacks of boxes, most marked Goodwill or Trash. "Holding on to every receipt anyone had ever given him? In duplicate?"

"Triplicate, actually. In fact, while you were cutting the grass, I found an entire stack of receipts from Hennessy Lawn. Who's Sage Hennessy?"

Chris nodded. "My cousin. He was around last summer, helping out for a bit. I think he cut your grandpa's lawn a few times."

"I found all the receipts right next to Granddad's old *TV Guides.* And every bit of salvageable wrapping paper anyone ever gave him."

"He still got all those salt and pepper shakers?" Chris grinned, remembering the first time he'd stopped by to check on Cormack. Natalie's grandfather had kept him for an hour, taking down each set of shakers from a shelf in the kitchen and giving Chris the complete history of salt and pepper shakers. Parts one, two, and three.

"Every last one," Natalie said. "What about you?"

"I'm more of a cheap plastic shakers kind of guy myself."

Natalie gave him an exasperated sigh, but behind it was a grin. "That's not what I meant."

Chris leaned back on his forearms, which not so subtly let him inch closer to her. "You don't have to call me doctor," he said. "I'm not that pompous."

"Still a smartass, I see."

"Stubborn, too. In case you were wondering."

"I wasn't."

God, she was gorgeous. Even with a tiny bit of pizza sauce on her chin. Especially with a tiny bit of pizza sauce on her chin. "You totally were," he said.

Natalie rolled her eyes. "For real, though. What about you? What have you been up to since..."

He waited a beat to see if she'd fill in those blanks. How she'd fill in those blanks. Would it be with something benign or something real? How would she describe that humid, dreamlike summer they'd spent wandering the woods? Would she mention the way she'd been silent the entire first day they'd spent together? Or how, after that, she'd talked for hours on end? It was as if she simply told him everything about the accident— every tiny, horrific detail—she could get past it. Maybe she'd mention the silence that had followed? Because their mouths and hands and hearts had been too busy with one another to talk.

"Since the last time I saw you?" she finally finished.

Chris blew out a breath. "Well, I took over the business about a year ago."

"Congrats."

He nodded. "It was more a necessity than anything. Things weren't going great financially, then my mom had some health problems, and my dad decided to retire."

That was the sanitized, edited-for-television version. The real-life, unrated version involved some shady business deals gone south, a trial separation between his parents, and a woman named Joan. It had taken everything Chris had, and then some, to turn things around.

"Still. You're twenty-eight and you own an entire business. That's impressive."

"Well, it's no Ph.D."

"Shut up and let me give you a compliment."

If he wasn't mistaken, that order came with a slight shift of her body toward his. Now, if he wanted, he could reach out and wipe that sauce right off her chin. And he definitely wanted.

"Here. You've got a little sauce." He brushed it away with his thumb, letting it linger there as her breath warmed his skin.

She looked away. "Thanks."

"Natalie..." He wasn't sure what to say. He didn't want to *say* anything.

"I should probably clean this up." She scrambled to standing before he could wrap his head around what had just happened. "Thanks for stopping by, Chris. For cutting the grass, too." She looked down at the pizza boxes in her hands. "Take care."

And when he stood to leave, that little nagging voice had come back full force. This time with a silent "I told you so" on repeat.

Chapter Three

"Natalie! I can't believe it's really you."

Natalie wanted to respond, but she was being suffocated in the mix of paint fumes and curly, purple-streaked hair. Far from the bony eleven-year-old she remembered, Katie Hennessy had grown into a curvy, feminine version of Chris. Which was to say she was gorgeous.

"It's really me." Natalie extricated herself from the hug. She'd never been a hugger. Even before... But especially not after. "How have you been?"

Katie pushed her way through the door and flopped down on the only remaining chair in the living room without waiting to be invited in. "Well, I just had sex in a storage room at the Painted Peacock, so things are looking up."

Natalie froze. "What?"

"Oh. The Painted Peacock. I work there. It's one of those places where you pay way too much money and then paint pottery someone already made. We fire it and a few days later, you come back and pick it up. Bowls, plates, tacky figurines. Stuff like that."

Well, that explained the smudge of purple across her left temple. "And you said you were having *sex* there."

"Storage room. We broke someone's teacup, but it was ugly anyway. I'll have to give her money back. Small price to pay. If you know what I mean." Katie winked.

Oh God. Katie might be twenty-one now, but she was still eleven in Natalie's mind. "Uh, yeah." Natalie laughed as if she knew exactly what Katie meant. And she did. In theory. But working on her Ph.D. meant Natalie met two types of guys:

dudes who still thought life was a giant frat party and men who spent so much time in the university's psychology building that they lost all sense of personal hygiene. It had been quite a while since she'd broken anyone's teacup.

"What are you doing here? Not that I'm not happy to see you," Natalie said. When the sound of "Dueling Banjos" had unexpectedly filled the living room, she'd rushed to the door. But the Hennessy on the other side wasn't the one she'd hoped to see.

Ever since Chris left two nights ago, all Natalie had done was pack boxes and wonder. She'd wondered if he was about to kiss her. She'd wondered if she should have kissed him. And if she had, would she have woken up beside him the next morning? Instead, she'd woken up to Cormack staring at her from the top of the dresser.

Katie's forehead wrinkled. "Chris didn't tell you?"

"Tell me what?"

"About Saved by the Paws?"

"Definitely didn't tell me about it," Natalie said.

"I told him to tell you. He must have forgot. Unless you guys were too busy *cutting grass*." Katie made air quotes and leaned back against the tattered brown recliner.

Natalie did her best to ignore the innuendo. "What's Saved by the Paws?"

"It's a dog rescue. I'm a volunteer there. Chris said you needed to find a home for your grandpa's dog?" She looked around the room. "Unless you already did?"

"No. He's outside. Hold on." Natalie walked through the mostly bare kitchen and opened the back door. There, in the middle of the fenced-in back yard, stood Cormack. On an old picnic table, staring into space. "Cormack, ready to come in?"

At the sound of her voice, the dog's ears perked, but he didn't move.

"Is that him?" Katie appeared beside her.

"The one and only."

"Hey, boy. Come here and let me see you." Katie took one step out onto the patio, and Cormack launched himself at her. While Natalie got the doggie version of the silent treatment, it appeared the Hennessys were some sort of dog celebrities.

"Sorry. He's usually more subdued."

"No worries," Katie said, as she gave Cormack a big scratch under the chin. "You must be the one I've heard so much about." Katie was venturing into full-on baby-talk mode, and the dog was eating it up. He rolled onto his back, letting her rub his belly.

"How old is he?" Katie asked.

"Five or six. He was a stray."

"And Chris said you can't have pets in your apartment?"

"No." Natalie sighed. "Plus, he hates me. So—"

"Chris does *not* hate you." Katie stopped petting the dog and winked at Natalie. "Actually—"

"No, the dog. He hates me," Natalie said. But heat prickled her face at the mere mention of Chris's feelings about her. No matter what they were.

"This guy? This guy doesn't hate you." Katie rubbed messy circles in Cormack's fur, and the dog responded with a case of upside-down wiggles.

"So you volunteer for this Saving the...?" Natalie asked.

"Saved by the Paws. Yep. Foster care coordinator, reporting for duty." Katie stopped petting the dog long enough to salute.

Little Katie Hennessy was not only having sexcapades in semi-public places, she was a foster care coordinator? Natalie wasn't sure what that entailed, but it sounded important. She could barely believe this was the same kid who used to be so shy she'd cried every day for the first month after her family had moved to Elm Creek.

"Does that mean you can help Cormack find a home?" Natalie asked. "I was actually thinking of asking Chris, but I guess he would have said something about it if he were interested."

"Trust me, my brother is interested." Katie looked her up and down. "In you *and* the dog. But he can't have the dog."

He can't have me, either. "Why not?"

"Let's see." Katie began ticking off the reasons on her fingers. "He lives in my parents' garage. My mom hates dogs—thus my intense passion for saving them. And he works eleven billion hours each week."

"Oh. I didn't know all that."

"Yep. Long story. So here's the good news and the bad news. The good news is, I can list him on our website—make him a cute little profile and take him to adoption events on the weekends."

"That's great news," Natalie said. "What's the bad news?"

"We're out of space in our foster homes, so you have keep him here."

"That's fine. I don't mind." She'd grown to like the old goat-dog, even if he didn't like her.

"And if he doesn't find a home before you leave, you'll probably need to take him to the shelter."

"Oh." Natalie bit the inside of her cheek and tried not to think about taking Cormack to the shelter and walking away.

"And he's a weird, older dog, and it's puppy season. So it's going to be tough." Katie rubbed the dog's ears and sighed. "Sorry, I wish there was more I could do."

Natalie felt like she'd stepped off the world's worst rollercoaster. High hopes, followed by a plunging blow, followed by feeling like she might throw up. There had to be another way. She'd find it.

"Can you make him the best profile ever?" she asked.

Katie squeezed her shoulder. "Absolutely. And we're having the first adoption event of the summer at the Painted Peacock this weekend. Bring him by around five o'clock, and we'll show him off."

"Thank you."

"Thank my brother. He promised to have one of the guys cut my lawn every week this summer. And I get to pick which guy. I can't decide if I should go for the obvious choice—his name is Chad; we sometimes fool around—or if I should take a smorgasbord approach."

Chris wasn't sure he'd ever understand his little sister. With the way she hopped from job to job and hobby to hobby and guy to guy, she made most "free spirits" seem like they were prisoners at Gitmo. But with her, there were two truths that never wavered: she was obsessed with dogs and she would do anything to avoid manual labor.

"You said Cormack would be here." Chris leaned against one wall of the Painted Peacock—a mural of the Boston Tea Party, starring peacocks. On the opposite wall, someone—he suspected his sister—had painted a version of *American Gothic*, again with peacocks.

Katie had organized some kind of kitschy singles mixer for dog lovers, and the place was starting to fill with canines and humans. All Chris knew was that Cormack was going to be here, and he'd been conned into helping as a result. Along with providing Katie with her choice of "lawn boys" each week.

"He's on the way," Katie said. "And we'll see where you're needed. Just give me a few minutes."

"You didn't bring him?" But he didn't need to wait for an answer to figure it out. Katie's shit-eating grin said it all.

"Nope."

"So Natalie's bringing him." He hadn't seen or heard from her all week, and he'd convinced himself—mostly, kind of, a little— that getting shut down was a good thing. Too many feelings. Too much baggage. Plus, she'd be leaving town in another week or so. The Elm Creek rumor mill was spinning with stories about some developer who wanted to buy the house, knock it down, and subdivide it for condos or something.

Which should have been good news for Chris. Corporate accounts were his bread and butter. If he could get a contract for the yard maintenance on a set of brand-new condos, he'd be able to move out of his parents' garage even sooner than anticipated.

"What about Natalie?" a familiar voice asked. A familiar voice that made him forget all about things like corporate accounts and condos and garage apartments.

"Hey," he said. "I was asking if you were bringing Cormack." He squatted to pet the dog's chest. And to avoid making eye contact.

She wore some kind of pink dress that showed off her legs and her arms and a hint of her chest. And every dude who'd showed up for this singles mixer was staring at her like she was a strawberry ice cream cone.

"Yeah. I guess I can just drop him off?" Natalie's voice shook a little, and when Chris looked up he saw the anxiety etched into the lines between her brows.

"Actually, the dogs are only going to be here for the first two hours. So if you want to hang out for a bit..." Katie nudged Chris as she spoke. "Maybe you guys can catch up some more or something. Paint a teacup?"

Natalie shook her head so hard, Chris worried she'd end up with whiplash. "That's okay," she said. "I'll wait in the car. Get out of your hair. It's packed in here anyway." She handed off the leash to Chris and did an about-face toward the door.

"What was that about?" Katie asked.

Chris bit the inside of his cheek. He knew exactly what it was about, but he didn't know how to explain it to his sister. "Do you really need me here, or...?" He jerked his head toward the door where Natalie had disappeared.

"Go."

He found her grandfather's old station wagon around the corner, but Natalie was nowhere in sight. Chris leaned against a light post and tried to figure out where she might have gone. He watched people wander hand in hand along the red brick streets of downtown. Some stopped into restaurants. A few ducked into the old movie theatre that always showed last season's movies. And one street over, a woman sat in Pumpkin Park, alone on a bench with her head in her hands.

Natalie.

He made his way over slowly, afraid she'd catch sight of him and run. But as he walked closer, she looked straight at him and didn't move. "Still happening, isn't it?" He lowered himself to the bench beside her. Close but not too close.

"Not for a long time. A really long time. But being back here..." Her hands shook. Her voice shook. Her legs shook.

"Natalie, look at me."

She did. "Everyone was staring at me."

"But not because of that," he said.

"It's always because of that." Her voice shot up a notch with every syllable.

Chris took a deep breath. That summer she'd had panic attack after panic attack. Turned out, being the only survivor of a horrific car accident would do that to a person. After a while, he'd gotten good at seeing the early signs. Sometimes he'd even been able to bring her down from the edge with a few well-placed questions or an offer to strip down and jump in the icy-cold creek together. But most times, he just held her while they both waited for her medication to kick in.

"Natalie, those people *were* looking at you. But not because of the accident. Most of them didn't even live here ten years ago," he said. "They were looking at you because it's impossible not to look at you. All the time, but especially in that dress. You're beautiful." He tucked a stray bit of hair behind her ear.

The shaking didn't stop.

"Can you get me out of here? I can't drive like this." Her dark eyes pleaded with him.

"Sure. I can drop you off at your grandpa's house if you want?" The house was so far on the outskirts of town that he'd have to immediately turn around and come get Cormack, but that was fine. If nothing else, it would give him an excuse to check on her once she'd had some time.

"Can we drive around for a little bit? I don't want to be by myself."

"Let's get out of here, Doc." He held out his hand, and she took it. "I know just where to go."

Fifteen minutes later, he'd loaded Natalie into the truck, turned up the music, and rolled down the windows. Fresh evening air moved in and out of the cab as they drove through the three-stoplight downtown area and made their way to the opposite side of Elm Creek. Sometime around the fourth round of "Fat Bottomed Girls," Natalie's shaking stilled to a dull quake now and again.

"How you doing over there?" he asked.

She turned down the music. "Wondering what you're trying to tell me with this song choice."

He laughed. With a tone like that, she couldn't be feeling too bad anymore. "Let one of the guys take this truck on a job last week. Gave it back with this CD stuck in the player, and it won't switch over to radio." He let himself glance over at her. "I remembered sometimes music helped before, so..."

"Helps a lot, actually. Thank you."

Chris stared back at the road. He didn't know how to ask all the things he wanted to know. How often she still had the attacks. Whether she'd ever found a medicine that didn't make her want to sleep for days. If she'd ever forgiven herself.

"Didn't seem to be as bad this time," he said.

"I've gotten better at handling them. You know, doctor of psychology and all. Plus, a lot of therapy. Medication. Exercise.

That kind of stuff. It's just different being here. Dealing with the house stuff on top of everything else."

"It's a lot."

"And I don't want anyone to adopt Cormack. I mean, I do because I don't want him to go to the shelter, but I don't, you know? I want to keep him, too."

"Makes sense."

"And I've been thinking a lot about..." Her voice shook at the end.

"About what?"

"About going to the cemetery." Now it wasn't only her voice that was shaking. "I never went before. That summer, it was all too much. And now it seems like this big thing. Huge, even. Looming over me while I'm here."

Natalie turned the music up—way up—again before he could respond. The wind picked up as the truck moved toward the outskirts of town. Buildings grew further apart, and Chris kept catching her scent on the breeze. She still smelled like apple shampoo, even after all these years, and it was like muscle memory or something, the way his dick reacted.

Boner memory, perhaps.

Which was stupid. Ridiculously stupid. She'd just stopped shaking thirty seconds ago, as they hit another replay of the song. And she'd made it abundantly clear that she wasn't interested in him. He rolled the windows up, praying that would stop the assault. *Get your shit together, Hennessy.*

"Where are we going?" she asked.

"It's a surprise."

"Oh, come on." She inched a little closer to him as she reached for the volume dial and turned down the music. "Are we even going anywhere?"

"We are."

"There's nothing on this side of town."

"This is a new and improved Elm Creek, Doc," he said.

"That is one thousand percent untrue."

Chris grinned as he turned off the main highway onto a bumpy gravel road. "Scout's honor."

"You were never in Scouts. In fact"—Natalie elbowed him—"you would have been the world's worst Boy Scout."

"That's offensive. I would have been a great Boy Scout."

"Right. If they needed someone to show them how to shotgun beers on their camping trips, you would have been an excellent Boy Scout."

"What can I say?" Chris pulled into the tiny parking lot and found the only available spot. "I've always been a man of many talents."

"Ha." Natalie shot him a wide smile, one that showed off her crooked incisor and made her eyes crinkle at the edges.

This was not helping his dick situation. At all.

"Wait," Natalie said. "Is this the bait shop? You brought me to John Jay's Bait Shop?"

He looked up at the old square building. A tiny white brick shop with bars on the windows and a heinous six-foot statue of a night crawler wearing sunglasses out front. "That I did."

"Because..."

"Because it's not a bait shop anymore. You're looking at John Jay's Famous Fried Chicken."

"Do they still sell worms?" Natalie unbuckled her seatbelt and leaned forward.

"Only fried."

"Shut up."

"You don't believe me?" He shut off the truck, letting silence settle in between them. He unbuckled his own seatbelt and turned toward her.

"About the worms?" Natalie pursed her lips. "No, I don't believe you."

"Would you like to bet on that?" He crossed his arms in front of his chest and leaned in closer. Close enough to see each time her eyes flickered with emotion. "We can go in."

"To the bait shop?"

Everything about her was lighter now—happy even. Chris reached out and tucked a strand of dark hair behind her ear. God, she was beautiful. And every time she got within fifty feet, he couldn't stop smiling.

"To the bait shop. And when we go in there and you see the fried worms, you have to eat one."

Natalie leaned toward him, bringing that damn apple scent with her, until they were closer in that truck that any two random people had a right to be. "That's it?" she whispered. "That's all you got, Hennessy?"

His pulse picked up, like it was doing sprints across the entire continent. Entire western hemisphere. Natalie fucking Green was coming on to him. Here, in a crowded parking lot, next to a human-sized worm statue.

And, like it or not, he loved every goddamn second of it.

"You have a better idea, Doc?"

"A few, actually. Want to hear them?"

Abso-fucking-lutely. He wanted to hear them here, next to her in the truck. He wanted to hear them as he kissed his way down her neck. He wanted to hear them as he stripped off this dress and went on a birthmark-hunting expedition. "Surprise me," he said.

Chapter Four

The freshly cut grass slid between her toes, soft and damp in the twilight. Her shoes hung from one hand, and her other held tight to Chris's. And she couldn't stop looking at him.

He was the same as he'd always been, but different. In a good way. The very best way, even. His dark hair stuck up a little in the front, and his shoulders filled out that button-down shirt like it had been sewn thread by thread for him. And his forearms were something straight out of copy of *Playgirl*.

Not that she'd hidden copies of *Playgirl* under her bed as teenager.

But his hands. They were going to do her in. Right here along the side of this old gravel road. Warm, soothing, rough. She couldn't stop thinking of them on her.

Maybe on her waist. Her face. Her neck. Between her thighs.

"You okay?" His voice cut through all her naughty thoughts.

She practically shuddered in an ill-fated attempt to send them fleeing. "Yeah, why?"

"You're just kinda quiet."

He was checking in with her, without saying it. Making sure their little trip into the bait-shop-turned-chicken-shack hadn't sent her into another panic spiral. It hadn't. Maybe it was because the place was so crowded that you couldn't see anyone, not really. Maybe it was because the scent of fresh-fried chicken was so overwhelming in there that people lost their minds. Maybe it was being there with him.

She squeezed his hand. "I'm fine. I mean, I'm still pissed that you won the bet, but..." She shrugged.

"I never said it was fried *earth*worms."

"Technicality." The restaurant—if you could call it that—had two lines that snaked halfway out the door. On the right side of the tiny shack, a sign hung from the ceiling. No words, just a drawing of a chicken wearing a chef's hat. On the left side, another sign displayed a drawing of a cupcake.

After they'd ordered their dinner, Chris had dragged her to the dessert line. And when they'd reached the front, they'd stood in front of a counter full of sweets. Oreos. Pies. Candies. "You buy it, we fry it," the guy behind the counter had said as he adjusted his hairnet.

Chris handed her a package of gummy worms and leaned close to her ear. "Sometimes, I wish I weren't so damn stubborn."

His warm breath on her skin had nearly made Natalie drop the bag of fried chicken in her hand. "Me too," she'd said.

And then, without ever saying a word about it, they'd been back in the truck, barreling toward the creek, fried chicken and fried gummy worms in hand.

Their creek.

"Stop here," she'd said. "It's so nice out. Let's walk the rest of the way."

As they walked the final distance to the spot where they'd first met, her phone buzzed against her thigh. She had to drop Chris's hand to pull it from the pocket of her dress.

"Hi, Katie. How's it going?"

Music blared in the background, filling the gaps between the sounds of glasses clanking. "Decent turnout. Some interest in Cormack, actually. But how are you? Are you okay?"

"Feeling better now." She glanced at Chris, who was watching her. Watching her like she mattered.

"My brother with you?"

"Yeah. Hold on." She handed the phone to Chris.

Now it was her turn to watch him. The sun had almost disappeared from the sky, and it sent soft light over his features as he gave his sister a series of one-word answers. By the time he handed the phone back, they'd almost made it to the creek. And she'd barely noticed.

"I guess we need to go back and get Cormack soon, huh?" she asked.

"Nope."

Her stomach twisted and tugged. Had she misheard? Was there someone there who wanted to take Cormack home? Would she never see him again? She fingers tightened around the straps of her sandals, the leather digging into her skin. "Is he getting adopted?"

Chris shook his head. "Katie said he could stay until the shop closes. Apparently, a dog who likes to stand perfectly still on top of the window displays brings in a lot of customers. And we need time, because I want to show you something."

Natalie laughed. "Funny. It feels like I've stood in this very spot before and heard that very pick-up line." And she probably had. She knew this creek like the back of her hand—better, even. She'd discovered it when she was nine or ten, when it was a short jaunt from her parents' old house. For a while, she and her sister had spent every free second playing here, barefoot and catching tadpoles in the inch of cold water that always filled the stream.

Eventually, they'd given it up. But after everything that had happened after the accident, she'd found her way back out there. And with it, found an eighteen-year-old Chris Hennessy. He'd just moved to Elm Creek with his parents and his younger sister, and he'd known nothing about her.

Which, back then, felt like everything.

Twenty-eight-year-old Chris Hennessy stepped closer, until the fabric of her dress brushed his legs. "Doc, you've gotta stop hitting on me." His voice came out a shade deeper and a fraction darker than normal. Somewhere inside of her, teenage age Natalie swooned. Meanwhile, adult Natalie couldn't resist seeing how much of an effect she could have.

She moved toward him, until it wasn't only the fabric of her dress pressed against him. "Why's that?" she whispered.

"What was the question again?" He ran a hand through her hair, letting his fingers come to a rest on the back of her neck. A tingle of anticipation rushed over her lips. Another tingle ran further south of her border.

Natalie wanted to close that oh-so-thin distance between them. But even more than that, she wanted to stretch this moment into three eternities. Take in every cricket chirping in the tall grass to her left. Feel the rush of cooling night air and the warmth of his breath against her. Taste the salt on his skin.

"What do you want to show me?" she said through a smile.

Honk! Honk! Honk!

The crunch of wheels on gravel and the constant thumping of a car horn sent Natalie tearing backward, heart racing—and not in the good, almost-kissing way. "What the—"

"Hennessy!" A bellowing voice took the place of the honking as a monstrosity of a rusted blue pick-up truck pulled up beside them. "What are you doing out here, boss?" The driver hung his arm out of the window. Dirt smudged the guy's forehead, and he looked like he'd been making mud pies all day. With one long nod in her direction, he turned back to Chris. "Don't answer that, man."

Chris stood up a little straighter. "Josh, this is Natalie. Natalie, Josh. He's one of our managers."

She forced a smile and a wave. "Hey."

"This the reason you look like a member of the walking dead every morning?" Josh asked Chris.

Natalie's cheeks warmed.

"I'm still your boss, Liventhall," Chris said. But the tone of his voice was more please-change-the-subject than about-to-be-fired.

"Whatever you say. Nice to meet you, Natalie. Are you guys headed to the house?"

Natalie opened her mouth to respond, but she realized she had no clue where they were headed—besides the world's longest almost-kiss.

Chris glanced at her. "Yeah."

"You want a ride?" Josh leaned over and the passenger door popped open. "I'm going to drop off some dirt. I promise not to stay." He winked at them, and Natalie wanted to crawl into her skin and disappear.

Chris looked at her, as if waiting for her cue. She wasn't exactly sold on the idea of climbing into this guy's truck. Especially since he kept leering at her like he'd caught them buck naked and writhing all over one another, instead of just standing a little closer than normal.

Okay, a lot closer.

"Whatever you think," she said.

A few minutes later, they sat on the faded, cracked truck seats, as Josh steered them from the bumpy main road to a twisting gravel lane. A comet trail of dust followed them, and Natalie couldn't quite figure out where they were headed. This road hadn't been here years ago.

"You gotta do something about this driveway," Josh said.

"I'm working on it."

He said something else over her head, but Natalie's brain didn't have the willpower to pay attention. Because right there in front of them, the bones of a beautiful log cabin grew up out of the ground, a few hundred yards from the creek.

"This is yours?" she whispered.

Chris nodded. "It's a work in progress."

"It's gorgeous," she said. She didn't say a lot of things, though. Like how, as an undergrad, she'd stumbled onto a magazine about log cabins in the student health center, of all places. And how, by the time she'd been called back to her weekly therapy appointment, Natalie had added "build a log cabin" to her *one day* list.

Along with things like "see the Grand Canyon," "run a marathon," and "learn to make her grandfather's spaghetti sauce."

Grief prickled her skin and eyes as she realized she'd never be able to accomplish the last one. At least, she couldn't learn it from her grandfather himself. Maybe he had a recipe somewhere around the house.

The driver's-side door slammed closed, and then it was just she and Chris inside the truck.

"Where'd you go?" he asked.

Everywhere. "Nowhere."

He looked at her for a long moment, like he was going to push further. "Want to eat then look around?"

"Absolutely."

The cabin didn't have finished floors or furniture, but it had a beautiful deck off the back, with a porch swing. They swung softly as they ate and fireflies flickered around them.

"When did you start this?" she asked.

"End of last year. I had a house in town, but I sold it so I could sink some money into Hennessy Lawn. My dad had pretty much run it into the ground. People owed him a ton of money, and he wasn't doing anything about it." He tensed. "So I moved back in with my parents for a little while, started cleaning things up with the business. One of the guys who owed us money offered me this lot to settle the debt."

She wiped her fingers on a napkin and watched the muscles in his face contract with whatever stress was underlying the memory. "Must have been a big debt."

He nodded. "Worked out, I guess. The house is slow going, but it's starting to pick up now that it's warm out."

"You're doing this all yourself?"

"I've got a contractor for the complicated stuff. And my cousin Adam's a carpenter. He's making a trip down in a few weeks. Going to help me with the cabinets and stuff."

"Wow. That's really great. Congrats." Her emotions felt like they had been piled into an ailing industrial-sized mixer. Roaring and blending and threatening to come spilling out of her carefully constructed bowl. She didn't know why this was affecting her so much.

"Hey, boss. Safe to come out?" Josh stood in the doorway, one hand over his eyes. "I unloaded all the dirt you wanted in the back."

Chris rolled his eyes. "You're fired."

"No, I'm not." Josh dropped his hand. "Not if you want the Babcock job to get done."

"Fine. You're fired after you finish the Babcock job." Chris raised an eyebrow.

"Sure, sure. Well, I'm out. Do you want a ride back, or...?"

Chris looked at her, brown eyes serious. "Want to stay for a while or ride back with this bozo?"

She had a million things to finish at the house. Packing, sorting, grieving. But he kept looking at her like that. Like she was more beautiful than this oh-so-beautiful house.

"Let's stay for a while," she said.

He knew there had to be plastic cups around here somewhere. He'd bought a giant stash of them way back when, expecting to use them to grab the occasional glass of water. He never expected to use them to serve Natalie Green a drink in his half-made house.

Of course, nothing about Natalie was expected.

"I swear they were just here," he muttered.

"Chris?"

"Yeah?" He spun, forgetting about the stupid cups and nearly losing his breath at the sight of her. Again.

Her long, dark hair fell in waves over her shoulders. And that dress. *Holy shit, that dress.* It put all her curves on perfect display. Like a present wrapped so beautifully he almost didn't want to unwrap it. Almost.

"I was thinking," she said.

"Sounds dangerous."

She took a step closer, her breasts against him as she breathed. And he wanted to feel more of them. A lot more. "Are you always such a smartass?" she asked.

"A solid ninety-five percent of the time." He snaked a hand around her waist, holding her against him. He wasn't sure if she'd pull away again—he never knew with Natalie—but he'd hold on to this moment, to her, for as long as possible.

"About our bet..." she said. It was then he noticed she held the grease-stained bag of gummy worms in one hand.

He pulled them from her grasp and tossed the bag over his shoulder. "I think you were right. I mean, I did win. But only on a technicality. I'm willing to entertain your terms." He couldn't resist touching the lock of hair that brushed her collarbone.

She smiled up at him. Sweet but seductive. All false, wide-eyed innocence. He'd seen that look a dozen times that summer. And he'd stashed the memory of it away somewhere, with all the other heartbreaks in his life. But now...now, that smile was enough to get him hard in ten seconds flat.

"Well, first you have to admit I won. None of this technicality nonsense." She slid her fingers under his shirt.

The skin-to-skin contact, even that tiny bit, was enough to make his brain short-circuit. He dipped his head, while his heart hammered in his chest. "How about I kiss you instead?"

"I might be amenable to that."

"Might?" Chris sank a hand into her hair, letting his thumb brush her cheek. She'd become happier and funnier and even more beautiful in the last decade. And now her lips were half an inch from his. But he didn't kiss her. Not yet. He wanted to feel that catch in her chest, when he closed the distance. Wanted to somehow feel that she wanted this as much as he did.

"I'm *definitely* amenable to that," she said.

"Good."

He breathed her breath between syllables. "I'm going to kiss you. A lot. Then I'm going unzip this dress, and kiss you some more. Here." He pulled his hand from her cheek and ran a finger along her neck. Then to her collarbone. "Here." He let his fingers fall lightly across her breast, savoring the way she sighed—almost imperceptibly—at his touch. "Here." His hand crossed the expanse of her stomach before coming to rest on her hip. He squeezed gently. "Here."

"Is that all?" she whispered.

He took his time, letting his hand slide down her thigh before catching the hem of her dress, then snaking it oh so slowly up to the soft lace of her panties. "Here. I'm definitely going to have to spend a long time kissing you here."

Chris rubbed small circles over the fabric, and Natalie's eyes fluttered closed. Her lips parted, and she let out a tiny moan. And finally, he breached that tiny distance between them. The second the warmth of her mouth met his, all teasing was over. She tasted like basil and honey, and he couldn't get enough.

His free hand slid up her side, gripping her closer to him. Natalie moaned into his mouth as their tongues pushed and pulled at one another, and all he cared about was making her moan like that again.

"Chris?" She pulled her mouth from his for a half second as she whispered his name, and he hated it. He hated that her mouth wasn't on his, so he kissed her again. Loving the pressure of her. The warmth of her. The way she rubbed against his thigh.

"Yeah?" he finally managed, once he needed to come up for air.

"Is there any place in this house that's not, you know, concrete?"

Chris looked over her shoulder at the rough floor. *Shit.* He obviously hadn't thought this through. Or rather, when he'd suggested this walk, he hadn't realized he would be so desperate to strip her naked, lay her down, and taste her.

"No. Floors come in next week." They could do it outside on the grass, the way they used to. But this was Natalie Green. By now she was probably used to being laid down in expensive feather beds and covered in rose petals or something. But if that was what she wanted, that was what he'd give her. Even if it meant they had to wait a little longer.

Even if the last thing he wanted to do was wait a little longer.

"We can head back toward the truck if you want. Stop by your place for a while."

Natalie let out a laugh and looked up at him. "Is that your way of saying you changed your mind about all the kissing?" Her tone was playful, but the tiny flicker in her gaze gave away her insecurity. He had no idea how someone this fucking sexy could ever be insecure.

He lifted her chin and laid a teasing kiss there. "Natalie, if you only knew."

"Knew what?"

"Knew how many times I've thought about *kissing* you in the last ten years. Knew how every girl always got compared to you." His voice came out rougher than he'd intended. "Knew how much restraint it's taking me not to pin you against this wall right now, just so I feel you tight around me. So I can hear you groan my name the way you used to."

God, his dick was going to spontaneously combust if he didn't cool it.

Her eyes fluttered closed, and her fingers traced the buttons on his shirt. This was decidedly not cooling it.

"Chris?"

"Hmm?" It was all he could manage when her fingers slid south to the button on his jeans.

This time the words were one hundred percent teasing. "I don't believe you."

"Are you feeling what's going on down there?"

They both looked down at the bulge in his pants. When Natalie looked back up at him, she tugged her bottom lip between her teeth. "I think I'm going to need some proof."

This girl was going to be the death of him. But it would be a good death, full of hot, wet sex, and he couldn't wait to get there. "Come on."

He led her back toward the porch, where the June breeze whipped her hair from side to side. The moon was out full force now, and her skin glowed in its light. "Sit." He pointed to the porch swing where they'd had dinner.

But he didn't give her time to do it on her own. He picked Natalie up and set her down softly, then reached both hands under her dress. He took his time, running his hands along her soft, smooth thighs as he kneeled between her knees. When he hit the fabric of her underwear, he hooked his fingers around them and tugged.

He pushed her dress up and pulled her hips toward him. The swing creaked in resistance, but when he parted her knees, there was none from Natalie. She was warm and wet, and the perfect curve of her nakedness was almost enough to drive him mad.

"Lean your head back," he ordered.

She closed her eyes and dropped her head so it lay over the back of the swing.

"God, you're perfect," he whispered against her thigh. And he whispered it against her folds, parting them with his fingers to give him exactly what he wanted. But he lost all words as he licked and caressed her, timing his movements with her breaths and moans. He slipped a finger inside her as he worked. Then two, adoring the way she bucked against him. Fucking loving the way she grabbed her own breasts, teasing her nipples through her dress.

"Chris." She practically panted his name, and it was the best music he'd ever heard. "I'm going to come."

"Fuck yes, you are." But he pulled back, changing his touch to something lighter. He was going to tease this orgasm out of her one screaming breath at a time. Because she was Natalie Green, and she deserved to be lavished and licked and fucked until he couldn't go on anymore.

"God. Yes. More, please. Please."

Chris pressed her knees up until she had one leg planted against the swing on either side of him. She was salty and sweet and everything he'd been missing for the last ten years. And with two more strokes of his tongue, she was trembling all around him. Calling out his name.

Natalie fucking Green.

Chapter Five

Something wet brushed her face, pulling Natalie from the dream where she and Chris fucked in the rain as lightning bolts hit the ground all around them. And then the wet thing hit her again—this time in a full-on dripping-wet lick.

"Cormack!" Chris's voice washed over her, and Natalie finally found the energy to peel open her eyelids.

They'd finally made it back to the truck and then to pick up the dog. And when they'd fallen into bed back at her grandfather's house, Natalie had never been so thoroughly exhausted and satisfied in her life. She didn't know what the hell they were doing, but she knew she liked it. A lot. And she wasn't going to let herself overthink it and freak out. Not now.

"Hey," she murmured. "What are you doing?"

He carried a plate in one hand and a glass of juice in the other. "Making you breakfast." He set the plate down on the bedside table, and the heavy scent of eggs and the sweet scent of jam made her mouth water.

Beside him, Cormack shifted his gaze between Chris, Natalie, and the food.

"Don't let him fool you," Chris said. "He already had his own plate of scrambled eggs." He still had that rumpled bedhead look. It made her want to stay in bed with him all day. Or maybe not in bed. The couch. The shower. Exploring. Taking their time. Then rushing through a hot quickie on the kitchen counter before they had to face the world.

A world that still waited for them beyond the doors of this house, full of the usual Elm Creek bullshit and memories she didn't want to face. A world where she had an appointment with

Alex to sign a bunch of paperwork for Granddad's estate. A world that was propelling her away from here for good.

"Doc, you look sad." Chris sat at the end of the bed and began crawling his way to the center, where she lay in her nest of blankets.

"I'm not," she lied.

"Are you sure?" He peeled back one layer of her covers as he hovered over her.

"Well, maybe a little sad." But the closer they came to skin-on-skin contact, the less sad she felt.

He pulled back another layer of covers, and Natalie shivered against the cool air. "What are you sad about? And more importantly"—he slid a hand under her t-shirt, grazing her side and stopping just short of her breast—"what can I do to help you cheer up?"

She knew she probably had crazy hair and smudged makeup under her eyes. But right then, with the way he was looking down at her, Natalie had never felt more beautiful. "I'm not sure." She arched her back a little, forcing his fingers to graze the underside of her breast. "Hmmm. That seemed to help a little."

"Interesting." Chris grinned and stroked her nipple with one rough thumb. "Maybe we should do a little experiment."

"For science."

"For science." He closed his mouth over hers, and all bets were off.

Natalie wrapped her legs around his waist and pulled him down on top of her. She needed to feel him against her. Inside her. "Chris?" she whispered, as his teeth grazed her neck.

"Hmmm?" His erection pressed against her, offering her a taste of what she wanted. But not nearly enough. It was like she was starving and only allowed to smell the fresh-out-of-the-oven cupcakes.

"Fuck me," she said. "Please."

He half moaned, half laughed against her. "Yes, ma'am."

A few hours later, sweat creeped across her brow as she shoved box after box along the living room wall. She needed to make the house look as presentable as possible. But even when Natalie stubbed her toe on a box and realized that—no matter how many internet remedies she tried—that old stain was not coming up off the hardwood, she was smiling. Smiling because she was exhausted and sore and completely lost in the memory of Chris's grin as he'd left that morning. He'd even loaded up Cormack and taken him off to work, with a promise to swing by later. Then he kissed her long and hard in the doorway before planting another, lighter kiss on her forehead.

And even though they'd both been amazing, it was that gentle forehead kiss that had her so smitten.

Ba-da-da-dum-da-da-dum-dun-duuuun.

Ba-da-da-dum-da-da-dum-dun-duuuun.

Natalie tried to wipe the just-had-my-G-spot-thoroughly-pleasured look off her face and opened the door.

"Well, well, well. Aren't you glowing?" Alex asked. "Maybe being out in the country air was exactly what you needed."

Natalie wrangled her laughter into submission. Country air wasn't quite what she'd needed. "Maybe."

For the next few minutes, they filled the room with chitchat. Niceties about St. Louis and her sister. It was so easy that, for a moment, Natalie considered asking about the one person who'd been in the back of her mind ever since she'd agreed to come back to Elm Creek. Natalie wanted to believe Mrs. Bradford couldn't hate her with the same level of blunt force she'd had ten years ago. Maybe time and distance had given the woman time to heal a few of the wounds Natalie had inflicted on her back then.

But before Natalie could muster up the courage to ask, Alex cleared her throat. "Well, great news. I don't think you're even going to need to list this one. We already have a very interested party."

"Wait. How interested? No one has even been out here to see it. It's a mess and needs repairs and we haven't even set a price and..." Her throat closed off and her stomach twisted into nervous knots. This was good news. Damn good news. So why did it feel like such a violation?

"People know this property, Natalie. It's been a fixture in Elm Creek for decades," Alex said. "He owns the Plaza Estates subdivision down the street. He's interested in making this property a part of the subdivision. Thinks he might be able to turn this into three separate lots."

"What? How would he fit two more houses on here?" Her voice came out high and scratchy, even though she tried and tried and *tried* to stay calm. This was the absolute best-case scenario. And she wasn't going to have to do any of the work she'd been so concerned about.

"Three. He'd need to knock this one down," Alex said.

"Wow." Natalie gulped in a lungful of air, but couldn't seem to get enough. "Knock it down?"

Alex dusted dog hair off her pants. "Is that an issue? You don't have to take it, you know. If you need more time to talk to your sister, we can turn down this offer and list it. If they're still interested, they'll offer again."

It was like her lungs hated her, hated oxygen. She forced them open and closed with a few deep breaths. This was stupid. Basically, Alex had gotten them a better-than-their-wildest dreams offer on the house, and Natalie needed to take it. Lindsey would want to take it. All these mixed-up emotions were only because she was all emotional and exhausted on account of the mind-altering sex. Once she'd had a nap, she'd realize what a great opportunity this was.

"No. It's great, Alex. Thank you. Lindsey is going to appreciate this so much. We both do."

For the next handful of minutes, she signed paper after paper to appoint Alex her official realtor-slash-attorney-slash-wizard. They chatted some more about prices and potential offers and how much longer she'd need before she could move out. "Not long. Maybe a week or so? I need to finish packing and make sure Cormack has a place to go."

"Now that we've got the paperwork, I expect we'll have an official offer this time tomorrow," Alex said. "So take care of as much as you can, as soon as you can."

"Will do." Natalie closed the door behind her and slid to the floor. The cool tiles sent a chill along her skin, and the hard wood of the door pressed against her back. This time tomorrow she would be one step closer to leaving Elm Creek for good.

Except it felt anything but good.

Chris hated Mondays. Not just because of the usual back-to-the-grind bullshit, either. He hated Mondays because those were the days that, without fail, he'd fight with his father. Sometimes it was a silent battle—two stubborn men full of resentments, keeping their words terse and their feelings locked inside. And sometimes it was a loud, raging battle where everything came out to play. His father's financial incompetence. The way he'd cheated on Chris's mother. How he'd put Hennessy Lawn so far in debt, Chris had to sell his house to fix it.

And on Mondays he had to eat dinner with the man.

Any other night, Chris could avoid him, coming and going out of the over-the-garage apartment without ever saying a word to the man. But Mondays were the one night Chris's mother insisted a family dinner. If he was going to live in their apartment rent free, he had to eat dinner with his parents and sister once a week. Those were the breaks.

After all, his mom said, if she'd been able to forgive his father, Chris should be able to forgive as well. But today, the prospect of forgiveness wasn't looking so hot.

"You finish the Landminer's job today?" his father asked.

"Nope." Chris heaped more potatoes onto his plate, hoping that the act of chewing would save him the pain of talking.

"They always want it done before the Fourth of July," his dad said.

"Mm-hmm," Chris muttered.

"Fourth of July is exactly one week away."

"I have a calendar."

"I don't know—"

Chris took a deep breath, trying to relax. But all the extra oxygen did was fuel the fire. "I've got it handled."

On the other side of the oblong table, Chris's mother stood and began gathering dishes—even though every one of them, including her, was still eating.

"Mom, sit down. Please," Chris said. He shot his sister a help-me look, then let his eyes rove the room, trying to get his temper under control. They landed on the cow, like they did every Monday night. A giant four-foot by four-foot canvas his sister had turned into a portrait of a black and white spotted cow—wearing a tutu and ballet shoes.

The thing was heinous, but his mom had loved it the second Katie brought it home from high school art class. Eighteen-year-old Katie was going through her goth phase then, and everything she wore had to be black, from her shoes to her lipstick.

Katie crammed a bite of salad into her mouth. "Mom, Chris has a dog at the apartment."

"Damn, Katie. Come on." Chris tossed his napkin on the table, trying to figure out why the hell his sister would pull such a dick move.

"What? Natalie said she—"

"Not now," Chris said. The last thing he wanted to do was bring Natalie into this.

"Please." His mom didn't yell or rub her temples or any of those things Chris would have expected. She did something worse. She started to cry.

Chris took the dishes from her and set them on the table. "Mom, please don't cry. It's just a dog. And I'm only watching it for a few hours. As soon as dinner's over, I'm taking it back home."

Even happy-go-way-too-lucky Katie looked alarmed. "It's a really nice dog, Mom. And I can bring over my Dyson tomorrow." She looked from Chris to their mother, wide-eyed with concern.

What the actual fuck was happening here?

"I'm so tired of the fighting and the tension," his mom said between sniffles.

Chris sighed. This wasn't about the dog at all. It was about his father. Again. "Mom, maybe Monday dinners aren't the best idea. Maybe—"

"Look, Linda." Chris's dad finally spoke up. "The crew need time to do it right. Chris needs some guidance. He's brand new at all this."

Yeah, if you counted quietly running the business for years while his dad spent afternoons screwing some lady from the Chamber of Commerce as new, Chris was new. If you counted sinking every last cent of his savings into saving Hennessy Lawn as new, he was new. If you counted turning a corner and making a profit for the first time in years as new, Chris was new. He shoved back his chair. "I said it's handled."

"Chris, please." His mother gave him that look, the one so full up with guilt he could probably drown in it. "Can't we all move on?"

"I've gotta go." He left, afraid he'd lash out at her, too. Sometimes—most times, really—he couldn't understand why she'd stayed with his father after he'd fucked up so many times.

By the time he grabbed Cormack and drove to Natalie's, his anger had calmed some. Two alarm now instead of four. Maybe if he kissed her, long and slow, it would take his anger down to a flicker. Hell, maybe a little naked time with *the* best ass in a fifty-mile radius would take him to pure Zen. Yes, that was it. He needed to see that birthmark, run his fingers through her hair, taste her, and everything would be fine.

"Hey." He slapped on a grin as soon as she opened the door. But it slid off at the frantic, panicked look on her face. "What's wrong?"

"What? Why?" Her expression shifted to a smile, but it was stiff. Cool.

It took him a minute to remember where he'd seen it before. That summer. Just before she'd taken off, she'd said everything was fine. And she said it with the same icy glaze in her eyes, even though everyone in all of Elm Creek knew she wasn't fine. How could anyone be fine after something like that?

"Natalie," he said. "What's going on?" He followed her into the house, where Cormack climbed onto a stack of boxes and lay down.

She bit her bottom lip—a move that less than twenty-four hours earlier had sent him into some kind of sex frenzy. Today, it made him want to wrap her in a warm blanket and keep her safe from whatever was shutting her down.

"I have a tentative offer on the house." Her voice was light and nonchalant.

"Wow."

"Yeah. I'll probably head back home in a few days."

The words—and the way she said them—made his stomach knot up. "I didn't realize it would be happening so soon. I guess I should have."

"Alex said people contacted her, I guess. The Elm Creek rumor mill and everything." She chewed on a nail. "Never stops churning. I guess this time it finally did some good."

He would *never* consider her leaving to be good. "Yeah."

"So I'm going to need some help with Cormack. I left a message for your sister, but I haven't heard back." She reached down and scratched the dog's head.

Maybe Katie hadn't been fucking with him over dinner. Maybe she'd known Natalie was leaving before he did. And that stung like a bitch. "It can take a while," he said.

"I know. I just...don't have a while."

He wanted to be the good guy who helped out. Who supported her. Who didn't pressure her to stay. Who didn't get unnecessarily attached to Natalie or the dog. But he wasn't, like it or not. "Well, I can ask. But Katie can't make families appear out of thin air. If she could, I'm sure she wouldn't be running the rescue in the first place."

"I didn't say—"

"You really can't take him back to St. Louis?" Chris felt the coals of that fire—the one that had started with his father—starting to catch. And the more he thought of poor old Cormack alone in a shelter, the hungrier the flames grew.

"Not unless I want to be evicted." She crossed her arms in front of her chest.

Chris had no idea why they were acting like this. No idea if they were fighting or ending things or just starting them. But he could feel a wall coming up around her, and another coming up around him. He wanted to kick them both down, or—preferably—kiss her until the walls crumbled at their feet.

"Natalie." He reached for her hand.

"I have a ton of stuff to do around here," she said, looking around the room. Never meeting his gaze.

"Yeah." He waited a beat to see if she'd ask for his company or at least his help.

Silence.

"Okay. Well. Have a good night." He made his way to the door and looked back at Natalie and Cormack. Yesterday they'd felt like they were his. Like he was theirs. Today... "I'll ask Katie to call you," he said.

"Chris, wait. I don't... There's so much hanging over me right now, and—"

But it was too late. He didn't want to end up as the same shut-out, angry, lovesick teenager he'd been all those years ago. He made his way toward the truck and refused to let himself look back. He'd already looked back far too much.

Chapter Six

Natalie wasn't sure when she'd finally decided to come out here. Sometime while tossing and turning all night she'd shored up her plans, and at the time it had seemed like a perfectly logical, perfectly good idea.

Now that she was here at the entrance to the Peaceful Elms Cemetery, with the dewy grass sticking to her ankles and the scent of freshly dug earth filling her nose, she couldn't figure out why she'd thought it was a good idea. For one, who came to a cemetery before seven o'clock on a Thursday morning anyway? Creeps and people whose grief was still oozing out of them, that was who. And Natalie wasn't keen on being either.

"Stupid idea." She turned back toward her car. She didn't even know where Candace was buried. She hadn't come to the funeral back then—not that she would have been welcome anyway. She wasn't ready to face Candace's family, and she definitely wasn't ready to watch her childhood best friend be lowered into the ground.

Even standing this close to the wrought iron gates was churning up all the things she'd thought long dissipated. Pain—the physical and the emotional that had followed her for years after they wrapped the car around the tree—hit her full force. Her once-broken foot throbbed as if she'd only just woken up in the hospital. Guilt—all kinds of it—pelted her in the face and lungs and gut. Guilt that they'd been drinking. Guilt that they'd taken Candace's mom's car without permission. Guilt that she'd let Candace get behind the wheel. Guilt that she'd been the one to walk away.

She leaned against the driver's-side door, warm morning sun on her face. Last night, all she could think about was Chris. The way he made her feel when they were together. Like they were a team. One that had mind-blowing sex and a dog that liked to climb on furniture, but a team nonetheless. The way his face had fallen when she'd told him about the offer on the house. The way that second of disappointment had turned to cool, stubborn anger.

Which was why, when she'd rolled over, wishing he was there tangled in the sheets beside her, she'd wondered if she should come here. If she could face all this—the toughest part about Elm Creek—maybe she could stay. Enjoy the creek and the Painted Peacock and fried gummy worms. Maybe Cormack wouldn't need to go anywhere. Maybe they could keep being a team.

Her phone buzzed. Chris.

Can we talk? Tonight?

It buzzed a second time. *Sorry if I woke you. Sorry I wasn't better about stuff yesterday.*

She smiled a little despite herself. Maybe she could do this after all. Maybe she could wander through this perpetually green field full of headstones until she made herself whole again. Or at least less broken.

And once she did, she could think about giving herself to someone else. Someone with dark hair and panty-dropping forearms and a way with goat-dogs. She slid the phone back into her pocket without replying and took a step forward.

"You can do this," she whispered. She took a second step. A third.

"Natalie? Natalie Green?"

Natalie started at the voice, her eyes jerking from side to side until they landed on the woman. She stood half-hidden behind a thick tree, her face puffy and her mouth set in a hard line.

"Mrs. Bradford." The tiny bit of courage Natalie had found circled the drain. She'd been ready to face her best friend's headstone. Not her friend's grieving mother.

"What are you doing here?" She dabbed her face with a wadded tissue.

Natalie swallowed hard. She thought of the way Chris grinned before he leaned in to kiss her. Cormack's graying chin. The house full of odd trinkets and love. *You can do this.* "I wanted to visit. Candace, I mean. Or her..." She couldn't bring herself to say the word *grave*. "I wanted to see you too, actually." She didn't know that last part was true until she said it. But there it was. "I'm so—"

"Please leave," Mrs. Bradford whispered. She was so far from the kind-eyed, bubbly woman she'd been before. Natalie could barely grasp that this was the same person.

She took a step backward. "Mrs. Bradford—"

The woman shook her head. "Leave."

Natalie's hands shook. Her chin shook. Even her insides shook. Her skin flashed cold and the earth seemed to be unsteady. One epic panic attack, coming up. "I don't want—"

"That's just it, Natalie. I don't care what you want." Mrs. Bradford's voice stayed an inch above a whisper. "You got everything, and Candace got nothing. So forgive me if I don't want to hear about what you want."

Natalie closed her eyes. The words were like venom ticking through her veins, making her heart pound so fast she thought it was sure to stop on the next beat. She jogged to her car and tore away, tears streaming down her face.

Once she was a safe distance from the cemetery, Natalie pulled over and buried her face in her hands. The pain pushed and pushed and pushed against her skin, until she was certain she'd explode from it. When that didn't happen, she pulled out her phone and stared at Chris's text asking her to meet tonight.

When her hands quit shaking long enough to function, she sent a single-word reply.

No.

She hit send, expecting the panic to lessen. Instead it only intensified, and her fingers kept moving, pushed on by her desperate need to make this all end. To get out of Elm Creek and quit causing everyone so much pain. "Alex?" she said. "Hey. I can be out by Monday."

Chris kept staring at his phone, waiting for some kind of explanation. But none came. He got spam emails and a reminder from his mother to swing by the pharmacy on his way home, but nothing from Natalie. Only that one syllable: no.

He'd been stupid. Worse than stupid. He'd been stupid *and* reckless, and now he was right back in the same position he'd been in ten years ago. He was in love with Natalie fucking Green, and she was on her way out again. This time forever, and he didn't have a damn clue how to fix it.

Or if it could even be fixed.

"Sonofabitch." He slammed the phone down on his desk, and with it a dozen Hennessy Lawn invoices went flying.

"Great to see you, too." Katie flounced in, covered in her usual mix of paint and dog hair.

He scrambled to pick up the pages. "Hey."

"Let me guess. It begins with Natalie and ends with Green."

He started to deny it, but it would have been a pointless exercise. "She's got an offer on the house."

"Yeah. I know. And?"

"And she's going to take it."

Katie tapped her foot. "And?"

"And I want her to stay."

"There it is. It's almost like you're a real grown-up. Using your words and everything."

"Fuck off, Katie."

"Hey. You called me, remember?"

He nodded. "Cormack. Have you had any interest in him?"

She flopped down into the worn fake-leather chair across from his desk. "We just got in a litter of lab puppies. Eight weeks old. They chew everything and poop everywhere. People love them."

"So, no interest in the slightly overweight six-year-old lab who thinks he's a goat?"

"None." She pulled her hair back and jammed one of his pencils into it. "I might have a foster home open next week, but no guarantees."

Chris blew out a hard breath. The thought of Cormack sitting confused and alone in some concrete bunker was too much to handle. "Okay, thanks."

"Have you told her?" Katie asked.

"About what?'

"Okay, bonehead. I'll spell it out for you. Have you told Natalie you want her to stay? That seems like the solution to a lot of potential problems here." His sister rolled her eyes, but Chris could tell she was being sincere. She wanted this to work out, too.

Goddamn, he loved his pesky little sister.

"I tried," he said. "She won't talk to me. Complete shutdown, like before."

"It doesn't have to be like before you know. Keep trying." She stood up and put one hand on his office door. "In the meantime, I might have an idea on the dog. Keep me posted, yeah?"

"Sure." Chris sat on his sister's words for a few minutes, turning them over and over in his head. Yes, Natalie had a history with Elm Creek, with him. One that included broken hearts and running away. But she was different now. Better. They both were.

And damn it, he didn't want her to leave.

By the time he reached Natalie's front stoop, his pompous bravery had come down a notch. Or three. But knowing she was on the other side of that door—knowing this might be the moment they finally got their shit together—that was enough to get him to press the doorbell.

Ba-da-da-dum-da-da-dum-dun-duuuun.

Ba-da-da-dum-da-da-dum-dun-duuuun.

The door swung open.

"Nat—"

"Chris?" It was Alex of the Brunching Babes. Definitely not Natalie.

"Hey. I'm looking for Natalie?" He jammed his hands into his pockets and tried to peer past her into the house. A flicker of a brown ponytail appeared in the hallway before it disappeared again. "Natalie?"

"She's had kind of a rough—" Her words fell off as she took in Chris's expression, and she took a step back. "Come on in."

With a few quick strides, Chris stood in the living room, where Natalie sat among a pile of boxes. Each and every one labeled "Goodwill." Nothing was left on the walls. The last bits of furniture were gone, their footprints still visible in the carpet.

"What's going on?" he asked.

"I'm packing."

"This is more than that," he said. "You're like a different person all of a sudden." And she was. Even her posture was different. Stick-straight and stiff, like she was on her way to the world's worst debutante ball.

"What did you want? Sorry, I have a ton of packing to do."

Chris took a deep breath and tried his damnedest not let her cool distance get under his skin. "Natalie. I think... No, I know..." Finally, he just sighed and let the words fall out. "Don't go. Please."

There. He'd said it. The words were shaky and less certain than he'd wanted, but they were there. Out there between them like a rope tied to shore. All she had to do was pull herself—pull them both—back in.

She froze. "What?"

He squatted beside her on the floor and brushed the escapee hairs from her face. Part of him wanted to demand answers and part wanted to scoop her up and feed her ice cream or something. Anything that would make her feel better. "I said don't go."

Slowly, she turned her face toward him. His gut flickered with hope. He wanted to see happiness there. That second before she threw herself into his arms and agreed to stay.

Her face flooded with tears. "No."

"No?"

"No." She rubbed at her eyes with her palms. "I can't."

"Why? Can't you do a dissertation from just about anywhere?"

"That's not the problem."

"Then what *is* the problem, Natalie? Exactly."

She shook her head. "I can't stay here."

"Why not?" He felt like a broken record. One that was about to spin off the table and shatter against a wall.

She sniffed. "I went to the cemetery today."

His eyes widened, and he reached out for her. "I would have gone with you," he whispered.

She ignored him. "She was there."

"Who was there?" But he knew. Of course he knew. Everyone knew Mrs. Bradford spent an hour every morning tending to the flowers and balloons surrounding her daughter's headstone. For the last decade, the woman had practically taken up residence at her daughter's grave.

"Candace's mom. She wouldn't let me see her. Wouldn't even let me see her *grave*." Natalie's entire face had turned red now, and all her features were contorted with pain.

"What do you mean? It's a public place, right?"

"She told me to leave. What was I supposed to do?" The sob that escaped her throat stabbed him straight in the chest.

"I didn't mean—"

"She blames me, Chris. Everyone blames me. Hell, even I blame me."

"I don't."

"What?" She looked up at him, and where he wanted to see peace or love, there was only disgust.

"I don't blame you," he said. "Yeah, you guys both did something stupid that night. But she was the one behind the wheel, Natalie."

"You don't understand." She hiccupped and sobbed simultaneously. "You can't."

"Explain it, then. Please."

"I *need* her to forgive me." She was nearly gasping for breath now between sobs, and he rubbed small circles on his back, trying to calm her.

"Mrs. Bradford?" he asked.

She nodded.

"Natalie." He took a deep breath and tried to figure out how to make her see what everyone else saw. Mrs. Bradford was an old, angry, bitter woman who'd decided to blame everyone and forgive no one. She'd blamed the school. All of her daughter's friends. The highway patrol. The list was endless. And every day since her daughter had died, she seemed more and more miserable. "Maybe you just need to forgive yourself."

He waited, heart pounding wildly, praying she would look up at him and agree. Praying his words would ease her pain.

"I can't stay here." She locked her gaze on his. "Please don't ask me to stay here," she whispered.

Chapter Seven

Four days. Ninety-six hours. That was how long it took her to pack up her granddad's eighty-four years of life. That was how long it took Natalie to stop shaking when she thought about the cold, sharp pain in Mrs. Bradford's eyes. That was how long it took before the pain of the run-in had subsided enough to make way for the pain that came with Chris's absence.

She'd begged him to leave her alone. Begged him like her life depended on it. And he had, even though the sadness in his features was heavy enough to sink a ship. But now, alone in this nearly empty house, all she wanted to do was call him. Ask him to bring over a bag of deep-fried gummy worms. Ask him to rub Cormack's belly and then kiss her so slowly she forgot herself.

"No. I'm not doing it," she told the dog. "It wouldn't be fair, right?"

Cormack barely raised his head from the floor. In Chris's absence, he'd reverted to lumpy rug status. But she didn't need the dog to answer. She knew she was right. It would be completely unfair to ask him to keep her company on her last night in town. Especially after he'd laid his heart out in front of her like that.

Don't go.

She had to go. There was no stopping the moving train now. Alex had all the ducks lined up to sell the property to the developer. Natalie didn't even need to be here for it. And because she was a saint, Alex was even going to take in Cormack until Katie found him a permanent home. Or maybe, in September when it was time to renew her lease, she could find someplace that allowed pets and bring him back to St. Louis.

If, a month ago, someone had told her she'd be willingly planning a trip back to Elm Creek, she would have laughed. Now, she mostly wanted to cry.

Across the room her phone buzzed on the counter, and her heart took off faster than her feet. *Chris. Please be Chris.*

"Natalie?" The female voice was decidedly not Chris's.

"Yes?"

"It's Katie Hennessy."

"How are you?" *How's your brother?*

"I just spent an hour naked in front of my ceramics wheel, so pretty good."

"Oh." Natalie cleared her throat. "What did you make?"

"Sweet, sweet love." Katie cackled. "That scene from *Ghost* has inspired *a lot* in my personal life."

Natalie scrambled for something to say, but she still couldn't picture Katie as anything but a gangly kid. "Thanks for calling me back," she finally said.

"Cormack?"

"Yeah. I'm, uh, not sure what Chris told you, but I'm headed out of town tomorrow. My friend Alex is going to let him stay there until—"

"No need."

Natalie glanced over at the dog lying completely still on his back, all four paws up in the air. "What do you mean?"

"Got a great application in on him this morning. I think it'll be a great fit. Can you bring him by my house tonight?"

"Tonight?" she squeaked. She wasn't ready to let him go tonight. She was supposed to let him go in the morning. And maybe not even for good. She absolutely, one hundred percent, could not bring him by tonight.

"That's what I said."

Natalie swallowed back all her hesitation. "Yeah, sure. What time?"

"How about seven o'clock? The fireworks don't start until nine, so that should give us plenty of time."

"Fireworks." Somehow in her frenzy of pain and packing, she'd forgotten it was the Fourth of July. "Right." She scribbled down the address Katie gave her and hung up in a daze. It was all really happening. Her final connection to Elm Creek was being severed, once and for all.

Chris had already changed his mind four times that afternoon and another four times that evening. But every time he talked himself out of it, he remembered the look on Natalie's face when she'd said she needed Mrs. Bradford to forgive her. He remembered the look on his mom's face when she'd cried over dinner.

Maybe his father didn't have quite the same level of pain in his eyes, but once he recognized it, Chris couldn't stop seeing it. Yes, his dad was a pushy old bastard. Yes, he'd fucked things up with Chris's mom. And yes, he'd nearly run the entire business into the ground. Maybe this small attempt at moving on would affect no one but Chris. But he needed to try.

Because damn if he was going to end up as bitter and cold as Mrs. Bradford.

And damn if he was going to keep adding to his mom's pain.

"Dad?"

"Yep? You got that Landminer job finished?"

"Yes. The guys finished it yesterday." Chris sat on the couch beside his old man. This was the closest they'd been in years. "I wanted to talk to you. But, at least in the beginning, I need to just talk. Uninterrupted."

His dad raised his eyebrows. "What's this about?"

"Dad."

His father sat back and crossed his arms over his chest. "Fine. Say it."

Chris felt his nostrils flare, but he refused to take the bait. "I forgive you," he said.

"Wha—"

Chris shook his head and powered through. "I'm going to try harder to forgive you. For the stuff with Mom, for the shady business deals, for all of it. I'm not saying we're ever going to be okay. I'm not saying I want to start spending 'quality time' together."

"Then what are you saying?"

"I guess I'm saying I don't want to be angry anymore."

His father stared off into space for a moment then looked back at him.

Chris's stomach tightened, preparing for the inevitable defense. Things like, "you had no right to be angry in the first place," or "what's between your mother and I is none of your concern."

"Okay," his dad said.

"Okay?"

He nodded. "I can accept that."

Chris sat in silence for a full five seconds, dumbfounded by this simple, two-syllable response. *Okay.*

"Chris?"

He blinked twice, trying to get his brain to function again. "Yeah?"

"Thank you," his dad said. Then he patted Chris on the shoulder and stood, leaving Chris alone on the couch. Feeling both lighter and heavier than he had in years.

Katie bobbed in, wearing some kind of smock thing with a finger-painted cow across the front. "Mom's in the kitchen drinking wine and making pies, so if ever there was a time to beg for a dog, it's now."

Chris pressed his hands into the couch and watched the tips of his fingers go white. "Okay."

"And then after..." Katie raised an eyebrow. "When Natalie comes by my house?"

He wanted Natalie to stay, to be with him. But only if she was happy. Only if she could learn to let go and to love Elm Creek as much as he loved her. "We'll see."

Chapter Eight

Natalie pulled the car into the driveway of Katie's ramshackle old house, and immediately the barking started. Not from Cormack, but from the inside.

"It's going to be okay, boy." She reached back and patted the dog on the nose. "Maybe you'll make some new friends tonight."

Cormack did *not* look impressed.

"You're going to have a great new family. I bet they have a kid you can chase. Or eat his homework. Whichever. And they probably have a great yard with lots of stuff for you to climb on, you old goat."

The dog raised one ear like he was actually listening, and Natalie's eyes filled with tears. *It's going to be okay. It's going to be okay.* With a deep breath, she clipped on his leash and led him out of the car. Noise came from around the back yard—the murmur of people talking, dishes clanking—but Natalie rang the front doorbell instead.

A chorus of barking and chaos later, Katie's head popped out of the front door. "You're here. Great! Can you go around that way?" She pointed to the gate along the side of the house. "I'll meet you back there. Bringing him through the house might be too crazy right now."

"How many dogs do you have?"

"Five. Six if you count the parrot that thinks he's a dog. Around the back?" Katie asked. She didn't have her usual collected demeanor. Her hair stood up in three different directions, and her eyes kept darting from Natalie to Cormack and back. Something was up.

"Sure."

With shaking hands, Natalie lifted the gate latch and walked into the back yard. She nearly bumped her head on a string of Christmas lights hanging between the roof and the fence. The rest of the place was full of Fourth of July party supplies. A cooler. A barbecue pit. Horseshoes. A guy carrying a case of beer.

A guy with forearms she could pick out of a lineup.

"Hi." She twisted the end of the leash between her fingers, as if by gripping it tight enough she could rein in her emotions. But it wasn't working. Lust and sadness and fear pinged around inside of her at a hundred miles an hour, and all she wanted to do was throw herself in those arms and silence the crazy.

"Hey." He kept his smile guarded, and she couldn't tell if he was happy to see her or not.

"I'm supposed to meet the people who want to adopt Cormack."

Chris set down the beer and stepped closer. But not close enough. Not as close as he would have a week ago. "You're looking at him."

Natalie's forehead crinkled as her mind struggled to keep up. "You? I thought—"

"The cabin's almost done, and I had a talk with my mom. As long as he stays in the garage apartment with me, it's fine."

"Seriously?"

He nodded. "Let's just say I buttered her up."

Natalie grinned. There was no one in the world Cormack loved as much as Chris. "What did you have to do? Promise to name your firstborn after her? Take a Mommy and Me knitting class?"

"Watch it, Doc." Finally, a real smile. "I'll sic my dog on you."

She laughed as she held out the leash. "I'd like to see you try."

Chris wrapped his fingers around the leash, then around her hand. Natalie's stomach slid to her knees.

"Can you stay for a while? Not forever." He held up his palms. "A few hours, maybe?"

She looked at his dark eyes. The bit of hair poking out from under his baseball cap. The tiny freckle on his neck. Looking at him made her so happy it hurt. "I can do a few hours," she said.

As he and Natalie helped set up for the annual Katie Hennessy Fourth of July blowout, all Chris could think about was the next step of the plan. Maybe it wouldn't work at all. Maybe Natalie would realize what was happening and speed out of town even faster than the last time.

But he had to try.

"Everything looks great," Natalie said as she rearranged the dessert table for the fourth time. Meanwhile, Cormack sniffed around the corner of the backyard.

"It does," Katie said. Then she looked back at him with a knowing glance. "I'll see you guys later." She slipped back into the house without another word.

"Wait. Where's she going?" Natalie asked.

He swallowed hard and took one long look at her. If this was the last time he saw Natalie Green, he wanted to remember everything about her. The way her shorts showed off her curvy legs. The way her smile was a bit higher on the right when she was confused. The way her ponytail slouched on the back of her head.

"She's staying," he said. "We aren't."

"We aren't?"

"We're taking a ride. Me, you, the goat-dog."

Her eyes sparkled. There. He wanted to remember that.

"Where are we going on this ride?" she asked.

For a moment he considered asking her to trust him blindly. But telling her required her trust him with her eyes wide open. "To the cemetery."

"Chris—"

"Mrs. Bradford won't be there. She's never there at night. And you deserve some closure, Natalie."

He waited. And waited. Watching her breathe. Watching her mull it over. Mull him over.

"You'll be there."

"The whole time. I promise. And so will Cormack. I mean, look at him. A fierce beast ready to ravage anyone who gets in your way."

They both turned to look at the dog, who was standing on a picnic table, staring into space.

"Okay," she said.

He took her hand. "Okay."

Chapter Nine

A familiar dread filled her entire body the second the iron gates of Peaceful Elms came into view. The grass was so green it practically glowed, and row after row of headstones filled the space—each a little shrine to its resident.

"You all right?" Chris asked

"I don't know." She honestly didn't. But she suspected she would soon. "You sure she's not going to be here?"

Chris didn't need her to clarify the *she* in this conversation. "She's here every morning. I think she spends most nights at the bar, honestly."

Natalie didn't know if this information made her feel better or worse. Probably worse, because that was her fault too. "Maybe we should just go. I don't want to cause her any more pain."

His expression went sad and serious. "What about *your* pain, Natalie? You didn't force her to get behind that wheel, you know."

"I know. But it doesn't feel that way." Her voice cracked at the edges, and she could feel the familiar hum of panic taking hold.

"Breathe."

She did, counting her inhales and exhales, reminding herself that the pounding in her chest was nerves, not an impending heart attack. "Chris, I don't know if I can do this."

He squeezed her hand and laid a kiss on her cheekbone. "You can. You don't have to if you don't want to, but if you want to do it, you can."

She wanted to do it, more than almost anything. She wanted to face her fear and grief and guilt head-on and come out stronger. Maybe even strong enough to stay a little longer. "Candace is over here, right?" She pointed to the tree where Mrs. Bradford had stood.

Chris nodded.

The sun seemed to sink a little further each second she waited. The moon had already showed its sliver, and the din of cicadas filled the silence. *I can do this.*

"Chris?" she asked.

"Yeah?"

"I'm sorry. For leaving town the way I did."

"Hey." He moved closer and ran his thumb along her cheek. "We were just kids. You didn't owe me anything."

"I did. At least a phone call or a goodbye. Something." She sniffled. "I'm sorry."

He kissed her temple. A solid kiss. A safe kiss. One she wanted to lean into and stay in forever. "Do you want some alone time, or...?" he asked.

"Yeah. A few minutes would be great." She offered him a small smile and took a tiny step inside the gates. That was all she could manage before her feet turned to lead.

"Natalie?"

She turned in the direction of his voice. "Yeah?"

"Tonight I talked to my dad. Because of something you said the other night. I just..." He fiddled with Cormack's leash. "I wanted to say thank you. So thank you." He stepped forward, kissed her lightly on the forehead, and walked toward a nearby bench with the dog.

Natalie stared blankly ahead, trying to process all this information—Chris had talked to his dad, that tiny kiss, the way it made her feel—but the thoughts overloaded her brain. First things first: she had to visit Candace. It had been ten years too long.

She took in the names engraved on the stones, noting ages and epitaphs of all kinds. Noting that the grounds were peaceful at dusk—beautiful, even. Finally, she arrived at the one she'd been looking for.

Candace Bradford.

Daughter, Sister, Friend.

Taken too soon.

Fresh flowers of every color surrounded the headstone, and a few fake ones as well. Two pinwheels caught the evening breeze and whirled, like a strange two-toy welcoming committee.

Natalie rested a hand on the cool stone. The top was rough while the rest was smooth. "I made it. Finally," she said. Already the tears pooled and blurred her vision. "You always said I was too on time for stuff, right?" She let out a barking laugh, which turned to a sob before it even left her chest.

Her friend—who loved pancakes and red lipstick, who collected fortunes from cookies and always chewed bubble gum—was here, under the ground. In a box. Probably wearing one of those Sunday school dresses she'd always hated. Natalie slid to her knees, feeling like her heart might fall out of her chest. And what a welcome relief that would be, because maybe then the pain would slow to a dull ache.

"Sometimes, I pick up the phone to call you." Natalie wiped at her face. "I don't know how to be without you, even now. I just feel like I'm stumbling all the time and waiting for you to pick me up."

She paused, as if somehow Candace would answer. Because Candace was gone, and it was her fault. "How were we so stupid?" she whispered. "I would give anything to change it. Anything."

And as the grief and regret welled up inside of her, Natalie forced herself through her foggy memories of the accident, like some kind of overdue penance. As if she could sharpen this constant, overwhelming ache inside of her and get some release.

That night, there'd been a baseball game, then a party, then the beer. Then the flashing lights and screams she'd only later realized had been clawing their way from her own throat.

There'd been the moment her mother had said, "Candace didn't make it, sweetie."

The moment the nurse had stuck the needle in her arm to calm her down.

Waking up in a fog and reliving it all over again, every day as if it were all fresh and new.

Her decision to run to her sister in St. Louis and never return.

And when Natalie's tears ran slower, she sat up and cried for all the fun times they'd had. Getting ready for prom. Sleepovers that lasted the entire weekend. Bickering like sisters. Forgiving each other as if nothing had ever gone wrong.

"I'm sorry, Candace," Natalie whispered. The sun was almost gone now. In the distance, lightning bugs flickered. "I'm so sorry."

The clanking of a collar filled the air between her sniffles.

"Natalie?" Chris's outline appeared above her. "You doing okay?"

She took a moment to take stock of herself. Exhausted, both physically and emotionally? Yep. Covered in dirt and snot while sitting on her best friend's grave? Yep. Feeling like she could really breathe for the first time in a decade?

Yes.

"I'm getting there," she said, reaching for the pen and blank Hennessy Lawn invoice she'd stolen from the truck. "I just need to do one more thing."

Chapter Ten

Chris pushed up the back door of the U-Haul and a half-dozen garbage bags fell down around him. "Doc, you know this is a cabin, right? Like, small house in the woods?" But he couldn't be mad. Not today.

The day he was moving into his built-from-scratch house.

With Cormack.

And Natalie fucking Green.

"It's not that much stuff. I promise." She pulled him toward her, and when they kissed, he forgot to breathe. Her mouth was hot and soft, and she tasted like the mint tea they'd grabbed on their way back from her apartment in St. Louis. Her *old* apartment in St. Louis.

Chris pushed up the bill of his baseball cap and nipped at her neck. "You wanna go test out the porch swing?"

"Isn't Katie on her way over with the dog?" she asked.

"I'll tell her not to come until later."

"Chris."

"What?" He slipped a hand under her shirt and ran his fingers along her ribcage. No matter how many times he got to do this—to touch her—he'd never fully believe it. And in the last two months, he'd done it hundreds of times.

At her grandfather's house, before she'd signed the paperwork herself and closed the deal.

At his tiny apartment above his parents' garage—where they'd tried to stay quiet, but he'd still ended up getting a fist bump from his dad the next morning.

At the cabin, as they'd picked out carpet and fixtures and furniture together—and made sure to christen every room. Twice.

And that Fourth of July night at the cemetery, when she'd left the apology letter for Mrs. Bradford tucked into a bouquet of flowers.

Neither of them were positive that the woman had read it, but recent rumor was that her mornings at the cemetery were growing shorter, and her trips to the bar fewer. So Chris liked to think she'd found the letter.

But, most importantly, Natalie had found something that night.

He'd sat there on the bench, watching her sob for an hour. He'd wanted more than anything to make her pain stop, but his instincts told him to give her this time to grieve. So he'd stayed away until her sobs had quieted.

And when she'd finally finished writing the note, she'd stood and looked him straight in the eye—a beautiful mess of hair and tears and blades of grass. "Ask me," she'd said. "Ask me one more time."

He'd leaned against her, breathing her in. Trying to memorize the way she fit against him. "Stay," he'd whispered against her ear.

She had. And tonight, after all the chaos of the move was over, he was going to ask her again. To stay forever, this time accompanied by the ring he'd picked out last week.

As soon as they tested out the porch swing one more time.

ABOUT THE AUTHOR

Amanda Heger is a writer, attorney, and bookworm. She lives in the Midwest with her unruly rescue dogs and a husband who encourages her delusions of grandeur. Amanda strongly believes Amy Poehler is her soul mate, and one of her life goals is to adopt a pig and name it Ron Swineson.

Also by Amanda:

Without Borders: A Wanderlove Novel

Semi-Scripted: A Wanderlove Novel (sneak peek in the back of this book!)

Visit her online at amandaheger.com.

Revved

by Harper St. George

Chapter One

Eight years earlier

Rachel Cambridge wasn't sure what she'd thought people would wear to illegal street races, but floral print sundresses were apparently not it. In a sea of denim and leather, she stood out like a...well, like a floral print sundress. An engine revved out on the street, the smell of burned rubber and exhaust hanging heavy in the humid night air. Dirty, unfamiliar smells. Excitement fluttered in her belly.

"This...um...this doesn't seem safe," said her friend, Emily, as she got out of the passenger side of the car. Emily's brow furrowed, and she tugged on a strand of her blond ponytail, looking toward the main street, where most of the crowd was gathering to wait for the next race to start.

Rachel had found a spot for her BMW coupe off a side street, in the back of one of the many vacant lots crammed full of spectators' cars. Glancing toward the street, she took in the businesses around them in various stages of abandonment and neglect. She'd never been to this part of Atlanta before. The races were on a back road near the airport, but so far removed from anything she recognized that they could've been in another city. "No, it's not safe. It's fun, which is the point." Smiling, she tugged the release on her seat and waited for the rest of her friends to climb out of the back.

After another look down at her dress, she picked up her denim jacket from the floor of the backseat and shrugged it on. It was snug and cut just below her breasts, more stylish than functional, but it was the best she could do to fit in. Not that it would matter. All four of her friends had gathered at the back of the car, seeming lost and like they'd just stepped out of a J.Crew ad.

God. They looked like prep school mean girls showing up to crash a party. A denim jacket wasn't going to disguise that.

"I thought the point was to meet hot guys," Kelsey said, the first to fall into step beside Rachel as she led the way out of the lot and up to the main street.

"That too. Maybe." Rachel grinned, catching herself as her sandals slid on the loose gravel at the side of the road, and a part of her hoped that anyone she met tonight would be more exciting than the boring boys at Westwood Prep.

"Maybe? Fuck that. You're talking to a guy tonight, Rach. I don't care that you're not looking for a boyfriend."

Rachel laughed and shook her head. With graduation coming up in a couple of months and college in the fall, she definitely didn't want to get involved with anyone. She didn't look over at Kelsey to argue the point—she was too busy taking in this new world they'd stumbled into, thanks to a tip from Kelsey's brother. People were packed along the cracked sidewalks and spilling out onto the little side street. All of them smiling—no, *beaming* with adrenaline—like they were exactly where they wanted to be. She'd never been exactly where she wanted to be. Never.

Women wore jeans or tight skirts—nothing floral—with their flashiest jewelry, like this was someplace special. Her diamond-studded earrings and pendant necklace were out of place. She tugged at her skirt, feeling like the intruder she was. She didn't belong here, but then she didn't quite belong in her world either.

A group of guys were swarming around two cars lined up under the street light where the side road met the main street, making her think they were preparing to race soon. One of the cars, a black muscle car with a white stripe down the middle, revved its engine, and she realized it was the same one she'd heard earlier. Its hood was raised, and a guy cocked his head out from under it to look at the boy in the driver's seat.

"Cut it!" he yelled. She got a glimpse of dark, wavy hair and a strong jaw before he disappeared back under the hood. It wasn't enough to tell anything, really, but her stomach gave a little flip just the same.

The boy turned off the engine and jumped out to stand by the front of the car.

The dark-haired guy pulled his head out and straightened as he closed the hood. "I thought I told you to tighten the fucking headers," he said to the boy at his side, but he didn't sound angry, only exasperated.

The boy shrugged, though why Rachel thought of him as a boy she didn't know. He was probably the same age as her, but he couldn't compare to the man at his side. *He* wore jeans that were low on his hips and a dark T-shirt that stretched tight across his wide shoulders and around his biceps, and had some kind of wrench clenched in his strong hand. The muscles of his forearm flexed as he tossed it into a case or something hidden on the ground behind him.

He was probably only a little older than her, closer to twenty than eighteen, but he was definitely a full-grown man.

"Holy shit, nice choice." Kelsey's voice came from near Rachel's ear where she'd leaned in to watch him. "I approve. Go talk to him."

Rachel shook her head. The idea was so outrageous she couldn't even consider it. He was so focused, so primal and sexy that she didn't think he'd be interested in her. "His girlfriend is probably here." The women standing near his car all wore a lot of makeup, stilettos, and their breasts were pushed up impossibly high, making Rachel feel like a kid playing dress-up. If that was what he went for, then she couldn't possibly compete. But although they watched him, not one of them approached him, and he was so intent walking around his car to check the tires that he didn't spare them a glance.

The rest of her friends caught up to them, and Kelsey brought them in on her plan to make Rachel talk to the guy, but she refused, and finally a race started and drew their attention to the main road. A couple of Hondas with blue and red lights glowing from their undercarriages took their places, engines revving. A girl in a tight skirt and thigh-high boots stood between them on the faded yellow line in the middle of the asphalt, holding a flag stretched tight above her head. The engines revved again, growing quiet just before she dropped the yellow fabric, and the drivers pressed the gas, fishtailing a bit as they sped past her.

The crowd exploded in cheers, but Rachel's guy barely noticed. He was too focused on his car. And it was his. She could tell by the reverent way he touched it, and when he sat in the driver's seat, he belonged there.

"Is it over? I can't tell who won." Emily wrinkled her nose as she stood on her tiptoes, trying to see down the road.

As a group, they moved a bit closer to the raceway, trying to get a clear view of the race. Rachel didn't notice until they'd already left her behind. In that rare moment when everyone seemed more intent on the race than what was happening on their little side street, she overcame her nerves and crossed the road to his car. Everything else in the world seemed still, except for the moths flying aimlessly under the streetlight and the two of them.

He'd gotten back out to lift open the trunk, and it was only after she'd approached that she realized he was changing his shirt. The T-shirt was gone and he was shrugging into a black button-up, but he paused when he caught her standing there. The sight of his lean-muscled chest made something pulse to life within her. He gave her a once-over, starting at her heeled sandals and ending at her face, before finishing pulling on his shirt.

"You lost, princess?" he asked as he started fastening the buttons from the bottom up. His hands were strong with thick, graceful fingers. His voice was so deep and rumbly, she felt it as she heard it. It was too dark even with the streetlight to see his eyes clearly, but she *felt* them on her.

She blushed because it was weirdly intimate, the way he was dressing while talking to her, but she liked it. For the first time in a long time, she was scared and nervous and doing something she wanted to do. "I'm Rachel. Are you racing?"

He kept watching her until he'd finished the last button and stepped forward, coming further into the circle of light. He had a smudge of dirt or oil on his right cheekbone. It didn't detract from his good looks at all. It made him seem gritty, maybe a little rough, and so much more real than anyone she knew. Like he knew all about life's hard edges and was willing to take them in his hands and smooth them out.

"Why? Wanna ride with me, princess?" It was a dare, softened by the hint of a drawl. The way the corner of his mouth turned up and his eyes flashed, she knew he intended to scare her off. That was exactly how she should react; she should turn away and leave him alone.

"Hennessy, you're up," someone called out.

Somewhere in the back of her mind she was aware that the other race had ended, that people were filtering back to the side street, but she couldn't look away from him. Every single part of her wanted to know how it would feel to sit in that car with him, to do something that hadn't been planned and then sanctioned by everyone she knew.

"Yes." The word surprised both of them.

He sobered, but then his mouth stretched into a genuine smile that crinkled the corners of his eyes and transformed his rugged looks into breathtakingly handsome. "Come on." He turned and walked over to open the passenger door for her, his eyes still daring her.

She nodded, unable to speak, unable to breath as her heart pounded. Something big was about to happen.

Sage opened his door to find Rachel standing there, the streetlight across the gravel lot behind her casting her in a golden glow. He'd known her for only three months, and just the sight of her standing in his doorway almost brought him to his knees. She'd been on his mind all day. Through the paperwork, the beeps of the monitors, his mom's tears, his dad's last, gasping breaths...she'd been there like a shadow in his mind.

Uncertain of her welcome, she gave him a shy smile. "I wanted to check that you're okay. I don't have to stay, but I wanted to see you."

He'd called her a few hours ago while he'd still been at the hospital to tell her. She'd offered to come over, but he'd told her no. Why had he told her no? Because this need for her scared the shit out of him, but he couldn't fight it anymore. He tried to clamp his teeth together and wrestle it into something manageable, but it was too damn strong. Burying one hand in the hair at the back of her head, he brought her against him, hoping that holding on to her would hold him together.

"Princess." He breathed her in. "I'm glad you're here." When he could finally draw in a steady breath, he pulled the door closed behind her and turned the deadbolt. Then he picked her up, and she slid her legs around his waist, her denim shorts riding up her smooth thighs. His hands went down to her ass to support her as he climbed the stairs to the small apartment above his garage. She didn't look at him again until he sat them down on the couch, with her straddling his lap.

"Are you okay?" she asked, taking his face between her hands, making him realize it had been a couple days since he'd shaved. Shit. He should probably do that.

He gave a nod. It was automatic. *Nod. Say that everything is going to be okay. Don't let them see how goddamned broken you are because they depend on you.*

But she didn't. Not like Isla and Cole, who needed a strong big brother. Not like his mom, who needed him to take care of the garage. Rachel didn't need that from him. Swallowing past the ache in his throat, he said, "I don't know what we're going to do without him." His voice was raw.

She didn't give him that look the nurses had, the one filled with pity. A few of his aunts and uncles had come to town, and the looks they gave him were even worse. Pity mixed with their own pain. Rachel knew his pain. With her he just saw his own pain reflected back at him, and maybe it was selfish, but it felt so good to have someone to share it with.

"Can I get you anything?" She looked toward his small kitchen tucked in the corner of the room.

"I just need you, princess."

She melted into his chest, and Sage wrapped his arms around her, pulling her tighter against him. She was so damn sweet and fit so effortlessly in his arms that he was having a hard time remembering how any other woman had felt against him. His hands stroked up and down her back as the sweet scent of the fancy shampoo she used reached his nose. He fucking loved that smell now.

From that first night, something in him had responded to her. He'd tried to write her off as a shallow rich girl, standing there in her sundress and heels, but there was nothing fake about her. There was no reason he shouldn't have called her tonight, except that he didn't know how to hold himself back from her anymore. He loved her. Every day he slipped a little deeper under her Rachel spell.

"Can you stay tonight?"

She nodded against his shoulder. "Is your mom okay? Cole and Isla?"

He relaxed, something about knowing he could hold on to her for the night setting him at ease. "Yeah, a couple of my dad's brothers and their wives came down earlier in the week, and they're staying with them. My cousin Chris is here too, but I had to get out of there." Normally, he would've stayed. Because they were the same age, he and Chris had gone through almost everything together. But the place had felt too crowded, and she hadn't been there. "I'll go back over in the morning."

He didn't mean to say more. He only wanted to hold her, touch her, but as his thumbs made tiny circles on the bare skin where her eyelet top had ridden up from the top of her shorts, he began to talk about what had happened at the hospital. Her hand came up to stroke the hair at the back of his neck, and he placed a kiss on her slender wrist, closing his eyes as he breathed in her scent. Her nails found the back of his head and raked gently against his scalp. There was something so comforting and peaceful about the gesture.

He told her about how scared he'd been watching his strong dad waste away to almost nothing the past few weeks. Sage would never forget how frail he'd looked. The man who'd raised him, taught him everything he knew about engines, had been a shadow of himself lying in that bed. His dad hadn't even been lucid at the end. There'd only been a shuddering breath and then it'd been over. His dad's life reduced to nothing.

How his mom couldn't handle it and had broken down. How every damn time Isla and Cole looked at him for reassurance, he knew he couldn't let them know even a hint of what he was feeling, because what reassurance could he give them if he was falling apart?

But Rachel already seemed to know. She nodded and stroked him in that tender way she had, and she didn't look disgusted when he admitted how lost he felt with the garage. He could fix engines, but he didn't know a damn thing about payroll or taxes.

She didn't care. She said he was smart and brave, and she wiped his useless tears and told him it was okay to cry.

Before he knew what he was doing, he'd wrapped his hand in her hair and pulled her mouth to his, needing to use her as a balm for the pain. Only when he was losing himself in her sweetness did he feel whole, and fuck, he needed to feel whole right now. He kissed her like he wanted to consume her, to drink in her sweetness.

When they ran out of air, she pulled back just enough to look at him in the dim light filtering in through the window from the street light. The depth of her stare made him feel like she could see down inside him all the way to his soul. She smiled, a gentle upward tilt of the left side of her mouth, and he groaned as he pressed his mouth to hers again. He couldn't get enough.

His hands moved up her smooth thighs until he found her cotton panties under the edge of her shorts. He hesitated, because he hadn't seen her all week and he didn't want her to think that sex was the only reason he needed her here, but she moved her hips, pressing herself against him. He could feel her heat through the denim of her shorts. Pressing open-mouthed kisses down her jaw line to her neck, he tasted her. God, he loved how she tasted. He squeezed her ass as his fingers made their way down between her legs. When he found the cotton there soaked, he groaned and couldn't resist letting his fingertips slip past the elastic to touch her.

"Christ," he said when her slick heat coated his fingers.

She tightened her grip on his hair and pushed back, arching into his touch. But her other hand went between them, past the waistband of his shorts, to find him hard and pulsing. He pressed a finger into her and almost lost it when she made that soft little grunt in the back of her throat. She didn't let go of him, though; she just squeezed and stroked him.

"Fuck, princess, I need to be inside you," he whispered against her ear.

She nodded, squeezing him again in her small hand. "Yes. God, yes."

Locking his arm around her waist, he stood and walked to the far corner of the room to his bed. He gently dropped her on the bedspread, and she sat there looking so damn sweet with the thin sleeve of her top drooping down off one shoulder that his cock pulsed.

Christ. She was his drug.

He pushed down his shorts, but couldn't look away from her as she shimmied out of her top and shorts. When she opened her arms to him, he fell into the cradle of her hips. Her soft curves fit themselves against him, and he lost himself in her arms, his face buried in her blond hair. He needed to feel connected to her tonight, needed to feel her skin on his.

Sage only realized he was crying again when her fingers brushed the tears away. Her mouth found his, and he responded without even thinking about it. Kissing her was so natural that it was instinct.

He meant to pull away, to go slower, but she made that little sound in the back of her throat again. The part moan, part whimper that drove him crazy.

"Sage, please," she whispered, sensing his hesitation, her hand going down to grip him.

Fuck, he needed her sweetness right now. He needed her to forget the giant hole left in his heart. He needed to bury himself in her and soak in all the good things she made him feel. Leaning over, he rifled in the drawer in his bedside table. Blindly finding the box of condoms, because he couldn't take his eyes from the beauty spread out beneath him, he fumbled inside but didn't feel a condom wrapper. Grabbing the box, he sat back on his knees and looked inside to find it empty.

"Son of a bitch." There were no condoms. They'd gone through the ones in his car and wallet. Dammit. He'd meant to pick up more, but with everything going on with his dad, he hadn't thought about it.

"What's wrong?" she asked, her blue eyes wide as she looked up at him. Her fingers gripped his hips as she shifted restlessly on the bed.

"Out of condoms."

She didn't miss a beat. She rose and wrapped her arms around him, placing a kiss to the center of his chest. "It doesn't matter. Please, Sage, I need you."

"Are—are you sure?" He had to ask, but he was already falling over her, because fuck if being inside her skin to skin didn't sound as close to heaven as he'd ever get.

"Yes." This time when she reached for his cock, there was nothing stopping her from leading him to her. As soon as her hot, tight heat started to close around him, he was lost. He pushed into her and closed his eyes as he took every damn thing she gave him.

He buried his face against her neck, breathing in her scent. "I love you, princess. I love you so much."

"I love you," she whispered back.

Chapter Two

Everything had gone wrong.

Rachel couldn't pull her eyes from the purplish-black smudge of toner that marred the side of her palm. Something about it had reminded her of him...of Sage. Of that one summer when everything had seemed so right, before it had gone so wrong. Even after eight years, thinking of him made her hurt. An ache built in her chest, but her mother's high-pitched, nasally voice wafting down the hallway pushed the memories away.

"Rachel!" It didn't matter where she was in the penthouse office suite. That voice always knew how to find her.

Rachel cringed and tossed the empty toner cartridge into the basket. After closing the door on the copier, she gathered up her fresh copies, and clutched them to her chest like body armor as she made her way to as her mother's office. It was filled with overbearing furniture that made the room feel dark, despite the wall of windows looking out over downtown Charlotte. "Hi, Mom."

"Sit down, Rachel." The woman was all business as she typed on her laptop, not even bothering to glance up.

Suppressing a sigh that would've smacked of self-pity, Rachel complied and approached the matched set of oxblood leather chairs. The giant mahogany desk would've dwarfed any other small-framed woman, but not her mother. Julianna Cambridge was a force to be reckoned with. From the roots of her blond hair, currently held back in a flawless French twist, to the tips of her perfect manicure, she exuded competence and power and...disapproval.

Her mother turned, glancing up at Rachel over the rim of her tortoiseshell reading glasses. One look at Rachel's appearance—hair blond and thick like her mother's, but not nearly as well managed in its limp knot at the back of her neck—and her mouth twisted down. Rachel did sigh then as she slipped down into a chair, placing the copies in her lap. She deserved a little self-pity.

"You look tired," her mother said as she whipped off her glasses with businesslike efficiency and set them on the green, overstuffed legal folder lying on her desk. The words MAXIM-SEGALL were typed on the tab.

"I am a little tired. I've stayed late all week to finish up the merger." Rachel nodded toward the folder. Maxim and Segall were steel conglomerates involved in a semi-hostile merger. Two of the three Segall heirs had sold their shares to Maxim, but the last one had been a holdout until Rachel managed to secure his signature the day before. She'd been proud of that victory, though it had rung hollow. All of her victories seemed to do that, affirming that she was making the right decision for her future.

At the thought, her pulse leaped like a dog pulling against its leash for freedom, so she took a deep breath to calm it. Not yet. She still had another week here.

Her mother raised her arched eyebrows, the same way she had when Rachel was a kid and had come home with a bad grade. That familiar tension tightened like a knot in her stomach, but something fierce had been coming to life inside her over the past couple of years, and it growled low and deep, refusing to be cowed. "You're making a horrible mistake."

They weren't talking about her appearance anymore. *This* was the reason she'd been called into her mother's office. They were going to talk about her "horrible mistake," the choice she'd made for her future, as if they hadn't already talked about it ad nauseam. Rachel took a deep breath, and made her voice as calm as she was capable. "I'm twenty-six. It's time I start figuring out what I want from my life."

Her mother smirked. It was the look that always said Rachel wasn't capable of making a decision on her own. And maybe once that had been true. Once, all that had been important was trying to smooth everything over after Hannah had died, and keeping the peace between her parents. But that wasn't working out for her anymore, and it was past time she take control of her own life.

"You're too young to know you're making a mistake."

"Maybe it's time I made some mistakes."

Her mother laughed. "Come tell me that in twenty years when you have no savings and no job."

Rachel fought the urge to roll her eyes at her mother's dramatics. She had a law degree. If this detour didn't work out, she'd find a job, though it might not be one her mother would consider worthy of her. Any job not in the family law firm wouldn't be worthy of a Cambridge, in her mother's opinion. "At some point you have to accept that I'm leaving. I'm moving back to Atlanta."

Her mother's frown deepened. "You haven't even given Daniel a chance. If you don't want to work, you might consider using your looks to your advantage. When you put yourself together, you're actually quite pretty."

Ugh. Daniel with his fish lips and no real conversation beyond his parents' yacht collection. "Mom, no."

"His parents loved you last summer at the beach house. They're open to the idea of you as a daughter-in—"

"Mom!" She could feel her voice rising, so she took another deep breath to steady herself. "I didn't go to college and law school just to find a guy to take care of me."

"People do it all the time."

"I'm not marrying Daniel. He's not my type."

The woman crossed her arms loosely across her chest. "Don't remind me of your *type*. I remember your unfortunate preference for trash."

She meant Sage. He was the only one Rachel had ever truly picked for herself. Since that had resulted in disaster, she'd always been careful to pick her boyfriends from the pool of approved candidates. As a result, there'd only been a few. But the only one who'd ever seemed *real* to her was Sage. Her heart twisted over on itself that her mother would refer to him as less than. "You never knew him."

"I didn't need to." Then she continued on with their conversation as if Sage had never been mentioned. "Daniel is from a well-connected family; he's handsome, and very smart. You need to start thinking of your future."

"This *is* the twenty-first century, and I *am* thinking of my future. This isn't about me not wanting to work. This place isn't me." She widened her arms to indicate the office suite, then grabbed the papers before they could topple from her lap. "I want to be a writer. I've wanted it for a long time...I thought this would make me happy, but it hasn't." *I don't belong here.* The thought had been with her for years, teasing at the edges of her consciousness. It had only become stronger once she'd allowed herself to embrace it. "It's time for me to do what I want. To try it." Not that her mother had acknowledged Rachel's new book deal.

"Is this about your father? Has he promised you something if you go back to Atlanta and work with him?"

She closed her eyes and counted to ten before she answered. "No. I'm moving there because it's home." It had always been this way. Her parents pitting their children against the other. When Hannah had died, it had been just Rachel left to turn herself into whatever they wanted her to be to please them and try to hold everything together. She couldn't do it anymore. Trying to believe that her mother's concern came from a good place, she continued to reassure her. "I'll be fine. I've worked every year since high school and I've saved every penny." Only now did she realize she'd been saving for her escape. "And I have the trust fund Grandma Rachel left me, and the advance I got wasn't too bad. I'll be fine." Not that her mother cared about her advance. She'd sold a three-book suspense series to a major publisher months ago, but had yet to hear a congratulations. To be fair, she'd yet to hear any praise for closing the merger, so she wasn't surprised. Praise was only doled out in their family as a means of control. Her mother was livid that that control was being taken from her.

"You'll be sorry. One day you'll want to come back, and I'm not sure I can risk another chance—"

"Mom, I love you, but this has to stop. If I come back, then I come back. If you give me another chance, then you do. If you don't, then that's on you." Taking the copies in her hands, she rose to her feet and smacked them down on her mother's desk. "I won't be manipulated anymore. I quit."

Her mother snorted a laugh, but sobered immediately. "Oh, stop with the dramatics."

Something nudged its way past the hurt and anger. It burst through the walls she'd built around herself like a seedling touched by the first rays of spring sunshine. It was relief, and it bloomed within her, crashing through the wall she'd built around herself. The weight of it falling was like shedding a suit of armor. "I won't do this anymore. I'm not Hannah, and no matter how hard I've tried to take her place...it's not working."

Disappointment was etched into every fine line on her mother's well-preserved face. "No, you're not Hannah." Something like pain flashed across her mother's eyes before it was controlled and extinguished, just like everything else that didn't belong in the woman's life.

There was nothing to say to that. They hadn't spoken of her sister's death in years. They never spoke about anything that really mattered. Rachel turned and walked out.

Four hours later, she was in her apartment surrounded by half-packed boxes she'd been working on all week. She'd opened a bottle of Pinot Grigio to celebrate her freedom, but somehow the alcohol had turned on her. She didn't feel much like celebrating when all she kept remembering was Sage the last time she'd seen him. She'd blame her mother for bringing him up, if only she hadn't been thinking about him a lot lately on her own.

Setting the almost empty bottle down on the rug beside her, she grabbed her phone from the end table and leaned back against the couch. She'd looked him up a couple of different times over the years. Mainly because she liked to torture herself with thoughts of what could've been had she not broken up with him. She realized it probably would've ended anyway with her so far away at college, but a small part of her still wondered if they could've made it work.

Holding her breath as she typed in his name, she didn't let it out until an image of him popped up. It was small and grainy, and he wore a baseball cap while sitting on the hood of a sports car with his team around him. He looked so happy. The article on the racing blog explained how he'd won an amateur race. There were a few other articles about other races, but there didn't seem to be much else. Aside from mention of his garage, he wasn't on social media.

She closed out the window and took another drink of wine. As she went to set the bottle down, something caught her eye. That faint smudge of gray ink on the bottom edge of her palm that had defied her attempt to completely wash it away. It made her think of Sage's hands, always marked with grease stains, and that ache returned to bloom across her chest. She'd loved his hands. They'd been so strong and capable, yet so gentle, and he'd always known just how to touch her. A tingle moved through her belly at the memory, making her breath catch and her thighs clench together. But it had been more than that with him. He was the only person she'd ever really been herself with.

What if she'd made a colossal mistake letting him go?

It was a mistake to let him go.

She giggled, even though it wasn't funny. Okay, maybe that meant she'd had too much wine. Setting the wine as far away as she could reach, she looked down at her phone again and scrolled to her contacts.

Sage Hennessy.

His number had been right there all this time, just waiting for her to delete it. She should've taken it out one of the times she'd changed phones. She never had, though she'd tried to forget it was there. It had been lurking, a silent reminder of who she once was and who she might've become.

Her thumb hovered over it, itching to press it. There was no way it was still his number. It had been eight long years, and she was stupid for keeping it. He must've moved on and was probably married with a couple of kids by now. Yeah, that suited him. He'd been close to his own dad. He'd want kids.

So why hadn't she moved on? Why did he always sneak up on her in those quiet moments when she was feeling lonely? The only time she hadn't felt lonely was when she'd been with him. Was she confusing loneliness for missing him?

It was a mistake to let him go.

This time she didn't giggle. Her stomach churned on the wine and the bag of popcorn she'd finished. She stared at his name until it blurred.

She'd call the number. Someone would probably answer and not even know him, because he'd have changed his number by now. That would be her sign to leave him alone and move on. On the off chance he answered, then she'd get to talk to him again, just once, to see if she'd made a giant mistake. Or maybe just to get some closure. She needed to do *something* so she'd stop thinking about him and get on with her life. Her infinitely better life without being under her mother's thumb and without the safety net of a steady income. Her heart stuttered a bit at that, so she pressed his name before she lost her nerve, and brought the phone up to her ear.

It rang and another irrational giggle threatened to escape. God, she was a little drunk. She bit her lip to make herself stop, and held her breath, expecting to hear someone answer and tell her they'd never heard of Sage. She caught sight of the smudge of ink on her hand as it rang again. That ache in her chest threatened to move up her throat, but she fought it.

"Yeah?" The voice that answered was deep and rumbly in her ear, though barely audible through the background noise of a car running and metal clanking. Sage's voice, unmistakable to her even after all these years. She closed her eyes as it echoed through her, causing her throat to tighten. She'd gone eight long years without hearing it. Eight years when she might've heard it every day had she not ruined them. What had she done?

"Just a minute," he said. He must've pressed the phone to his chest, because everything was a little muffled, but she could hear him telling someone to quiet down. Another voice yelled back, and then there was a round of laughter. The sounds retreated, and she figured he must be walking away. She imagined him walking to the office he used just off the service area of the garage. A door closed, and she could hear the leftover smile in his voice when he said, "Sorry about that. This is Sage."

Oh my God!

Her heart broke free of its stupor and sent blood rushing through her ears. The phone slipped out of her hand, and she stared at it lying on the floor. She'd been so convinced he wouldn't answer that she hadn't thought ahead. What the hell was she supposed to say to him?

"Hello?" the voice said from the phone on the rug next to her leg.

She fumbled to pick it up, debated ending the call, but ended up jerking it up to her ear. "Sage?"

He was quiet. There was nothing on his end but that engine in the background muffled behind a closed door. Then finally, "Rachel?"

She closed her eyes in decadent pleasure as his voice moved through her. She had no idea how he'd guessed it was her just by her saying his name. "Yeah, it's me."

There was a second of silence again before he sucked in a deep breath and asked, "Are you okay?"

She smiled. Of course that would be his response. He'd only ever wanted to take care of her. Everything inside her warmed. It was like coming home to a blanket and a cozy fire after a day playing in the snow. "I'm fine. I just...well, I found your old number and thought I'd call—"

He hung up. The engine noise went away and there was nothing.

Dumbfounded, Rachel sat there for a minute still holding the phone to her ear. It hurt. There was no denying the pain that ripped through her when he shut her out. But another part of her, the reckless part, the part that was fed up with the old Rachel who tried to please everyone, was smiling.

The opposite of love wasn't hate—it was indifference. He wasn't indifferent. He was still hurting, which meant he still cared...at least a little.

Maybe they didn't have a chance anymore. Maybe she should let it go. But something in her needed to see him, to tell him in person how sorry she was for leaving.

Sage Hennessy stared down at his phone, anger vibrating through him. The last time he'd talked to her he'd thrown his phone against the wall when they hung up, and then stomped it with his boot. The last time he'd been hurt, because she'd broken him like he hadn't meant anything to her. This time he didn't know why he was angry.

Oh, yeah he did. He was angry because just for a second there, just after she'd said his name and he'd known it was her, he'd been happy. For just that sliver of time, his stupid heart had remembered how good it felt to hear her say his name. What a goddamned idiot his heart had turned out to be.

He didn't break his phone again. He just blocked her number and slid it back into the pocket of his jeans. Apparently nothing he'd done over the years had helped rip every little piece of her from his heart. Perfect.

Fucking Rachel Cambridge.

He could've gone the rest of his life without hearing from her again. Sucking in a breath, he pushed his hands through the sides of his hair, tugging slightly in the back. The minor discomfort wasn't enough to combat the phantom pain in his chest. It was there like an echo. An echo that had lasted eight fucking years and showed no signs of fading out. It just rattled around, waiting for something to bounce off so it could take flight again and give him hell.

He let out the breath and leaned back against the edge of his desk, arms crossed over his chest, trying to figure out what the hell had made her think he'd want to hear from her. Maybe she'd gotten bored and decided she needed to slum it again. To make him feel like a king, only to swat him away and tell him he wasn't good enough for her.

Christ. A handful of words from her and he was already a mess. Nope. He wasn't going there with her again.

Once was enough.

Someone rapped their knuckles against his office door just before pushing it open. His friend Rob stood there holding his own phone. "Hey, man, I gotta get home. Sara will kick my ass if I'm late tonight."

Sage only realized then that the engine of his GT350 had stopped. They'd been replacing the intake manifold to get it ready for the race tomorrow.

"Yeah, no problem." He straightened and ran a hand through his hair, trying to look like he hadn't been having a pity party in his office. "Tell her thanks for letting you come out before date night."

Rob grinned. "Fuck off."

Sage forced a laugh. Rob and Sara had gotten married and had a baby all in the same year. He was surprised Rob came out as much as he did. They never did much on Friday nights but tinker with their damn cars and drink beer, but fuck if staying home with a woman he loved didn't hold its own unique appeal.

"I'll be at the track bright and early in the morning," Rob said.

"Thanks, man. I know you will." Sage headed back out to the garage with his friend on his heels. Rob worked at the garage and had headed up Sage's pit crew when he'd started racing on the amateur circuit. Sage did well, but he'd never viewed racing as anything more than a hobby. His real passion was playing with engines, squeezing all the power out of them that he possibly could.

Not that he didn't have other passions. Rachel had been one of them. She'd been hunger, thirst, and every other goddamned need rolled into one. And the way she'd said his name on the phone—soft and sweet, with just a hint of that rasp that used to drive him crazy—had brought it all back. He'd thought he'd purged her from his system, but it turned out she was there to stay.

"Hey...you okay?"

Sage nodded, not trusting himself to speak.

"Who called you?"

Nope. He wasn't fucking going there. Rob had been around when Sage had dated Rachel, and he knew how it had ended. No way was Sage going to open the door for that heart-to-heart. "Wrong number," he said, and walked over to lower the hood of his car. The guys had already begun to put away their tools and start on the pizza. The party was winding down.

He slid into the driver's seat, pulled forward out of the garage, and drove the gravel path to the warehouse on the lot next door. It had belonged to a guy who'd owned a small chain of automotive supply stores, and he'd kept his overstocked inventory there. Sage had bought it when the guy had retired a few years ago. He used it for the restoration jobs he'd started taking on and as a place to keep his two racecars.

His life was good. He was racing and working on engines. The only things he'd ever wanted to do with his life, except for having a family. He'd always imagined himself as a dad, having his kids hang out in the garage after school, showing them how to work on engines just like his dad had shown him and his younger brother and sister. Even his sister, Isla, had gotten lessons on cars whether she'd wanted them or not. He hadn't found a woman yet he wanted to share that life with, but he assumed he would one day.

Once he'd thought Rachel had been that woman for him. But what the hell had he known as a stupid twenty-year-old? It had taken him years to stop picturing her face when he thought about the future.

Years.

He pulled into his parking space in the warehouse-turned-garage and cut the engine.

Fucking Rachel Cambridge.

Chapter Three

A week later, Rachel was convinced this was possibly the worst idea she'd ever had. Sage wasn't going to be happy to see her. It bothered her, though she understood. If their situations were reversed, she'd probably feel the same. Only that would never happen, because Sage wouldn't have treated her the way she'd treated him. He never would've said she wasn't good enough for him.

Rachel smoothed a hand over her tank dress. It was late on a Saturday, the sun making its way down past the oak trees that lined the grassy area between the parking lot and the side street. The garage was a neatly built block building painted a creamy color, with a restored, old-fashioned gas pump sitting out front under a sign that read "Hennessy Automotive." Perched like it was on the edge of a residential neighborhood, it reminded her of a picturesque scene from the 1950s. The light over the sign was dark now. The garage had been closed for an hour, according to the sign on the door, but a couple of guys were still there tinkering. One of them had directed her to the warehouse on the next lot. She stood there now, losing her nerve, debating whether to turn around and go. Sage had made it pretty clear he didn't want to talk to her.

Metal clanked inside the steel building, so she paused just beside the open roll-up door to make sure he was alone. Bob Dylan singing "New Morning" drifted out from inside, but she heard Sage's own mumbled singing underneath Dylan's. Something in her stomach fluttered at the sound. She'd always loved the husky texture of his voice, the way it could reach in and touch places deep inside her. Taking a hesitant step forward, she caught sight of him squatting next to the fender of a classic car. The sanding block he held dripped water as he ran it smoothly along the side of the car.

She wasn't quite prepared for how he'd changed. He had the same dark hair falling forward over his forehead, the same tanned skin covering muscular forearms, the same strong, capable hands. His thick, graceful fingers smoothed along the edge of the area he'd just sanded. When he straightened and leaned back, cocking his head to the side to look at it, her gaze was drawn to his shoulders. He'd always been solid, but he seemed even broader now, filling out his Hennessy Automotive T-shirt with a thickness that hadn't quite been there before. She drew in a breath and held it as his hand moved to the back of his neck, brushing aside the thick waves of his hair to massage the muscle. Her fingertips tingled as she remembered running them through his soft hair, and how he'd loved it.

She must've made a sound, because he turned, his eyes going wide when he saw her. For a second neither of them spoke. Rachel couldn't have spoken had she tried. Everything inside her was too busy waking up. Her heart sped. Her stomach fluttered like it was trying to keep up, and her skin prickled in awareness of him.

He recovered first, and his stormy blue eyes shuttered immediately. "You lost, princess?"

She didn't know if he realized that was the first thing he'd ever said to her, but her heart tripped over itself all the same. He didn't sound as friendly as he had that first time. Finally managing to breathe out, she smiled and said, "Hey."

His eyes narrowed and he rose to his full height, boots scuffing across the concrete floor as he set the sanding block on the nearby workbench and picked up a towel to dry his hands. She couldn't help the way she watched the muscles bunch and flex under the cotton of his T-shirt. A large fan whirred above their heads, circulating the air a bit, but the neck of his shirt was a darker blue, wet with sweat from the humid summer air. A smudge of dirt marked his left bicep, emphasizing how well developed that particular muscle was.

A long-buried memory of him surfaced. It was a hot Sunday afternoon and he'd been shirtless, muscles glistening in the sun while he tinkered with his car. She'd kissed his shoulder, swiping her tongue along the saltiness of his skin. He hadn't worked for much longer after that. They'd spent the rest of the day in his bed.

Her mouth went dry at the memory, so she swallowed a few times and tried to make herself seem like a normal person. Damn. She'd somehow forgotten how consuming their chemistry had been.

She'd expected him to be angry, but his scowl was doing things to her. Bad things like the anxiety twisting her into knots on the inside. Good things like the butterflies fluttering in her belly and the way the muscles clenched deep in her core. She made herself look back at his face when he tossed the towel onto the workbench and turned down the music coming from the speaker on a shelf near his head, but even that was a mistake. He wasn't beautiful. His nose had a Roman curve, and his brows were angry. But his cheekbones were perfect slashes under the skin of his cheeks and his lips were full, pretty in a masculine way. Somehow the combination came together in an attractiveness enhanced by the rugged flaws. It didn't hurt that she remembered how gentle he could be, and how amazing it felt to have all of that blue-eyed intensity focused on her.

God, he *was* beautiful.

"How are you?" Belatedly remembering the package in her hand, she stepped further into the open space of the warehouse garage and held it out to him. He seemed on the verge of telling her to leave, so she hoped her peace offering could buy her a few minutes. "I brought you this."

When he didn't take it, she stepped closer and set it on the workbench.

His eyes never left her face. "Why are you here, Rachel?"

Damn, she'd never had the full force of his anger on her before. Well, at least not where she could see it. She'd broken up with him over the phone. She forced herself not to shift her feet as she tucked her hair behind her ear and moistened her lips. "I wanted to see you, to see how you are. The garage looks great. You're doing well for yourself. One of the guys"—she pointed toward the garage in case he had any doubts who—"told me you'd expanded here a couple of years ago."

She'd been too focused on him to notice earlier, but now she paused to take in the large warehouse. There were shelving units in back filled with parts, and she counted seven classic cars in various stages of restoration scattered throughout at different workstations. She knew she was rambling so he wouldn't make her leave, but she couldn't seem to stop. "So you've started restoring cars like you always talked about. I'm glad it worked out. You deserve to...have things...work out." Nice segue.

He breathed in through his nose, and his hand came up to run over the day's growth of stubble on his chin. He clearly did not know what to make of her. She couldn't blame him. Now that she was here, she had no idea what she'd planned to say. Again. And she couldn't keep her eyes to herself. She didn't mean to, but they followed the movement of his hand, catching on his full bottom lip. A shiver of awareness worked its way through her middle, and she had to force herself to meet his gaze again.

"Is this the part where we talk about what we've been up to and laugh about old times?"

Only a few feet separated them, but it might as well have been a deep chasm. That was how unreachable he seemed. He was so hurt. Her chest tightened at the same time that tiny seed of hope that had brought her here dug its roots in deeper. He wouldn't still be hurting if he didn't care. Right? "Sage, I came to apologize...for what happened, for the way I ended things. It was thoughtless and stupid."

"Apologize." He said it like he was mulling it over, like it had never occurred to him. "That was, what...eight years ago? It doesn't matter." Finally looking away from her, he picked up the sanding block and pulled off the sandpaper, tossing it into the trash at the end of the workbench.

It did matter. He tried to hide it, but the pain was still there in his eyes.

"It matters to me." She chewed her bottom lip and watched him do everything he could to avoid her and the gift sitting inches away from the tools scattered across the work surface. She didn't blame him, but his neglect still stung. "And I think it matters to you. You seemed upset on the phone, so I—"

"So you what?" He dropped the pack of sandpaper he'd been returning to the shelf and turned back to look at her. "You thought it'd be a good idea to show up here?" He didn't raise his voice, but his eyes were hot.

She shook her head. "No, I knew it was a pretty bad idea. But I wanted to let you know, in case you'd been hurt, that it wasn't your fault. You didn't do anything wrong back then. It was me."

He snorted a laugh. "You made it pretty fucking clear I did a lot wrong. I didn't go to your prep school. I didn't have parents with money. I wasn't what you wanted."

She closed her eyes as she remembered that phone conversation. She hadn't even had the guts to say those awful things to him in person. Because none of them had mattered, and she'd known that if she saw him and had to say those hurtful things to his face that she couldn't do it. She would've broken. "That's just it, though. None of that was true. Not a single word of it."

"That's where you're wrong, princess. Every damn word of it was true." He stared down at the woman who'd walked out of his life nearly eight years ago. She was a little curvier, and her hair was shorter than the girl he'd known. There were probably other changes that he couldn't see. She'd graduated law school—he knew because he'd looked her up a few times online—and she'd seen more of the world. But despite how she must've grown and changed, that sweetness he'd always loved about her was still there in her eyes. He'd expected that to be long gone, but it was there shining out at him, making him miss her more than he'd realized.

"But none of those are the reason I couldn't be with you anymore."

"I'm a grown man, Rachel, and it was a long time ago. It doesn't matter." Sage took a breath and let it out again, nice and slow. Turning back to the tools spread out on the workbench, he began sorting them back into their slots so he could get out of there. "Look, I'm sorry I hung up on you. That was a dick move. I'm not mad at you."

"Please, Sage." She reached out and touched his arm, and it was like a bolt of lightning shooting through him. His gaze closed in on her touch, riveted to her soft palm on his forearm. When he could finally breathe again, he looked up at her face, and fuck if she wasn't smiling. Her lips tilted up in that sweet smile of hers that did things to him he didn't want to acknowledge. It always had.

"Please, just let me explain," she said.

Under the guise of thinking over her request, he moved his arm and stepped back, putting some much-needed distance between them. The way she said "please" had him remembering the way she'd said it when she'd been under him. Fuck. That had been so long ago that he should've forgotten all about it. He ran a hand over his jaw. "You telling me if my family had lived on the north side and had an office in one of those tall Buckhead buildings that you still would have broken it off?"

She blushed and looked down. "You scared me, Sage. I didn't know how to be with you and be who I thought I was meant to be."

"What does that mean? Who were you meant to be?"

"Hannah?" She shrugged and glanced up at him. "I'm not sure."

Her sister had died before he'd met Rachel, and he'd known about her, but he had no idea what she was talking about. "What about Rachel? I liked her."

"After Hannah died, everything sort of fell apart. My parents were barely speaking, and my grades, which had never been great, only got worse. When I lost her, it felt like I'd lost everything. My whole family broke down. I just needed so badly to keep everything together that I made myself become her." She paused, and her bottom lip trembled as she took in a breath. His chest tightened, but he fought it off and looked away. "*She* was supposed to follow in my parents' footsteps. Not me. But I did anyway, because that's what everyone wanted. That's what made everyone happy. And I hated every damn second of it. I hated everything until you came along."

It made sense, but some part deep inside him wanted to tell her thanks for coming by, but he was fine. He wanted to be fine without her. Hell, he *was* fine without her. He ran a business, had expanded a business, bought a house, dated occasionally. His life was great. Yet there'd always been this hollow in his chest. It ached now, and he couldn't stop himself from running a hand over it.

"I was only happy when I was with you, Sage. Please believe that. You were good for me, and I couldn't see it then."

That ache expanded, pushing the air out of his lungs. He couldn't believe her. He couldn't believe he'd been good for her. If he did, that ache would take over. If that were true and she'd still pushed him away... "I don't believe you." Moving away from her, he grabbed the bucket he'd been using for the wet sanding and tossed the dirty water out onto the gravel. He'd been finishing up when she'd come in, and now he just wanted to go. It had been an early morning and he was supposed to meet the guys for a drink. "Just go. You've said your piece."

"Please let me—"

The words spewed out of him before he could even think of shutting them down. "I fucking loved you, Rachel. Why? If I was so good for you, how could you tear us apart like that?"

She looked stricken, her mouth tight, her eyes shining with pain, and he cursed himself for nearly losing it. No matter what had happened, it was too long ago to even matter now. And yet...it did. His fingers clenched around the handle of the bucket. Every nerve in his body waited to hear what she would say.

Nothing had prepared him for her actual words.

"I...I thought I was pregnant."

For a second the room went quiet. There was only the sound of his own blood whooshing in his ears. A million thoughts poured through his mind at once, but the only one that mattered—the only one he could grab on to and make sense of—was that she'd never told him. Despite how close he thought they'd been, she'd never shared that with him.

He closed his eyes as he remembered the only night they'd been together without using protection. The night his dad had died. It had been reckless and stupid, but he'd been in too much pain and too in love with her to think straight. It didn't excuse anything, not the least of which was that she'd had to face that on her own. She'd never said anything, so he'd assumed they'd been fine. "What happened?"

"I never took a test, but I was two weeks late before I started my period, and convinced I was pregnant." She stood there with her arms crossed over her chest, looking lost and unsure, and damn if he didn't want to hold her. "I was too scared to take a test, and too scared to tell you."

"Why were you scared to tell me?" His voice was raw.

"Because I didn't know what you'd say."

He sucked in a breath to fight the ache in his throat. "It was my fault. I would've been there for you, Rach."

"I know you would." She nodded, a sheen of tears in her eyes. "And that's why I couldn't tell you. I didn't know what to do, and it scared me because there was a part of me that wanted it to be real. Some stupid part of me wanted to have your baby, so I wouldn't have a reason not to be with you anymore. So that it'd be taken out of my hands." She breathed in and swallowed a few times before continuing. "That scared me. I knew then that I couldn't stay with you, because I was afraid if I did I'd give up everything else I thought I wanted."

Sage ran a hand through his hair. He'd always thought she'd used him, that he'd been nothing more than a few months of fun. Never in his wildest dreams had he thought that she'd lied when she told him she didn't want to see him anymore. He'd believed her when she'd said she didn't want him, that he wasn't good enough. If what she was saying now was true—and he found himself believing her whether he wanted to or not—then she'd thrown away what they'd had. It had been real, but she'd walked anyway.

Maybe he shared a little of that blame. Dropping the bucket, he walked the distance that separated them and put a hand on her shoulder. The urge to touch her was too strong to ignore, and a shoulder was nice and impersonal. He hoped she didn't realize how his fingers shook. "I'm sorry for that night...upstairs." He nodded toward the garage and the apartment upstairs, where he'd lived the night she'd come to him and he'd been so careless. He'd never been with a woman without a condom. Never. "I should've been careful, and I'm sorry you had to face the consequences alone."

"It's my fault, too."

He'd gone eight years without touching her. Eight long years without feeling her skin, but everything in him remembered. Everything came alive. Heat and awareness flickered between them. Her eyes widened, and he knew she felt it too. Just like he knew she was remembering what had happened in his bed that night.

Chapter Four

That night had changed everything. "I love you" had come to them so easily afterward. Rachel had mentioned him to her mother, which hadn't gone over at all how she'd imagined. Though looking back now, she could see she'd been stupid to think her mother would understand. She hadn't, and she never would.

But Rachel didn't care anymore. She'd worked hard over the last year to extricate herself from her family, and it had all paid off when she'd moved into her tiny duplex just a few miles away from Sage's garage earlier that week. It was far away from North Atlanta and where she'd grown up. She was closer to Sage now, but it remained to be seen if he wanted anything to do with her.

She ached to touch him, to push his hair back off his forehead and slide her arms around him. Once, those actions would've been automatic to her, but she had no right to touch him now. Despite how many years had passed, it still *felt* like she had that right, which was strange. He wasn't hers to touch and comfort, and God that was so wrong. For the first time, the full impact of the hurt she'd caused both of them set in, threatening to squeeze the air from her lungs.

Dear God, what had she done to them? She fought back tears and swallowed past the lump in her throat. She wouldn't beg him or look weak. If he allowed her a second chance, she'd take it, but if he wanted her gone she'd have to walk away.

"That night..." His eyes hadn't lost any of their intensity as they held hers, though his hand dropped back to his side.

"It was eight years ago today. I remember." She'd always remembered the anniversary of his dad's death. Every year.

"That's why I brought you this." She nodded to the package wrapped in the plain brown paper they used at the store where she'd bought it.

He followed her gaze and hesitated, but he didn't seem angry anymore, or like he was about to tell her to leave. Taking that as encouragement, she picked up the gift and tried handing it to him again. This time he accepted it. He held her gaze with his as he took it, his fingers coming so close to hers that her skin tingled in awareness.

"You didn't have to get me anything," he said, a reluctant smile tugging at the corner of his mouth.

"I saw it and thought of you and wanted you to have it."

He nodded, but he was looking down at the package now as his fingers tore at the tape. As he tugged the paper away, his mouth fell open a little when he saw the box containing the 1/18 die-cast model car. "This is a '67 Shelby. You just happened to see this and think of me?"

She shrugged. "Well, I called around to a few places, and then I went and saw it. Thought of you the entire time."

"I can't take this. It's too much." He shook his head and tried to hand it back to her.

"It's yours. I know your dad used to get them for you, and it'd go well with your collection." He still had some in a large display case in the waiting area of the garage. She'd been relieved that she hadn't seen a '67 Shelby there, though he probably had some at home too, wherever he lived now. He was doing so well, he'd probably moved out of that tiny apartment. She wanted to ask, but it really wasn't any of her business.

"Thanks." He took a couple of steps until he could set the box on the workbench. He didn't say anything else right away, and she couldn't read anything from his expression. When he finally turned back to face her, she stepped away and pressed her hips back against the pristine, unsanded fender near the hood of the car he'd been working on. He stood there watching her, and then crossed his arms over his chest. "Why are you here?" he finally asked.

"Like I said, to explain what happened." She tried not to shift under his scrutiny.

He raised a hand to his chin, his fingertips scraping against the dark stubble there. She couldn't help but remember what it felt like beneath her own fingers, so she clenched her fists together and stuck them behind her back.

"But why? Why now?"

She chewed her bottom lip as she debated just how much to tell him. She didn't want to come off as pathetic, because how else would it sound to someone like him, someone who'd been as independent as he'd been? She was just now, at twenty-six, moving out from under the thumbs of her parents. But she'd decided that honesty was the only way forward, especially with him, when dishonesty had only come between them. She took a deep breath and launched into the shortened version of how she'd gotten brave enough to write a suspense novel after graduating law school. It had landed her a modest publishing deal, and she'd finally stood up to her parents, quit her job, and moved back to Atlanta.

"I hadn't actually thought about calling you. I mean, I've thought about you a lot, but I knew you didn't want to hear from me and that it would be a bad idea. I'd planned to send you a card or something explaining things, but my last day at work I stood up to my mother and it felt good. *Really* good." God, it really had. That weight lifting from her chest after so many years had been unbelievable. She smiled. "I'd kept your number on my phone and decided if I was being bold, that I might as well try it. And you know the rest—here I am."

He was silent for so long that she wasn't sure he would respond. "Why are you here, princess?" he asked again, correctly believing there was more. The words were spoken softly but with such feeling that she caught her breath to stop a gasp from escaping. His stormy blue eyes looked right down into her soul and burned where they touched.

She knew what he was asking. It was now or never.

Steeling herself for rejection, she stepped as close to him as she dared, near enough that she could feel the heat from his body. The scent of grease and sweat shouldn't be so appealing, but because they were a part of him, a part of Sage, she breathed them in, almost savoring them. Her heart fluttered and the muscles deep in her belly clenched in anticipation. "I want to give us another chance, Sage," she said, laying her hand on his forearm.

He hissed in a breath as if she'd physically hurt him. She wasn't sure if it was because of her words or her touch. The sound made her wince, and she closed her eyes because she was too much of a coward to look at him, while her fingers gently squeezed the hard muscle beneath them, craving the feel of him. But the backs of his fingers sliding over the smooth skin of her cheek made her open her eyes again in surprise. His eyes were burning, unsettled, as he looked down into hers. He'd leaned his hips back against the workbench, making the nine-inch height difference between them nearly disappear. Just one push up on her toes and that gap would be gone completely.

"I'm not sure I can," he whispered, but he drew a little closer to her and parted his lips.

His answer wasn't unexpected. She'd broken both of their hearts, and she couldn't expect forgiveness right away. But that sounded a lot like a goodbye. If they said goodbye, they'd go their separate ways and never run into each other again. She could feel her time with him slipping away. Her hand slid up his arm, tightening a little around the hard muscle of his bicep, and she rose up on her toes until his mouth was just a breath away. "Then let's start with a kiss. One kiss, and I promise I'll leave you alone until you decide the time is right...if you decide the time is right."

He made a sound in the back of his throat, half groan, half growl, and closed his mouth over hers. It wasn't soft and tender, but desperate and almost angry. She didn't care. It felt like coming home, and she ached for him so badly that she wanted any piece of him he was willing to share. She opened for him, and his tongue swept into her mouth, stroking against her own. His taste and smell flooded her senses. They were both so achingly familiar, both so needed. She hadn't realized until just this second how deprived of him she'd been, like a single flower in the sands of the Sahara desperate for rain.

And oh was it raining. His arm wrapped around her waist, pulling her up the length of his thigh to get her closer, while his mouth continued to take hers. She'd had boyfriends in college and law school, but none of them had kissed her like this, like they *needed* to kiss her. Like they might die if they didn't taste her. Not one of them. Only Sage had ever been so focused on her. Only Sage had ever known just how to get to her.

She wrapped her arms around his wide shoulders—so much thicker than she remembered—and curled her fingers in the wavy hair at the back of his head. She wasn't sure if she was holding on or trying to get as close to him as possible. Definitely both. Everything inside her had liquefied so that she couldn't stand on her own, and she wanted to feel him against her. If she only got one kiss, she was going to make it count.

Sage pulled back just enough to breathe. All he managed to do was breathe even more of her into him. That expensive shampoo she still used, the sweet mint of her breath, the salt of her skin...all of it combined into a scent that was uniquely hers. And he remembered it. Goddamn how he remembered it. The familiar feel of her in his arms, her scent and taste, brought back a flood of memories he thought he'd locked away for good.

But she'd walked into his garage and busted that lock all to pieces.

He opened his eyes to see her sky-blue ones staring up at him. It was like looking into them eight years ago. He closed his eyes again, but that only made him picture her more clearly. Her face flushed, her eyes wide as she said his name in that soft way she had, and pulled him back into her.

Christ.

He was already hard and straining more against his poor zipper with every heartbeat. He should let her go, but his arm only tightened around her waist, while his fingers tightened on her hip, stubbornly refusing to listen to his brain. She was fuller there than she'd been, soft but firm at the same time. His eyes shot open and he was staring at the thin white cotton of her dress. The small row of buttons that hid her breasts from him. They looked so fragile that he imagined one firm tug would pop them all open. But first he'd feel her from the outside, watch as the grease on his hands dirtied up the white, to mark her in some primal way he didn't even fully understand.

That wasn't right. She'd made it clear she didn't want to be dirtied up by him, that she deserved someone who didn't come home every day with grease under his nails. Whatever he felt about her, she deserved what she wanted.

He made himself look into her eyes again and had to stifle his groan at the look of want in them. At least that hadn't changed. It still only took one spark to ignite them. He couldn't resist touching her one last time. Moving his right hand from the edge of the workbench and shifting his stance wider to balance their weight, he brought his fingertips up to her cheek. Her skin was soft and nearly flawless. She was so beautiful that it damn near hurt him to look at her, to know that she'd been his and wanted to be again. But he couldn't trust her. He couldn't let her in again.

His calloused fingers must scrape her softer skin, but she didn't seem to mind. She leaned into him, his hand cupping her cheek and his thumb moving over her bottom lip as she blinked up at him, her wide eyes so fucking open and bare to him that he felt that wall he'd built up start to crumble.

"Please, Sage," she whispered against his thumb.

He knew what she was asking. More. And he clenched his teeth against the wave of need that poured through him in response. His erection pressed painfully against the zipper, making him shift to alleviate the pressure a little. But then she moved. She left one hand resting at the back of his neck, ready to pull him in for another kiss, while the other trailed down his chest and stomach. His blood roared through his veins and his gaze centered on his thumb pressed against the pretty pink of her lips.

It wasn't a conscious thought. His thumb just pressed a little, making a way for itself as her lips parted for it. Then the tip of his thumb sank into her heat, and she closed around him. His dick pulsed, begging to get to her, to sink into her exactly the same way. He took a breath in between his teeth when her tongue flicked over the tip of his thumb. Before she could do more, he pulled it out, but was fascinated by the trail of wetness his thumb left on her lips and chin as he moved his hand down her neck. His knuckles settled just over the slight rise of her breasts at the low neck of her dress.

"Why, princess?" He kept asking because he needed to know why she was here. Why she wanted him after all these years. Why she hadn't been able to move on.

"Because I love you. I never stopped."

A bolt of sheer pain speared its way through him. He didn't love her. It wasn't possible after all these years, and yet...as they sank in, her words were like a salve to a wound he'd been bandaging with work, racing, and beer. Her hand somehow found its way under his shirt and her palm pressed against his bare stomach. Something inside him pulled to get free, to relish every scrap of affection she was willing to dole out to him. Then she rose up on her toes again, and her soft, warm lips touched his.

The tip of her tongue brushed against his bottom lip, and he was like a drowning man fighting for a life preserver as he turned into it.

His grabbed her hips with both hands and pushed her back against the '65 GTO. His mouth devoured hers as he dragged her up his leg and ground her against his thigh. She gasped against his mouth and pulled at his shirt. He leaned back just far enough to grab the bottom with one hand and bring the T-shirt up over his head, tossing it away. He didn't miss how she stared at him in appreciation, and he couldn't help the swell of pride along with the swell of blood that went right to his cock.

He kissed her again as his hand did what it had wanted to do for a while now, touch her breast. When his thumb brushed over her nipple through the cotton of her dress and bra, she moaned. It was low, soft, and feminine, and it did things to him. She'd definitely filled out there, the soft flesh just filling his hand. Short of breath, he broke the kiss and bent her back over the hood of the car to bury his face in her neck, seeking out the sweet skin he knew he'd find there. His teeth scraped her ear, and she arched her hips into him as both of his hands went to those fragile buttons. He'd been right. One good tug and the dress popped open all the way down to her navel.

He couldn't resist rising enough to take in the beautiful sight of her body. She was all lightly tanned skin and toned muscle. Because he was lost and knew there was no turning back, he pulled the lace of her bra down until her nipples were free and tucked the fabric beneath her breasts. They sat there like an offering, pushed up above the bra. He groaned as he sucked one pink nipple deep into his mouth. He'd never get enough of her.

It was full night outside now, and with the light coming from overhead, anyone could look inside and tell what they were doing, and he'd still let this go too far. The front of the garage didn't face the street. But he didn't want anyone else to see her, and after he'd tasted her other nipple, he jerked away and walked over to the roll-up door. He couldn't look away from her, though, and she watched him. Her hands were pressed to the candy-apple red hood of the car beneath her. She didn't make a move to cover herself. Blindly, he reached over and pressed the button that made the door slowly begin to roll closed before going back to her.

As he walked back to her, she shrugged out of the dress so it fell around her waist, caught between the car and her hips. Gently, almost reverently, he ran his hands up the smooth skin of her stomach to cup her breasts. He dragged his gaze away from the perfect mounds to watch her face as he moved his thumbs over her nipples. She caught her breath and her eyes half closed. He let his right hand fall down past her stomach and over her hip to her thigh, dragging the skirt of her dress up so he could touch her.

Sage knew he'd find her wet, but he needed to feel it for himself. She gasped as his fingers found the thin cotton and lace of her panties at the juncture of her thighs. She'd already soaked through them. Shoving his knee between her thighs, he forced them wider and pressed two fingers against her clit, rubbing her through the wet fabric. She closed her eyes and grabbed on to his shoulders, pulling him closer.

He couldn't wait any longer to really touch her, and slipped his fingers beneath the cotton, stroking the delicate flesh of her pussy. She was so wet and swollen that she coated him. "Ah, princess," he whispered, and moved his other hand to her back to hold her close. His head dipped to hers and he placed a kiss on her temple as he closed his eyes to keep a handle on his control so he wouldn't take her right now. Instead, he circled her entrance a few times with his fingertips, until her hips started to move against him, before pushing his fingers inside her.

She moaned and clenched him hard, so hard he had to fight not to come in his jeans as he imagined it was his cock she gripped so tight. He didn't know which one of them he was trying to drive crazy, but something in him made him go slow when all he wanted was to go fast. Maybe it was that he wanted to savor every second of her, because it would probably be for the last time.

It didn't matter what he wanted, because she had other ideas. He knew what they were when she cupped him through his jeans and squeezed. "Now, Sage." Her hot breath tickled his ear, and he couldn't hold back anymore. He was lost to her. As he fumbled in his pocket for his wallet and retrieved the condom, she unbuckled his belt and then his button and zipper. Before he realized it, her hand was inside his boxer briefs and her fingers were wrapping around him. He closed his eyes and wavered on his feet for a second before tossing his wallet to the ground and ripping the foil of the condom open with his teeth.

She pushed his jeans down past his hips, and he sprang free. He fucking loved the look on her face as she took him in, her eyes practically glowing with lust and appreciation. But when she started to kneel at his feet, he stopped her. As much as he loved the memory of her mouth on him, he wanted her, *needed* to be in her when he came. *Needed* to feel her come around him, with him.

"I need to be inside you."

Her eyes darted to him, burning with a need that matched his own. "Yes." He couldn't look away from them as he rolled the condom on and grabbed her hips to pull her against him. Hands under her thighs, he picked her up and adjusted her on the car before settling between them. He'd forgotten about her panties, and in a moment of sheer frustration that something was keeping her from him, he tore at them, hearing a rip at the side where the delicate lace had held them together. And then there was nothing between them, and he slid into her. Just the head, until she lifted her hips for more and he pushed in all the way. They both groaned as he slid home.

He leaned her back until she was lying on the hood. Holding himself up over her with one hand, he couldn't look away from the sight of her. She was sweet and beautiful and all the things that were too good to be true in the world, but she'd broken them. He didn't know if he could give her free rein on his heart again, but he could give her this. He could give them this.

He pulled out almost completely then pushed back into her tight heat and savored her gasp. She felt amazing around him. Fucking perfect. "Sage." His name came out on a moan, and he remembered how it sounded when she called it out as she came, his cock buried deep within her. He groaned and clenched his teeth as a drop of come seeped out the tip of his shaft, pressure coiling at the base, his balls already tingling with the need to come. Not yet.

His arm went around her hips, dragging her onto him while he pounded into her. Her small breasts bounced with each thrust, and he couldn't decide which sight was more beautiful. Those perfect breasts or her face, flushed with arousal. Her fingernails bit into his hips, and he knew she was close, the pain mercifully taking the edge off his pleasure as he fucked her. But the tide quickly turned, and as she met his thrusts, the pressure began to build at the base of his spine and the pain of her nails only spurred him on.

His whole world narrowed to Rachel beneath him. Her scent, her sounds, her tight, wet heat clenching him, and he couldn't hold himself back anymore. He fell over her, needing to feel every inch of her skin against his. He grabbed a handful of her blond hair and held her still as moved in her, but she loved it. She loved him. She whispered it against his neck, and then shouted it when her body trembled, clenching tight around him. Throwing her head back, she cried out his name. He gave up the fight to hold back and buried himself inside her one last time. Coming with a groan wrenched from deep within him, he held her tight as he poured himself into her.

Chapter Five

They stayed still for a long time, waiting for their heartbeats to return to normal. Sage was still connected to her, and he couldn't help but savor that for a little longer. Her hands moved over his shoulders and held him tighter. He closed his eyes and allowed the peace that came along with that to settle within him. It had always been like this with her. So peaceful when it was over.

Finally, when his breathing slowed, he rose up enough to look down at her. A bead of sweat trailed down his brow, and she ran her thumb along its path. He had to fight himself not to turn and kiss her palm. It seemed like such an easy, natural thing to do, to kiss her, to stroke her.

The one kiss she'd asked for had gotten out of hand. The way he was feeling now, he'd be ready for round two in a couple of minutes. He tried to regret not stopping when he'd known he should've, but he couldn't find regret anywhere. There were a lot of other emotions tumbling around inside him, but that wasn't one of them. Right now, he was wondering how it could still be so good between them. He'd had other women since Rachel. Hell, after she'd walked away he'd tried to drown himself in women and work, but he hadn't found anything like what they'd had together.

"Rachel." He figured he must look as confused as he felt.

She smiled. "Sage."

They stayed that way, breaths mingling as they stared, both of them stunned by what had happened. Finally, he knew he had to say something, so he rose up and tried to tell her how he hadn't meant for that to happen. "I'm—"

"Don't say you're sorry." She gave him another hesitant smile and pushed his hair back off his forehead. "We both wanted it. We're adults. It's okay. But don't regret it."

He nodded and pulled away from her finally. Taking care of the condom, he tossed it into the trash and adjusted his jeans. He tried not to watch her as she sat up on the edge of the hood and closed the top of her dress, but she was so damn sexy sitting there that he had trouble looking away. Her hair was a mess and her face was still flushed. He couldn't help but feel a swell of satisfaction that he'd done that to her.

The truth was he didn't know what to say to her. He wanted to walk over and pull her into his arms, to feel her body relax into him. Fuck, he *wanted* to take her home and do it all over again in his bed. But he wouldn't. Not now. Maybe not ever. He couldn't go through the hell she'd put him in all over again.

When he turned back to her, his eyes practically devoured her as he reached out and helped her to the ground. "I don't..." He ran a hand down her arm when he let go of her and gave a short, humorless laugh at his own awkwardness. "I don't know where we go from here."

She wasn't awkward at all as she reached over to touch his hand. Just that one touch made his knees tremble and all the blood in his body head south again. "I understand if you need time."

"Yeah." He nodded and put his hands in his pockets. It was the only way he could make sure he wouldn't touch her again. "I'm gonna need some time."

She nodded and dipped her head, so he couldn't see her expression. He didn't want to hurt her, but he needed her to go so he could start thinking straight again. Following her to the door at the front, he reached past her to unlock the deadbolt and open the door for her. "Thanks for the model," he said when she stopped next to him. "And for remembering."

His breath caught when she touched his bare chest. It wasn't much, a light touch, but enough to set his heart racing again. "Bye, Sage." She leaned up and pressed a kiss on his cheek, and then she was gone, walking across the lot to a car parked under the ring of light cast off by the streetlight. He wasn't sure what he'd expected. A Beamer, maybe, like her old one, or some other luxury car. He hadn't expected a redesigned Dodge Challenger.

"Nice car," he called just loud enough for her to hear over the light traffic going by.

She turned and gave him a playful smile. "Thanks. It was a present for graduating law school."

"Your parents bought you that?"

"No." Shaking her head, she pushed her hair back over her shoulder, and he was caught by the subtle, feminine gesture. Christ, he'd missed her. "My dad bought me another BMW, but I traded it in. He wasn't happy."

He was dumbstruck by that. Maybe she was figuring out who she was.

"You'll have to come ride with me sometime," she said, and continued walking toward her car.

He was smiling as he watched her go, his gaze on her ass until she disappeared around her car. He waited until she'd driven out onto the street before he closed the door and leaned against it, his legs too weak to hold him up anymore.

Fucking Rachel Cambridge.

Sage leaned over the table, lining up his shot. Holding the cue lightly in his hand, he pulled back and aimed for the cue ball. It hit the eightball with a satisfying whack that sent the white one flying off into the corner pocket. Dammit. He'd scratched on the last shot. Something he never did. His friend, Shawn, gave a whoop of victory and started giving high fives to the group.

"Dude, what the fuck was that?" Rob laughed from where he stood with his arm draped across his wife's shoulder.

Sage shook his head and put his cue back in its slot on the wall before taking out his wallet. He withdrew a twenty and slapped it on the green felt of the table with a smile. "Don't get used to winning. I'll still kick your ass on the track next week."

"Hey, don't forget my beer. The bet was twenty dollars and a beer," Shawn said as he picked up the twenty and held it up to more cheers. Shawn raced his own car on the circuit and had started coming to Sage a few years ago for upgrades. They'd been ragging each other ever since. It was Friday night and there wasn't a race tomorrow, so they'd all come to the bar after work.

"Yeah, yeah." Sage threw up his hand and accepted the backslaps as he made his way to the bar in the front. Shawn couldn't play pool for shit, so Sage would be hearing about this one for a while. His concentration had been shot to hell all week, ever since he'd seen Rachel.

He ran a hand over his hair as he passed through the wide hallway that connected the room in the back to the bar in the front of the old converted mill. Posters of metal bands and beer signs covered the exposed brick walls. The music was louder up front, because a band had set up in the corner and the female lead was singing "Rebel Yell" by Billy Idol.

Rachel had been on his mind almost constantly. He couldn't believe that he'd held her, been inside her. Just the thought made his dick pulse, and he gritted his teeth as he fought for self-control. He still hadn't forgiven her for leaving, but that hadn't stopped him reliving those minutes in the garage with her all week. How fucking sweet she was, and how he drowned looking into her pretty blue eyes.

It was a little slow for a Friday night, so he managed to get one of the last stools at the bar. The pretty brunette tending bar was pouring a whiskey, but she smiled and caught his eye when she saw him. "Hey, haven't seen you around lately."

"Hey, Shay." She'd started working here a couple months ago, and they'd flirted some. She'd even mentioned she wasn't seeing anyone the last time they'd talked. She was pretty, tall and slender, with legs that had made him imagine them wrapped around him more than once. Tonight he looked at her and felt...empty.

Giving him a wink, she walked away to deliver the drink but came back soon and leaned forward on the bar. "How you doing tonight?" The arms and neck of her T-shirt had been strategically torn away, leaving a tear between her breasts that revealed a generous amount of olive skin. She was gorgeous and giving off all kinds of signals that she wouldn't turn him down. He should ask her to go home with him and spend the rest of the night forgetting Rachel. The only problem was that she wasn't Rachel.

Fuck.

Scrubbing his hand over his face, he asked, "Can I get two IPAs?"

"Two?" She raised a brow and reached into the fridge under the bar for two bottles.

"Lost a bet." He grinned, scratching at the stubble around his mouth, remembering he hadn't shaved in a couple days.

Shay laughed and opened each bottle before setting them in front of him. She opened her mouth to probably ask about the bet, but Rob took the stool beside him.

"Can I have one of those, Shay?" he asked.

"Sure thing." She grabbed another and set it down, but a customer down the bar drew her attention and pulled her away.

"So what's going on with you?" Rob asked, spinning the bottle in a slow circle between his fingers, his gaze on the label.

"What do you mean?" Sage took a long pull of his beer and set it down.

"You lost to Shawn. That asshole can barely tell the difference between stripes and solids."

Sage shrugged and held the bottle to his mouth again. "He's not that bad."

"This got to do with Rachel Cambridge?"

Sage choked on his beer, chest heaving as he tried to force air back into his lungs. "What?"

Rob gave a grin and shrugged. "The guys told me a pretty blonde came by to see you last weekend. And then there was that 'wrong number' a couple weeks back. I took a guess."

Well, shit, this was exactly what Sage didn't want to happen. If he didn't have to talk about her, he could keep her his secret and not deal with the complications she'd bring. Coughing once more, he set down his beer and rubbed his palms on his jeans. "It's none of your business."

"No." Rob didn't seem too offended. "But you've been distracted this week. What did she want?"

He started to tell him it was none of his business again, but not talking about her hadn't helped her go away. Fuck it. "She apologized...for leaving the way she did, saying the things she'd said."

Rob took a deep breath and let it out in a slow hiss before taking another drink of his beer. "That was harsh...the way she left. She tell you why?"

Sage nodded, running his finger along one of the water rings left by the bottle on bar. He couldn't stop hearing her tell him why.

Some stupid part of me wanted to have your baby, so I wouldn't have a reason not to be with you anymore.

What if it had been real? What if she'd had his baby and they'd spent all these years together? He liked the idea of having kids with her. Shit. He didn't know a damn thing about her now. He knew the Rachel he'd loved, but that didn't mean she was the same. She might've changed. It didn't seem like she'd changed much, though. She'd felt the same, looked at him the same, touched him the same. He scrubbed another hand over his face to block out the memory.

"She did. Part of me understands." He did understand. She'd scared him too. What they'd had had been out of control. Too much, too fast. "But part of me can't forget." That was the thing. He didn't know how big that part was.

"Maybe you don't have to forget, but the past is the past. It doesn't matter now. You've moved on."

Sage stared at his hands on the bar. He hadn't moved on at all. That ache for her was there, still thumping around in his chest.

Rob didn't say anything else for a minute, but after he took another pull on his beer, he said, "Or maybe you could just talk to her, see what happens."

Sage nodded, and Rob got to his feet. "Shawn's getting antsy for his beer," he said, and picked up the one Sage had bought for their friend. "Better take it to him." Then he walked away to the pool tables in back.

Sage picked up his beer again and downed it all. Shay had made her way over by that point. "Need another?"

"No, thanks." He took out his wallet to grab enough money for the three beers.

She took the empty bottle away and wiped down the bar in front of him. "You seem sad. You okay?"

Shaking his head, he gave her a half-smile. "I don't know." Hell, he didn't know if he'd ever be okay again.

She tugged her bottom lip with her teeth and gave him a shy smile. "You could come over later...if you want. We could talk about it."

His hand paused in placing the bills on the bar. She was fucking gorgeous with her doe eyes and her breasts practically falling out of her top. Before Rachel, he might've said yes. But now...fuck, she just wasn't Rachel. She wasn't who he wanted. "Thanks, Shay. I appreciate it, but I can't."

"Oh." Her face fell, but then she smiled. "So it's girl trouble, then?"

"Yeah."

She nodded and picked up his money. "I hope she knows how lucky she is."

Sage gave a token laugh, and walked back to say goodbye. He didn't feel like being out anymore. He'd managed not to look Rachel up online all week, but he wanted to know more about her. And maybe Rob was right. Maybe he didn't have to forget everything. Maybe they could just talk and see what happened.

Chapter Six

Moving back to Atlanta had been easier than she'd thought it would be. She'd spent most of the past two weeks setting up the extra bedroom in her duplex as an office. Her mom hadn't called to check in, which wasn't unexpected. Rachel knew she'd have to be the first one to offer an olive branch, but she wasn't ready yet. Her dad had come by her new place, though, and brought her a stack of files. He'd offered her part-time freelance work. It was his way of looking out for her, and while she appreciated the gesture, she hoped she'd be able to focus on her third book, which was due in six months. However, it was nice to know she had a backup source of income if she needed it.

She'd reconnected with some of her old friends, but with the exception of Kelsey, she didn't think they'd be hanging out very much. She wasn't like them. She didn't want all the things that they wanted. For the first time in her life, that was okay with her.

The only thing she wanted right now was Sage. But it had been two weeks since she'd seen him at his garage, and he hadn't called. She'd done her best to forget, but it was impossible to forget him and how well they worked together. So she'd settled on not thinking about him too often. It mostly worked.

It wasn't working as she said goodbye to the librarian and the small group of readers who'd stayed late after her reading at the library. There hadn't been a large crowd, but it had been a respectable showing as she'd read passages from her first book and answered questions. A part of her had hoped to see him there, but she knew it was stupid. He didn't even know about the reading or her book.

Still. She couldn't help the feeling of melancholy that came over her as she walked down the stone steps outside the library in Midtown. It was early evening, and the sun had long been blocked by the tall buildings around them, but the air was still humid and heavy.

"Hey, princess." The deep voice with the light drawl came from just ahead. She looked up to see Sage leaning there against the railing at the bottom of the steps. Wearing jeans and a button-up with the sleeves rolled up over his forearms, he looked so good her stomach gave a little flip. "Would you sign my book?" Smiling, he held up a copy of her paperback.

She laughed. "You did not buy my book."

"Read it, too."

Coming to a stop on the wide step just above the ground, she pressed a hand to her belly as she tried to make herself believe this didn't mean what she wanted so badly for it to mean. When she'd walked out of his garage she'd been convinced that that would be the last she'd see of him.

"I did," he said when he saw the disbelief that must have been on her face. "You're a great writer, and I really enjoyed it. You were smart to base it on your days in law school. I could see a lot of you in the main character. And I didn't guess who the killer was. Total surprise."

"Thanks." She felt herself blush, though she didn't quite know why. It was something she'd heard before from others. Maybe it was just that it was him, and having Sage read the words that had been pulled from deep within her was a little more intimate than she'd realized.

"You're a good speaker, too. It sounded like one of the books my mom listens to when you read from it."

Her heart stopped beating for a full second. "You were inside? In the library?"

He nodded. "I hid out in the stacks. I didn't want to interfere."

She couldn't believe he'd come. He was standing right in front of her, and she still couldn't believe he was there. She knew she should say something, but her mind was racing too fast.

He shifted a bit from one foot to the other, clearly a little nervous. "Are you busy right now? Come have a beer with me?" He looked so hopeful that there was no way she was saying no.

"Sure, okay." About a million questions churned through her brain as he led her to a pub just two doors down on the corner. It had patio seating and a long bar that stretched the length of the restaurant.

His hand pressed against her lower back, and he answered one of the most pressing questions. "I'm sorry it's taken me so long."

She nodded, and he didn't continue right away as he opened the door for her and followed her to two stools at the bar. They each ordered Sweetwater 420 on draft, and she waited for the bartender to leave them before even daring to look at him. He was watching her, his eyes softer, easier than when she'd left him, and her heart fluttered in response.

"I've been thinking a lot about what you said. Leaving your job and your parents the way you did." His throat moved as he swallowed before he picked up his glass and took a drink.

She wasn't entirely sure which way this conversation was headed. This was Sage; with the exception of hanging up on her, he'd always been fair with her. If he didn't want to see her again, she wouldn't put it past him to show up and tell her that in person. He wouldn't take the easy way out like she had. He didn't say anything for so long that nerves made her say what she knew he was thinking. "I know. It's pathetic it's taken me this long. Most people do that in college. Not at twenty-six."

"It's not pathetic. It's brave."

She forced a laugh. "Oh, it is. It's fine. I'm just happy that I'm free now."

"It's not pathetic. It took courage to stand up to them, to walk away from the pressure and demands. Not everyone could've done that. Some people live their whole lives like that."

This was why she'd loved him. He'd always made her feel good about herself, even when she probably didn't deserve it. Being with him was always so easy. "Not you, though. You've taken what you wanted."

He gave her a tiny hint of a smile that made her stomach flip over. "I got lucky, princess. My dad wanted me to take over the garage, and it just so happens that's where I belong."

"But you've done so well. You've expanded the garage and you have your racing."

He nodded. "Only because of my parents. I fit here. Your sister's life wasn't a good fit for you. Maybe your parents weren't a good fit. But I'm really glad you've found your place now. Give it a few years and I bet you surprise yourself."

She bit her lip, trying not to let the gigantic smile she was holding back stretch across her face, because he hadn't said the words yet. But the words he *had* said were so good, more than she deserved. "How are your mom and your brother and sister?"

"Good. Mom helps out in the office a couple of days a week. Cole graduated with a degree in engineering, and Isla graduates next year. Journalism. She wants to move to New York."

"Sounds like they've turned out well, and a lot of that is because of you." He'd sacrificed hope of further education for himself by working nonstop at the garage to keep it going so they could go to college. She couldn't help but think back to that night she'd called him, how she'd said she couldn't see herself with someone who wasn't going to college. What an idiot. "I'm sorry if I made that harder for you in any way. I was so stu—"

"You don't have to apologize anymore."

"I do. I just can't stress enough how much I didn't mean that—"

"Hey." He grabbed her hand and laced his fingers with hers on her lap. "I know. I've been thinking about it a lot, and I know you didn't. It's in the past. We can't change what happened."

"I know, but I did an awful thing. You were so perfect, and I made you feel like you were nothing. I'm sorry."

He smiled and turned to face her fully, his free hand moving up to touch her cheek. "We were young. Despite what happened, we never stopped caring. There's still something between us. Now let's start from here."

She stared up at him, heart pounding in her chest. "Where do we go from here?"

His thumb stroked across her skin. "I thought we'd start with getting a table and talking more about your book. I'd love to hear your inspiration for it and the other books you have planned. Maybe afterward you can come by my house and see the projects I'm working on."

"You bought a house?"

"Yeah, a craftsman just a few streets over from the garage. It needed a little work. My cousin Adam's a carpenter. He came down from Boston and helped get me started."

He'd talked about his cousins a lot back when they'd dated. She'd always loved his stories, and been a little envious of his close family. "I'd love to see your house." His smile widened, an easy smile that warmed her from the inside out. It was difficult to believe that he could be hers again. "And have dinner with you."

His gaze stroked her face before he leaned forward a little at the time, giving her time to move away, until finally his lips touched hers. It was a gentle kiss, just a brushing of lips, but everything inside her came alive just the same. She reached up and cupped his jaw, relishing the solid feel of him beneath her palm. She was never giving him up again.

"I missed you, princess."

ABOUT THE AUTHOR

Harper St. George was raised in the rural backwoods of Alabama and along the tranquil coast of northwest Florida. It was a setting filled with stories of the old days that instilled in her a love of history, romance, and adventure. By high school, she had discovered the historical romance novel which combined all of those elements into one perfect package. She has been hooked ever since.

She lives in Florida with her husband and two young children. When not writing, she can be found devouring her husband's amazing cooking and reading. She would love to hear from you. You can connect with her online at harperstgeorge.com.

Also by Harper:

His Abductor's Desire

Her Forbidden Gunslinger

Enslaved by the Viking (Viking Warriors #1)

One Night with the Viking (Viking Warriors #2)

The Innocent and the Outlaw (sneak peek in the back of this book!)

Nailed

by Tara Wyatt

Chapter One

"You did what?" Adam Hennessy pushed a hand through his hair, his grip tightening on his phone. The late August sun beat down on him, and he wiped at his sweaty brow with the back of his hand. He toyed with the hammer in his tool belt, waiting for Jared to explain himself.

"I backed my Jeep into my neighbor's backyard. Took out her fence and her deck."

"How the hell did you do that?"

"I was backing into my driveway, and I hit the gas instead of the brake. I panicked, and instead of taking my foot off the gas, I just, I dunno, I kept going, and I swerved to avoid my house. Went straight into her yard."

Adam blew out a slow breath, shaking his head. "Jesus Christ. I love you, man, but you're a fuckin' terrible driver, you know that?"

"Thanks, asshole."

Cradling the phone between his ear and his shoulder, Adam reached into his cooler for a bottle of water. He'd been working for hours now, sweating through his T-shirt. "But you're okay?"

"Yeah. Neighbor lady just about took my nuts off, though."

Adam snorted, twisting the cap off his water bottle and taking a long pull before answering. "You drove right into her yard. What did you expect? A welcoming committee and a fuckin' parade?"

Adam smiled at his own smartassed joke, but Jared didn't laugh. "Hennessy, seriously. This chick's scary. She tore a strip off me and threw a pot of flowers at my head. She was flipping out, man. Wicked gross mental fit."

Adam laughed, shaking his head at his friend, knowing full well that Jared was laying it on thick. He'd known him for almost thirty years—they'd become fast friends on the first day of kindergarten—and Jared was a lot of things. Loyal. Hardworking. A good friend. A bit of an asshole. And a chronic exaggerator. "Can't say I blame her."

Jared paused before continuing. "So, listen. Don't get mad."

Adam tensed, the muscles in his shoulders stiffening as he paused, the water bottle halfway to his mouth. "Christ, there's more?"

"She was yelling at me and throwing shit, and I...I promised her you'd fix it."

Adam sighed heavily, tilting his head back and closing his eyes against the sun beating down from directly above him. He scuffed the tip of his steel-toed work boot against a two-by-four lying on the ground in front of him beside his open tool chest. "Let me get this straight. You promised the dragon lady I'd fix the fence and deck that *you* drove through." His voice was flat, irritation rolling through him.

"She was gonna kill me. I had no choice. I panicked."

"Yeah, I'm sensing a theme here." He rubbed the cool plastic exterior of the water bottle across his forehead, drops trickling down over his sweaty face. As much as he loved his job—building things, making something from raw pieces, bringing it together in a perfect meld of functionality and beauty—he couldn't wait to pack it in for the day. A shower, a cold beer, and his couch were all calling his name.

In his empty house. Where all he had to eat were takeout leftovers.

"So you'll do it?" Jared asked.

"I'm booked solid right now, man. I can't. Besides, I don't do pro bono work. I'm not a fuckin' lawyer."

"Yeah, no. I understand. It's not like I let you crash with me when your ex-wife kicked you out last year or nothin'."

Well, shit.

The leaves of the maple tree in his client's Back Bay yard rustled softly above him, the breeze drying the thin layer of sweat clinging to his skin. It was so damn muggy out that he might as well have been swimming in the ocean. He pulled at his sweat-darkened blue T-shirt, emblazoned with his "Hennessy Carpentry" logo, fanning the cotton away from his skin, just trying to move the air. He stared at the intricate lattice he'd assembled that adorned the top of the red cedar tongue-and-groove fence he'd spent the past three days putting up.

Goddammit, he did owe Jared a favor—a big one—for the way he'd let Adam stay with him after his marriage had gone down in flames over a year ago.

"Adam? You there?"

"Yeah, I'm here. I'll swing by her place tomorrow, see what I can do. Text me the address."

"Thanks, man. I really appreciate it. Oh, and Hennessy?"

"Yeah?" Adam took another sip from his water bottle before dumping the rest over the back of his head and down his neck.

"You might want to wear a cup."

Charlie Grant stared at her computer screen, her fingers poised over the keyboard as the cursor blinked back at her expectantly. Dust motes swirled idly around her in the morning sun streaming in through the window above her desk. The sunlight bathed the room in a warm, cozy glow, the cheeriness of the morning totally out of sync with her current mood. She pulled her hands away from the keyboard and chewed on a thumbnail, fighting the urge to open her web browser. If she did, she'd go straight to Facebook, and then Twitter, and then ESPN.com, checking out last night's scores instead of working on her column. Which was due tomorrow. And she had...five words so far.

She flipped through her coffee-ringed notebook, staring at the notes she'd taken during the last Red Sox game, wondering if she was on the wrong track with this week's column. She'd planned on doing a profile of Dave Rossum, the Sox's star relief pitcher, but it wasn't coming together. Although she had lots of notes, all of her ideas felt flat. Uninspired and uninteresting. She rolled her neck, trying to work out some of the tension gathered in her muscles. Her chest tightened, and she knew it was anxiety. Pressure.

She'd taken over the *Boston Globe*'s weekly Red Sox column at the start of the season four months ago, and each column needed to be better than the last. Even though it was the twenty-first century, and gender equality blah blah blah, the truth was that women still weren't entirely welcome in sports journalism, especially not twenty-eight-year-olds with limited experience. So, with each column, Charlie felt the need to prove herself. To shut them all up with how well written and insightful it was. To show them that her gender and age didn't matter. Each column was a step forward in her career, a building block for the future she envisioned for herself.

Taking a deep breath, she shook out her hands, knocking over a stack of papers and magazines and an empty beer bottle from her cluttered desk. She rolled her chair back to retrieve the spilled items, the wheels crunching over the chip crumbs she'd spilled the other day and hadn't cleaned up.

Charlie could do lots of things. Was good at lots of things. She could write. She could run for three or four miles and barely break a sweat. She was kind to dogs and children. She could sing, better than most. She could teach her mother how to use a smartphone. She was amazing at catching food in her mouth.

So with all of those skills, who needed to be domestic? She didn't have time for that other stuff—cooking, cleaning, organizing, whatever the hell it was people did on Pinterest. And by not having time, Charlie meant she couldn't give less of a shit.

"Pfft. Pinterest," she said, righting the beer bottle and putting it back exactly where it had been perched on her desk. A few months ago, one of the editors—a penis-having editor, of course—at the *Globe* had suggested she "branch out" and write a "women's interest" piece on social media trends, including Pinterest. Within minutes, Charlie had been knee-deep in articles on how to have a perfectly organized pantry, and she'd told the editor that she'd be sticking to sports, thanks.

A perfectly organized pantry. Seriously. Charlie could think of about six hundred things she'd rather be doing with her spare time besides alphabetizing spice jars. Like having sex. Watching baseball. Hiking. Sleeping. Making friends with the hobos who lived at the dump.

She hadn't done a master's in journalism at Northwestern to write about things she wasn't passionate about. She'd always known she wanted to be a sports journalist, chronicling the glorious highs and the heartbreaking lows of her favorite athletes. She loved writing about a game, or an athlete, or a team, and finding the narrative hook that would take the story from mere reporting to a memorable, emotional, and compelling tale. Connecting fans with their heroes through words on a page.

It was alchemy, doing that, and on the days when it came together, it was beautiful.

Today was not one of those days.

"Uggggggghhhhhhhh." She tapped her forehead against the edge of her desk as her brain ran away down a procrastination rabbit hole. Sitting up, she rolled her chair back toward the desk, more chips crunching as she went. She contemplated digging the vacuum out, and that was when she knew she was well and truly stuck on what to write.

Her doorbell rang, echoing through the quiet house, and she frowned, not expecting any visitors. She rubbed a hand over her makeup-free face and tightened her messy ponytail before pushing out of her chair. As she walked down the stairs to the main level of her grandfather's old house, she adjusted her faded blue T-shirt, trying to smooth out the wrinkles. At least it was clean, despite the fact that she'd pulled it from the pile of dirty laundry littering her bedroom floor. Crossing the last few feet to the front door, she hastily retied the drawstring holding up her black-and-gold Boston Bruins flannel pants.

Pressing up onto her toes, she peered through the peephole and stilled, not quite able to believe who was standing on her front porch. Her heart pushed up into her throat as her fingers curled against the oak door, her nails scratching helplessly against the wood. She swallowed, her pulse hammering in her temples, and watched as the asshole on her front porch rang her doorbell for a second time. How the hell had he gotten her address?

He raised his fist to knock, and she flung the door open, not wanting to feel the rap of his fist against the wood. He froze, his big hand still in the air, and as he stared at her, it dropped slowly to his side. If you'd asked her six months ago, this wasn't at all how Charlie would've predicted her first face-to-face meeting with her online crush would go. Not. At. All.

She leaned against the doorjamb and crossed her arms in front of her. Her heart beat against her ribs, hurt and anger warming her skin. "Adam Hennessy. So. You *are* alive."

He stared at her, his mouth agape. "Charlie?" His eyes raked over her body, and she hugged herself a little tighter. For a second, she wished she were wearing something other than a worn T-shirt and flannel pants, and then she hated herself a tiny bit for feeling that way. He didn't deserve *anything* from her. He deserved nothing, which was exactly what he'd given her.

"What the hell are you doing here?" she asked, meeting his gaze. His light blue eyes held hers, and he rubbed a hand over his mouth. The pads of his fingers rasped against his closely cropped light brown beard, the soft bristling sound prickling over her. He looked even better in person than in the photos from his profile. He was taller—at least six foot one, seeing as he had a good half a foot on her—and broader than she'd expected, with mouthwateringly sculpted arms and huge, strong hands. He ran one of those hands through his short, light brown hair, leaving it slightly disheveled. His white T-shirt stretched across his chest as he moved, the muscles bunching and flexing beneath the cotton. The breeze shifted, and she caught the faint scent of clean laundry and sporty aftershave. Her stomach did a slow turn, flopping over on itself, and she hugged herself tighter.

Silence stretched between them for several moments, broken only by the rustling leaves of the maple tree in her front yard and the birds chattering merrily from somewhere nearby. A horn blared in the distance, several streets over, and all she could do was stare. For once in her life, words were failing her. She didn't know if she wanted to laugh, or cry, or slap him, or just keep staring. Why the hell did he have to look so good? She clamped her teeth together, her chest burning as the wave of humiliation and hurt came crashing back over her.

Six months ago, she'd foolishly thought they'd had a connection. Thought she'd found someone kind and smart and funny. She'd thought that maybe, just maybe, she'd found the person who could help her put the shredded pieces of her heart back together.

But he'd proven her wrong.

It had been several months since Jeff had left everything she had to give—her heart, her confidence, her trust—battered and broken, and she'd decided that it was time to move on. That she wouldn't let that heartbreak dictate the rest of her life. So she'd joined OkCupid, and while she'd found her share of losers on the site, Adam had seemed different. He hadn't immediately asked her to send him topless pics, or if she liked anal, or sent her a dick pic, so right from the start, he'd been miles ahead of ninety percent of the other guys who'd messaged her.

Six months later, she still remembered his opening volley. He'd said, "Hey. So, I have nothing clever to say. Awkward, right? I just wanted to message you because you seem cute and fun and cool. I also question what the fuck is wrong with our society that someone like you has to be on this site, but I'm on here too, so... Yeah. I'm terrible at this. Hi."

They'd messaged back and forth for weeks, getting to know each other, talking about anything and everything, and God, she'd liked him so much. He'd seemed too good to be true: gorgeous, and funny, and smart, and sweet. Finally, after hundreds and hundreds of messages, he'd asked her to meet him for coffee at Fiore's Bakery, and she'd agreed.

Her skin prickled as she remembered sitting in Fiore's Bakery by herself for an hour, watching the sky darken from purple dusk to velvety winter darkness. Waiting. Willing to give him the benefit of the doubt. But he hadn't shown. He'd stood her up, and she'd left, walking home alone in the cold, the wind whipping at her hair and stinging her cheeks.

She'd messaged him as soon as she'd gotten home, even though she felt like a fool for letting history repeat itself. Once again, she'd put herself out there, had let herself feel things, had let herself believe that a seemingly great guy would be into her, only to come crashing back down to reality.

At least he hadn't waited until they were engaged to reject her, though. He did have that going for him over Jeff.

He'd never responded to her "what the hell, dude?" message, and his profile had disappeared from the site. He'd ghosted; she'd never heard from him again. She'd deleted her own profile from the site after that. Now, here he stood, six months later, on her front porch. Staring at her. Looking ridiculously hot in his stupid white T-shirt and stupid jeans. With his stupidly sexy face.

Finally, after several long moments, he answered her question. "I'm here to look at your deck and fence. I'm a friend of Jared's—

your neighbor—and he asked me to come by. He feels terrible about what happened."

And what about you? Do you *feel terrible?* The words bounced around her skull, but she held them in, trying to convince herself that his answer wouldn't matter, because she didn't care.

"Why am I not surprised you're friends with that asshat?"

"I'm just here to help." He watched her warily. Her eyes dipped down over his body, taking in the small "Hennessy Carpentry" logo over his left pec. A very well-developed pec. The fact that she was ogling his chest made her angrier, both at him and at herself, and she ground her teeth together, tension radiating through her jaw.

"I don't want your help. I don't want anything to do with you."

He closed his eyes for a second and sighed, his arms limp at his sides. "Charlie, I...I'm really sorry. I owe you an explanation."

A wave of hurt crashed into her, stealing her breath, and she channeled that hurt into anger. "I don't want your explanation, or your apology. Get the hell off my porch." She spun on her heel and slammed her door in his face.

Chapter Two

Adam sat in his truck, staring at Charlie's house. It was a lovely, if somewhat worn, twentieth-century colonial revival with sky-blue siding, white shutters, and oversized windows. The door she'd just slammed in his face was oak and in need of some TLC. He tipped his head back against the headrest and turned the keys in the ignition, cranking the air conditioning. It wasn't even ten in the morning, but the air was already stifling in the cab of his truck.

Jared's neighbor was Charlie Grant. Shit. What were the fuckin' odds? She'd been even prettier in person. Prettier, and so hurt. She'd try to play it off as anger, but he'd seen the hurt flashing in her eyes. He deserved all of it, that hurt and that anger, asshole that he was.

After he'd moved out of Jared's and gotten his own place, getting his shit together, he'd joined the online dating site, feeling like it was what he was *supposed* to do. Thinking that maybe he could meet someone, get laid. Move on, somehow. But he hadn't been prepared for Charlie and the easy connection they'd forged. He'd still been working through the damage caused by the breakdown of his marriage, and he hadn't been ready for a relationship; he'd been too emotionally drained from the divorce. Really, he should've been focused on figuring out who he was, post-divorce, what he wanted, all that shit. But he'd liked Charlie so much that he'd kept talking to her, getting himself in a little deeper with each online conversation. He'd waited for weeks, hoping he'd feel ready. She'd made him want to feel ready.

It had all come to head when one night, after a few beers, he'd asked her out during one of their chats. And then he'd panicked.

He'd known Charlie wasn't going to be someone he could have a casual fling with, and he hadn't been in a place to offer anything more, as much as he might've wanted to.

She was smart, and funny, and sarcastic, and so damn cute. Just talking to her made him feel so fucking good, and he hadn't known what to do with any of that.

So he'd stood her up and deleted his profile. Real fucking mature.

He drummed his fingers on the steering wheel, replaying what had just happened. How shocked and then hurt she'd been to see him. How cute she'd looked in her pajamas, her reddish-brown hair thrown up in a messy ponytail. How she'd wrapped her slender arms around herself, as though seeing him caused her physical pain. Hell, after the way he'd led her on and then stood her up, maybe it did. He couldn't blame her for slamming the door in his face before he could explain.

He sat up a bit straighter, squinting at her house as an idea took root. He cut the ignition and stepped out of his truck, the scents of fresh-cut grass and hot pavement mingling in the air. Hands on his hips, he peered up at the house before wandering around to the side and into the backyard, letting himself in through the gate that didn't latch properly.

He let out a low whistle as he observed the damage that Jared had done, taking out the entire section of fence that separated his backyard from Charlie's, as well as destroying her deck. Tire tracks covered the grass between the two heaps of splintered boards. Crouching down, he examined what remained of the deck and saw that the wood was old and rotting in some places. Even before Jared had rammed his Jeep into it, it had already been falling apart.

He paced the yard, trying to figure out if he could replace the missing section of fencing, or if the entire thing needed to be redone. He glanced from the fence to her deck, his mind already whirring with ideas and designs.

He wasn't sure he deserved her forgiveness, but this was his chance to make up for the way he'd treated her. She might not want to hear his apology or his explanation, but he could try to show her. With wood and nails and sweat, maybe he could make her see how much he regretted hurting her. At the time, he'd been so caught up in himself that it hadn't really occurred to him that she *would* be hurt when he didn't show. It came back to that whole emotionally drained thing. But she was hurt, and he was an asshole.

He hadn't realized just how bad he felt until he'd seen her standing in front of him, in the flesh, scowling at him. A wave of shame had rocked him, stealing his breath for a second, followed quickly by a hot, sharp pang of lust. A part of him had wanted to cup her delicate face, drink in those pretty brown eyes, tell her he was sorry, and kiss her until she forgot she was hurting. He knew he had no right to any of that, but he wanted it just the same.

God, he'd made such a huge, fucking colossal mistake, and not just because she'd been even cuter in person.

"Hey! Get the hell out of my backyard!" Charlie appeared in a second-floor window, a deep frown creasing her pretty face.

He planted his hands on his hips, squinting up at her. "Don't you want me to fix this?"

She stared at him, and his words hung between them, heavy with meaning. "No. I want you to get off my property."

He held his hands out at his sides. "Charlie, I'm sorry. I'm an asshole."

She sighed and shook her head, her voice losing some of its sharpness. "I'm sorry you're an asshole, too, Adam."

It was hard to tell from his vantage point, but he thought maybe something in the line of her shoulders softened, and a tiny seed of hope took root in his chest. A cicada buzzed, humming its warm summer song. He wiped at the sweat forming along his hairline with the back of his hand.

"Let me do this. I want to fix this," he said, gesturing around her backyard.

"And I want you to go. How many times do I have to ask you to get off my property?"

"Charlie, I just—" But he didn't get the chance to finish his thought because he was too busy dodging the sneaker that came flying at him from the window. "Hey! What the hell's wrong with you? I'm trying to help you out here!" he yelled, irritation flaring up through him. He was being nice, attempting to make amends, and she was chucking Nikes at him.

And fuck if the twisted part of him didn't like it, just a little. Her anger was about her being hurt, yes, but it was also about protecting herself. She was strong. Gutsy, and nobody's doormat.

It was really fucking appealing, flying sneakers and all.

"*Me?* What the hell's wrong with *you*? What kind of person stands someone up and then ghosts on them after weeks of messages? Huh? And now you think you get to stand there, say you're sorry, and that it's *fine*? That I'll just let you—"

This time he cut her off. "I'm sorry, Charlie! Fuck, I'm real fuckin' sorry, okay? It was a stupid, dick move."

Another shoe came flying out the window, landing with a heavy thunk in the grass beside him. He jammed his hands back onto his hips and blew out a long, slow breath through his nose as we waited to see if more footwear was about to rain down on him. Charlie reappeared in the window, her cheeks flushed.

He held out his hands at his sides again. "All right. I'm gonna go. Mainly because I don't want to get brained with a shoe." He pointed up at her. "But I'll be back tomorrow. I'm not giving up, Charlie. I'm gonna make this right."

He hadn't realized just how much he'd hurt her, and it gutted him. He wanted, more than anything, to try to make up for the shitty way he'd treated her. He'd try again tomorrow. If after that, she still wanted nothing to do with him, wouldn't accept his help and let him make amends, he'd go. But he had to try, just one more time.

The next morning, Charlie stood under the hot shower spray, rolling her shoulders and trying to work out some of the tension that had gathered over the past twenty-four hours. After Adam left, she'd spent the rest of the day restless and on edge, finally submitting her column around midnight.

Adam. God. It had been weeks, maybe even months since she'd last thought of him, and then boom. There he was. In that stupid tight white T-shirt. With those hands. And those blue eyes. And the beard. And the pleasant, deep voice. And the muscles.

Damn him.

She grabbed the shampoo and squirted a little mound into her palm, lathering it through her hair as she played everything back through her mind. And not just what had happened yesterday, but everything. The cute, fun messages. How excited she'd been when he'd asked her out. The humiliating disappointment when he hadn't shown and had disappeared from the face of the earth without a word.

I'm sorry, Charlie! Fuck, I'm real fuckin' sorry, okay? It was a stupid, dick move.

His words echoed through her mind, bouncing around her skull. She couldn't help but wonder if he was sorry that he'd hurt her or sorry that she was mad, because they were two completely separate things. A part of her wanted to believe it was the former, but the more realistic part of her knew it was most likely the latter.

"Fucking men," she said, her voice echoing off the shower tiles. A loud knocking sounded through the house, and she froze, tilting her head as she listened. The knocking continued, and she turned the shower off, stepping out and grabbing a towel from the rack. The doorbell rang, chiming through the silent house. She wrapped the towel tightly around herself, grinding her teeth together. Stomping into her bedroom, she crossed the worn hardwood floor to the window, water dripping down her legs as she went. If that asshole had actually come back, she'd have to find something more substantial than a shoe to throw at him. Maybe a frying pan.

She yanked the blinds up, and her frown dropped away, her eyebrows shooting up when she saw the UPS truck sitting in her driveway. The driver headed away from her front door and back toward his truck.

"Shit!" In the wake of the stress of barely finishing her column on time and Adam's sudden reappearance, she'd forgotten about the materials she'd requested from the Giamatti Research Center at the Baseball Hall of Fame. The files contained copies of rare interview transcripts from Red Sox greats like Cy Young, Babe Ruth, Wade Boggs, Bobby Doerr, and tons of others, and she needed them for the book proposal she'd been working on for months now.

Gripping the towel where the fabric overlapped between her breasts, she sprinted for the front door, flying down the stairs. She flung the door open and ran out onto the front porch. The front door slammed behind her, rattling the windowpanes.

"Hey! Wait!" she yelled, waving one arm frantically at the UPS guy. He'd just started to back out of her driveway, and he stopped, putting the big brown truck back in park. After she signed for her delivery, he unloaded the three sealed boxes onto her porch. Eager to dig into her treasures, she headed for the front door, planning to get dressed first, and then haul the boxes inside.

She closed her hand around the black wrought iron knob and slammed her shoulder into the door when it didn't budge. Panic shot through her, dancing like electricity over her skin, and she tried the knob again, rattling it and pushing against the door, but the door didn't move.

She'd locked herself out. Wearing nothing but a towel.

"Nononononononono," she chanted as she tried the knob several more times. "Fuck!" She kicked at the door in frustration and then instantly regretted it when her bare toes made contact with the wood. Pain shot across her foot. "Shit!" She hopped on one foot, clutching her throbbing toes in one hand. The towel started to slip. "*Fucking shit!*" Dropping her foot, she scrambled to grab her towel before she flashed the entire neighborhood.

She leaned her back against the door and forced herself to take several deep breaths as she tried to figure out how she was going to get back inside. Maybe she'd left the back door unlocked. Or maybe she could break in through a window. She spotted a pair of flip-flops under the bench on her porch, and the tiniest bit of relief trickled through her. Slipping them on, she felt a little bit less naked. Still, like, *super* naked, but at least she wouldn't step on bugs. Or a rusty nail. God, and then she'd get tetanus. Which sounded just about right, given how the past couple of days had gone.

She knew it was probably futile, but she walked around the side of the house and into her backyard. Gingerly, she picked a path through the debris of her deck, making her way to the back door that led to the kitchen. The door was a few feet above the ground, and she clutched the towel around herself as she reached up to grasp the knob. She tried it, but it was locked. Of course. At least it was warm and sunny out. If this were a movie, it'd start raining, or things would somehow get worse, just for comedic effect.

"Charlie?" came Adam's voice from several feet behind her.

She wasn't laughing.

Chapter Three

Adam stood still, unable to tear his eyes off Charlie's smooth, creamy skin, dotted with pale brown freckles. Charlie, in nothing but a towel, her hair soaking wet, was pretty much the last thing he'd expected to see when he'd pulled his truck into her driveway and walked into her backyard.

But then he'd always liked surprises.

Her shoulders tensed at the sound of his voice and she turned slowly, clutching the light blue towel around herself, her knuckles white. Two pale strips—tan lines—streaked down over her shoulders, disappearing into the towel.

"What are you doing here?" she asked, tucking a strand of damp hair behind her ear, a scowl on her face. His fingers twitched, wanting to repeat the movement.

Despite the scowl, she took a tentative step toward him, the towel riding up slightly as she stepped around the broken boards, the muscles in her toned legs flexing. A drop of water fell from her hair and onto her arm, sliding slowly down. Her eyes met his, and she bit her lip as she studied him.

Fuck, he wanted a second chance. And it wasn't only because his jeans were getting tighter by the second. Sure, that was part of it, but it was more than that. It was just Charlie. The woman he'd started to fall for without even meeting in person. She was strong, and funny, and didn't take anyone's shit. She was smart, and passionate, and hardworking. She was hurt and angry right now, but he could handle her prickly. In fact, he didn't mind prickly Charlie. Not at all.

"I told you I'd be back today," he said, shoving his hands in his back pockets, not knowing what else to do with them.

"Ha, well, excuse *me* if I didn't exactly take that at face value."
She sniffed and adjusted her towel.

He tipped his head. "Fair enough. So, uh, what's with the
towel?"

"I..." She gestured helplessly and then quickly returned her
hand to the towel with a wide-eyed grimace, apparently afraid to
hold it one-handed. Something in Adam's chest tightened and
then warmed, and he looked down, hiding his smile. When he
glanced back up, her bottom lip was caught between her teeth
again.

God. So fucking cute.

"I locked myself out."

"In a towel?"

She sighed impatiently. "The UPS guy was here, and I needed
to sign for the delivery."

He rocked on his heels. "Must've been important."

"It is. It's research material for a book proposal."

"The one about the Red Sox greats?" She'd told him her idea
during one of their chats. "You're doing it?"

She nodded, a tiny smile tugging up the corner of her mouth.
"Yeah. I am."

"That's so cool, Charlie. Seriously. It sounded like a great idea
when you told me about it."

She started to smile wider, and then caught herself. The smile
dropped off her face. "Don't. Don't do that."

He frowned, not following. "Do what?"

"Be nice to me." She said it as though he were doing
something wrong, her nostrils flaring.

His frown deepened, one eyebrow arching up. "You want me
to be a dick?" he asked, unable to keep the note of frustration
from creeping into his voice.

She snorted. "No, I want you to go."

He yanked his hands out of his back pockets and jammed
them onto his hips. "You're real stubborn, you know that?"

She muttered something about the pot and the kettle.

He shook his head, glancing down at his work boots for a second, and then up at her house, torn between leaving out of sheer frustration, and staying out of a confusing jumble of things. Guilt, sure, but something else too. Something deeper and warmer than the guilt he felt over hurting her. Over putting that wariness in her eyes. "I can help you."

"I told you yesterday, I don't want your help." She paused before continuing, her fingers curling even tighter into the towel. *Lucky terrycloth.* "I don't need your help."

He nodded and rubbed a hand over his mouth, deciding to call her bluff. "So then let's hear it."

Her brows knitted together. "Hear what?"

"Your plan to get back in your house." He studied her, eyebrows raised. "I assume you have one. Seeing as you don't need my help."

"I...I'll just go to the neighbors and call a locksmith."

He tilted his head, considering, and shrugged. "Yeah, I guess that works. Assuming your neighbors are home. And who knows how long it'll take the locksmith to come? Could be an hour. Could be longer. And you're not exactly dressed. Leaves a lot to be desired, as far as plans go."

She took another step closer to him, a challenge flashing in her brown eyes. "Oh, yeah? What's your plan?"

"Pretty simple, really. I go get my ladder, climb up to your open window," he said, pointing up toward the second floor of her house, "and I let you in. You're inside in under five minutes, and then I can get to work."

"Get to work?"

He nodded. "Yeah, fixing all this."

Her nostrils flared again, and damn if that wasn't cute, too. "I told you, I don't need you to fix it."

"Yeah, well, I sorta promised Jared, and he's a good buddy. I wouldn't want to let him down." He shrugged, trying to make the words sound lighter than they felt.

She took another step toward him, only a few inches away now. "Funny, I would've thought letting people down was your specialty. You didn't have any issues doing it to me."

Guilt slammed into him, and he curled his hands into fists at his sides. It was the only way he could stop himself from touching her, which he was pretty fucking sure wouldn't go over well. But he could see how much he'd hurt her, and he wanted to soothe the pain he'd caused. The need to touch her was guilt, and regret, and lust, all rolled into a confusing knot that sat right in the center of his chest. "Charlie. I'm so sorry. I know I said it yesterday, but yelling it kinda takes some of the meaning out of it. So, I'm telling you now that I'm really sorry for standing you up, and I'm sorry for going silent. You deserved better than that. I hate that I hurt you."

For several moments her eyes held his, and he waited, giving her space, giving her time, to process his apology. Finally, she spoke, her voice quiet. "Why?"

A heaviness sat on his shoulders because he knew he owed her the truth. "I didn't tell you this, but I was going through a divorce. I wasn't ready to date."

She frowned, some of the warmth leaving her eyes. "Then why were you on a dating site?"

He blew out a breath and shook his head. "Because I'm an idiot."

"Finally, something we can agree on." But she smiled the tiniest hint of a smile as she spoke. "Why didn't you tell me?"

He shrugged. "I don't know. I guess I wanted you to know me without the baggage."

"I get that. For the record, it wouldn't have changed anything." She shuffled her foot, looking down as she spoke.

He nodded, relieved that she hadn't rejected his apology. "I'll go get my ladder."

"I told you, I don't need your help." Although she was still being stubborn, her voice had taken on a teasing tone. He ignored her and strode around her house and out to her driveway, unhitching the ladder from his truck. He hefted the ladder over his shoulder and walked back into the backyard, and everything—his skin, his muscles, his jeans—tightened at the fresh sight of Charlie in her faded blue towel and flip-flops. Her toenails were painted a navy blue, and the freckles that dotted her shoulders and arms also trailed down her legs, a light brown constellation against her pale skin.

He swung the ladder down and extended it to its full length, aligning it below the open window, and found himself wondering how much of her skin those freckles covered. If they trailed across her back, over her small breasts, and down her flat stomach. If she'd like it if he kissed them all, a tiny apology for every single one.

Charlie's arms were crossed in front of her as she watched him, one eyebrow raised. "You don't listen very well, do you?"

He adjusted the ladder, making sure it was secure, and spoke without looking at her. "No, I heard you. You don't need my help."

"Right."

He leaned against the house, crossing his arms over his chest and tipping his chin at the ladder. "So go on, then, hot stuff."

Her cheeks flushed, and goddamn did he like that, the sight of her cheeks going pink because of him. Her mouth opened and shut, firming into a thin line. The buzz of a lawnmower started in a nearby yard, vibrating through the still, humid air.

She cleared her throat and squared her shoulders and then tucked the ends of her towel against her chest. And then she stepped up onto the bottom rung of his ladder.

Immediately, he was behind her, his hands at her waist as he gently lifted her down. "Charlie. God. I was kidding." He spoke the words into the back of her head, his hands still on her. She was warm and soft through the terrycloth, and she tipped her head down. Her damp hair fell forward, exposing her delicate nape. She took a shaky breath that he felt through his entire body and she eased back against him, her back flush with his chest. His fingers flexed into her, and she gasped softly. She could probably feel his heart pounding against her shoulder blade.

"Your jokes need work," she said, her voice breathy, almost snatched away by the lawnmower's drone.

God. All those freckles. He wanted to taste every single one.

Reluctantly, he stepped away from her and climbed up the ladder before he did something stupid, like put his mouth on her skin.

He reached the top of the ladder and wasn't surprised to find the window screen missing. It was the same window she'd thrown shoes at him from yesterday, after all. Sticking his head in, he took in the messy room and carefully stepped inside. His foot knocked over a pile of *Sports Illustrated* magazines from what he assumed was Charlie's desk. Swinging his other leg over the sill, he turned and bumped into a stack of banker's boxes piled beside the window. He squeezed around the desk, stumbling when one of his boots snagged in the spaghetti factory of cords snaking across the floor.

Charlie's desk was piled high with papers, magazines, file folders, and books, all engulfing her laptop in a fortress of clutter. Several dirty plates, a couple of mugs, a glass, and a few empty beer bottles occupied any free space between the other items. The rest of the office wasn't much better. The bookcase was overflowing and leaning slightly to one side, ready to give out under the weight of the books stuffed on its shelves. An old plaid couch sat against the far wall, a full laundry basket, a pizza box and more random crap covering it. Dusty sports memorabilia filled the walls.

He strode back to the window. "Your office is really messy," he called down to her, and she glared up at him, the scowl firmly back in place. Fuck, but that scowl made him want to tease her even more.

"Would you just get down here and let me in?"

He leaned against the windowsill. "You want me to come down there? Why?" He paused, smiling down at her. "So I can *help* you by letting you in?"

"Hennessy, I swear to God," she said, her face flushing again.

He laughed. He couldn't help it. He also knew he shouldn't push it, and hurried downstairs to let her inside. Flipping the deadbolt on the kitchen door, he flung it open and held out his hand to her. Because the deck was gone, there was now an awkward step up from the backyard into the house.

She stared at his hand for at least three heartbeats before shuffling forward. With a heavy sigh, she placed her hand in his. At the contact, his entire body warmed, his gut tightening. Her hand curled into his, impossibly soft and small against his work-roughened skin. She stepped up into the house, her eyes glued to where her hand disappeared into his. The edge of her flip-flop caught on the doorsill, and she stumbled forward. Acting on instinct, his arms shot out to catch her, and she tumbled into him, her towel slipping and falling to the floor.

"Close your eyes!" she shouted, her voice high-pitched and panicked as she crashed into his chest. He screwed his eyes shut tight and wrapped his arms around her, steadying her against him. His hands splayed across her bare back, and he couldn't stop the low groan from escaping his throat. Her skin was warm and smooth beneath his palms, and fuck, she smelled so good. Hot and sweet, like sunshine and honey.

She sucked in a breath, and her bare breasts pressed against his chest. He could feel her hardened nipples through his T-shirt, and he pressed his eyes closed even tighter. He wasn't sure how long they stood like that, with his arms around her, her naked body pressed against his, neither of them speaking.

"Adam?" she said, and it took everything he had to keep his eyes closed.

"Yeah." He dipped his head, just a little.

"Let go of me."

Immediately, he dropped his hands to his sides and turned away from her. He heard the rustle of the towel as she picked it up off the floor and wrapped it around herself.

"You kept your eyes closed," she said, and he didn't miss the note of disbelief in her voice.

He glanced over his shoulder, and, seeing that the towel was back in place, turned around to face her. "Yeah. You asked me to."

She swallowed, her throat working, and her eyes met his. Something impossible to read flickered across her face before she cleared her throat. "I'm not paying you to fix the deck or the fence."

He nodded, unable to stop the smile from spreading across his face. "I know." And it was fine with him, because he didn't want money. No, he wanted something better.

A second chance.

Charlie cranked up the dial on her small desk fan, not caring about the papers the mechanical breeze sent fluttering to the floor. The air in her office was stifling. A trickle of sweat slid down between her breasts, and she blew a stray strand of hair out of her eyes. Her feet propped up on the tiny bit of available real estate on her desk, she returned her attention to the research file in her lap.

The high-pitched whine of a saw cut through the afternoon's silence, and her gaze slid back to the window. Again.

After the towel incident two days ago, she'd barely been able to look at Adam. She just kept replaying it in her mind over and over again. And the worst part was that it wasn't humiliation she felt. No, that'd be way too sensible.

Every time she replayed it, she felt pure, unadulterated lust, her stomach dipping and swirling as though she were on the world's tallest, steepest roller coaster, about to rocket down that first hill.

She squirmed in her seat as she remembered the feel of his hard body against hers, his huge hands on her back. They were so big, so strong and rough, and she'd wanted more of them. Wanted to know what they'd feel like in her hair, cupping her face, on her breasts.

Inside her.

She squirmed again, clenching her thighs together in an effort to stifle the warm, heavy throb settling there. She knew, given their brief history, that she shouldn't want him, and yet...he'd kept his eyes closed. And he was fixing the damage his friend had done, free of charge.

And he'd apologized. More than once.

And unless he'd had a long, thick tool of some kind stashed in his jeans pocket, he'd reacted to having her pressed naked against him.

It was that last idea that she couldn't seem to shake, and she pushed out of her chair, tossing the folder on her desk.

She shouldn't want him. She shouldn't want anything to do with him. Not only had he proven himself untrustworthy, but she knew—better than most, probably—that even a man as hot as Adam Hennessy wasn't worth the risk.

When her now ex-fiancé Jeff had told her the day before their wedding that he wasn't in love with her, that he was in love with someone else, she'd fallen apart. Suddenly, the future she'd thought she had was gone, and she'd felt lost. Broken. Empty. In hindsight, there'd been red flags. He'd worked late more nights than not, putting space between them. He'd barely been interested in sex as the wedding approached. Jeff hadn't wanted anything to do with planning the wedding, and had grown more and more distant as the date had neared. He'd rolled his eyes at her enthusiasm, and she'd chalked it up to dudes just not being into wedding stuff. But it had been a symptom of a much deeper problem—he hadn't wanted to spend his life with her. The woman he'd chosen over her was prettier, more feminine. More likable, at least according to Jeff. And while Charlie was pretty damn comfortable with who she was, that betrayal, that rejection, had hit hard and sunk deep.

Thankfully, she'd had her family and her friends to lean on, and she'd spent months putting herself back together. She was still standing, but she wasn't the same. It was as though her broken pieces had been reassembled slightly off-center, some of the cracks still visible.

Adam, if she let him, could shatter her, and that was terrifying, because she wasn't sure she had the strength to put herself back together a second time.

But she could want to *do* him without actually dating him, right? Sex wasn't love, and the idea of enjoying his gorgeous body while keeping her heart locked away held some appeal. Oh, hell. A lot of appeal.

She sauntered over to the window and rested her chin in her hand as she watched him work, her butt perched on the edge of her desk. He'd spent the first day cleaning up the backyard, hauling away all the broken pieces of wood with two other crew members. Then he'd set about tearing down the old, rickety fence while his crew leveled the ground where her deck had been, pouring concrete and anchoring what she assumed were the main support posts for the new deck.

Now, late in the afternoon, his crew had already finished up, but Adam stood in the middle of the yard, feeding boards through a table saw. He tossed the newly separated halves onto the ground beside the saw and picked up a water bottle. After draining it, he crushed the empty plastic in his hand, his long, thick fingers curling around it.

Goddamn. Those hands.

Adam grabbed the hem of his T-shirt and pulled it up, wiping at his sweaty face with it and exposing a flat, muscular stomach dusted with light brown hair. Even worse, he had those damn cut lines along his hips, with the muscles arrowing down in a V and disappearing into his jeans. The muscles in his arms flexed as he wiped at his brow, and Charlie touched her mouth to make sure she wasn't drooling.

"Hi, Charlie," he called without looking up.

"Just making sure you're not slacking off," she yelled down, unable to help the smile from stretching across her lips. "I have no issues getting my whip out."

He turned to face her, pointing up at her. "Hey, I'm not intimidated by you just because you have mean eyebrows and know more about baseball than me."

She frowned and narrowed her eyes at him. "I have mean eyebrows?"

"Yeah. They're all..." He angled his index fingers over his own eyebrows, pointing them on a downward tilt toward his nose. And then he smiled and pointed up at her again. "Like that."

She smiled into her palm, hiding it from him as warmth flooded her at his teasing. "Yeah, well, you have a mean...whatever. Go to hell."

He laughed and wiped at his brow again with the back of his hand. "Pretty sure I'm already there. It's gotta be ninety-five fuckin' degrees out here."

And then, his eyes holding hers, he reached behind him and yanked his shirt off with a tug, tossing it down beside his crumpled water bottle. Her mouth went dry as she studied his hard, defined body, unable to tear her eyes away from the feast of skin and muscle and *man* before her. A dusting of light brown hair covered his defined pecs, and...oh, God. He had tattoos.

Charlie had several weaknesses when it came to men. Blue eyes. Killer smiles. Nice beards. Muscles. Tattoos.

Stupid, sexy Adam checked every single box.

An American flag covered the inside of his right bicep, and an American classic-style anchor sat below word "loyalty" on his left bicep. What looked like a dragon adorned his right pec. He turned, giving her an eyeful of his broad back, and she burst out laughing, unable to help herself. A large tattoo about the size of her hand covered his left shoulder blade. And it was ridiculous: a cartoon cupcake with muscled arms, and what appeared to be the words "stud muffin" etched below it in a semicircle.

"That's the worst tattoo I've ever seen," she called down.

He looked up and winked, his eyes crinkling as he smiled, and her stomach flipped over on itself.

Terrible tattoo or not, with his strong body, gorgeously masculine hands, and easy confidence, Adam Hennessy looked like a man who'd be fantastic in bed, and Charlie knew she was in deep trouble, because damn did she want to find out.

Chapter Four

The heat wave was killing him.

That was what Adam kept telling himself as he worked, slamming nails into place as he mounted the last of the fencing. Normally, he used a nail gun—it was faster, more efficient—but today, even though the heat was sweltering, he found himself needing an outlet for the energy pumping through his veins, hot and fast. His skin felt too tight, as though his bones strained against his muscles.

Rivulets of sweat streaked down his torso, making his T-shirt cling to his skin, and he dropped the hammer, trading it for the bottle of water on the ground beside him. He closed his eyes as he swallowed, not caring that the water wasn't cold, and his mind spun with the image of creamy skin, dotted with freckles. Warm, soft flesh beneath his hands, yielding to the pressure of his touch. Charlie's naked body pressed against his.

The pressure built, tightening his chest until he could feel every pulse of his heart, and he finished the water. It was a feeling he wasn't used to, this *wanting*.

It was the heat, he tried to convince himself.

And the fact that he wanted to fuck Charlie until neither of them could walk.

Yeah, there was that. But mainly, it was the heat. And he needed to believe that, because besides a little light teasing, she'd kept her distance since the towel incident. He wasn't sure if that was his cue to leave her alone, or flirt with her more.

The truth was, he hadn't dated much since the divorce. A little, sure, but just enough to know that he had no fucking clue what he was doing. He felt like a car-crash victim relearning how to walk after an accident. Unused muscles had atrophied, making for some unsteady steps.

He'd been with Melissa for ten years. He'd met her right when she'd finished college—they'd both been twenty-three. They'd dated for five years before he'd asked her to marry him. Engaged for a year, then married for four before it had fallen apart over a year ago now.

It wasn't that either of them had done anything wrong. No one had cheated, or lost all their money, or anything like that. It had been an accumulation of the smallest things—a collection of slights and resentments on both sides—that had festered with time and bad communication. They'd grown apart and fallen out of love. There'd been almost no animosity between them when they'd realized it was over.

Didn't mean that it hadn't fucking hurt, though. He'd failed Melissa, because although he'd cared for her, ultimately, he hadn't been what she'd needed. Slowly, he'd watched what they'd once had die, watched until neither of them could deny that it was over. Even as amicable as things had been, the divorce had been so damn *hard*. And he knew that part of the reason he'd chickened out on his date with Charlie was because he was fucking scared of the same thing happening again.

"Hey, man. Nice to see she hasn't killed you." Jared sauntered up to the newly installed fence separating his yard from Charlie's, leaning his arms against the white oak.

Adam shot Jared a look, one eyebrow raised. "You know, you're gonna owe me a couple thou for materials when I'm done here."

"I thought you were working for free." Jared frowned, tilting his head.

"I am. Still gotta pay for the materials, though, man."

Jared blew out a breath. "Fine. Yeah. Let me know when you're done."

"Don't worry. I will." Adam picked the hammer back up and dropped a handful of nails into the pouch of his tool belt.

Jared tilted his head toward Charlie's house. The windows were open, and David Bowie floated out, the music hanging in the thick, muggy air. She'd been playing his greatest hits for the past hour, and Adam wasn't complaining. "How's it going with the dragon lady?"

Adam hammered a nail home. "Her name's Charlie. Don't call her that."

Jared held his hands up. "Hey, you're the one who gave her the nickname."

Adam lined up another nail and drove it into the oak, fastening the board in place. "Yeah, well. That was before I knew her."

Jared huffed out a breath and nodded. "I get it. She's cute. You got a thing for the drag—" He cut himself off when Adam shot daggers at him with his eyes. "For Charlie."

Adam shrugged, sinking another nail. "Maybe, yeah."

"I told you about how she almost took my nuts off, right?"

"You did. And if I recall, I said I didn't blame her." Slam, another nail in. "Stand by what I said."

"Hey, they're your nuts. You want 'em shredded off, I guess that's your prerogative."

Adam smiled as he lined up another nail. He couldn't deny that the idea of Charlie's hands on his balls was an appealing one. "I like her. She brings me lemonade and makes fun of my tattoos."

Jared blinked slowly before giving his head a shake. "Whatever, man. They're your boys." And with that, he walked back toward his house, waving over his shoulder.

Adam scooped up more nails and dropped them into his tool belt just as the back door of Charlie's house swung open. She stepped out, a basket of laundry propped against her hip. He watched her over his shoulder as she crossed to the small clothesline in the far corner of her yard. She wore a skintight red-and-white striped tank top and a tiny pair of denim shorts, her hair up in a ponytail, as usual.

Freckles on full display.

Giving his head a small shake, he turned his attention back to the fence, lining up another nail.

"Am I making it hard?" she called, and he smashed the hammer into his thumb.

"*Fuck! Motherfucking shit-ass fucker!*" He dropped the hammer and pulled his hand against his chest, his thumb throbbing as pain shot through his hand and up his arm.

Charlie dropped the basket of laundry and came running over, one hand pressed to her mouth. She wrapped her fingers around his arm and pulled his hand away from his chest. "Let me see." She cradled his hand in hers, peering down at his thumb. He'd split the skin over his knuckle, and a stream of blood trickled from the wound. "Shit. Come inside. I have a first-aid kit." She grabbed his good hand, the one he hadn't clumsily smashed a hammer into at her probably unintended innuendo.

His pulse beat thickly, thrumming in his temples, his chest, his injured hand. He pulled air into his lungs and pushed it back out again through his nose, letting her lead him into the kitchen. She let go of his hand as they entered the house, and he was surprised at the disappointment he felt.

She turned the faucet on, streaming cold water into the sink. "Wash it off, and I'll go find the first-aid kit."

Doing as he was told, he stuck his throbbing, bloody thumb under the water, watching as the blood swirled away down the drain. She was back within moments, a beat-up white tin clutched in her hands. She hopped up on the counter beside the sink and turned the faucet off. Taking his hand, she patted it dry with a paper towel before digging into the dented tin.

"That thing looks ancient. Anything you've got in there must be expired."

She pulled out a tube of antibiotic ointment. "Are you worried this is gonna sting?"

"I know it's not going to sting. I just don't want my thumb to fall off when it gets infected from using Korean War-era Neosporin."

"Baby," she said, glancing up at him as she dabbed the ointment on his thumb.

He wanted to make another smartassed comment, but he was too focused on the feel of her fingers on him to do anything but breathe.

She bit her lip as she applied a butterfly bandage over the cut and then slipped down off the counter. Yanking open the freezer, she rummaged around inside before tossing him a small bag of frozen vegetables. "Do you want some Advil?" she asked, turning and leaning against the counter beside the fridge, studying him as he arranged the cold bag around his throbbing thumb.

"I'll be fine. Thanks for the"—he peered down at the bag—"turnips."

"Thanks. I don't like turnips, so you can keep that." She hopped back up on the counter beside him again, and something hot beat through his body, chasing away the pain in his hand. "You sure you're okay?"

"Yeah. This may come as a surprise to you, but that's not the first time I've hit myself with a hammer. Probably won't be the last, either."

She nodded, her eyes on his hands. Silence hung between them as late afternoon sunshine streamed in through the window.

"What did you mean when you asked me if you were making it hard?" he asked, inching closer.

She waved a hand through the air. One of the straps of her tank top slipped down, and his eyes traced the line of her collarbone and shoulder. "Oh. Uh, I just hoped I wasn't distracting you. I know how annoyed I get when I'm working and I get interrupted."

"Oh. Yeah. No. It's fine. It's your backyard, Charlie."

She looked down for a second and nodded, not saying anything.

He readjusted the bag and glanced around the kitchen, taking in the harvest-gold appliances, the dated cabinets, and the worn linoleum. "So, when you bought this place, were you planning to fix it up?"

She inched a bit closer to him, and the light in her eyes changed, a sadness creeping in. "Um, no. This is my grandfather's house. He moved to Florida last fall and let me have it. I needed a place to go."

He licked his lips and shifted against the counter. "You know, I stayed with Jared for a few months last spring," he said, tipping his head toward Jared's house. "Guess we just missed each other."

"Seems to happen with us." She flashed him a tiny smile.

"How come you needed a place to go?" He erased another inch between them, close enough now to feel the warmth coming off her skin. His heart slammed into his ribs, and he licked his lips.

She stared at his mouth before answering. "I'd been living with someone, and it didn't work out." She ducked her head, and he had the feeling there was more to the story than she was letting on.

"I'm sorry."

She smiled sadly, the corners of her mouth barely turning up as her lips pressed together. "Thanks." She gestured around her, her hand sweeping through the air and encompassing the clutter throughout the house. "I haven't gone through his stuff yet. He said I could put whatever I wanted into storage. I only added my crap to the mess. I didn't really sort through a lot of it after the breakup. I guess I just haven't felt ready."

"I get that. But sometimes..." He shrugged and leaned a bit closer. "Sometimes you'll never be ready for something. You just have to do it. Take that leap and hope a net will appear." He wasn't entirely sure that he was still talking about her clutter.

She looked up and met his gaze, and the seconds stretched out like something warm and sticky, slow and sweet. She rubbed the palms of her hands over her denim shorts, a sweep of her hands up and down her thighs. Swallowing, she nodded. "I should get back to work." She bit her lip, still rubbing her thighs, and something kicked in his gut, making him hyperaware of his own body. Each breath in and out. Each throb of his heart in his chest. Her eyes trailed down his body, and heat seared through him.

Before he could talk himself out of it, he tossed the bag of vegetables in the sink and moved in front of her. He pressed his hands against the counter on either side of her, caging her in. "Thank you for the first aid," he said, and her eyebrows rose, as though his words surprised her. He knew he should probably back off, but he couldn't. Not with her so close, her warm, sweet scent invading his nostrils and humming through him like a chorus of cicadas.

"You're...uh...you're welcome," she said, swallowing thickly as her eyes skated up and down his body again. Her gaze slid back to his and she sucked in a deep breath, her chest rising and falling, almost touching his. "You...you have a weird look on your face. What are you thinking about?" Her voice was a husky whisper, and her eyes dropped down to his mouth again.

"This," he said, and dipped his head. She sucked in a sharp breath as his lips brushed hers, gentle and slow. He pulled back after a second, trying to gauge her reaction. She threaded her fingers through his hair and pulled his mouth back to hers with a soft moan, and this time there was nothing gentle or slow about the kiss. He closed his mouth over hers, and she opened for him with a quiet whimper. Her tongue slid against his, and he wound his arms around her waist, pulling her closer. He kissed her hungrily, his hands skimming from her waist and up her back. Heat flared across his skin as she nipped at his bottom lip, soothing the bite with her tongue.

He groaned against her mouth and caressed her tongue with his, exploring the sweetness of her mouth. He'd kissed other women since his divorce, but none of those kisses had felt like this one, hot and hungry and *right*. He loosened her ponytail and tangled his fingers in her hair, tilting her head back and deepening the kiss, wanting more. Needing more of her. Of Charlie, and everything she had to offer. Of everything she'd let him have.

Her hands slid down his back and then up his arms, her fingers curling into his biceps as he kissed her slow and deep. Electricity shot down his spine, heat pulsing and flaring through him as his quickly hardening cock pressed against the fly of his jeans.

She moaned and wrapped her legs around his hips, pulling him closer as she wound her arms around his shoulders.

He knew he had to break the kiss, because he was dangerously close to hauling her off the counter and getting her naked as fast as he could. And as much as he wanted that, he knew that they should probably stop. Baby steps.

After allowing himself the luxury of a few more seconds of Charlie's mouth on his, he pulled away, cupping her face and leaning his forehead against hers. Out of the corner of his eye, he saw the bandage on his thumb and realized he'd completely forgotten about the dull throbbing in his hand, too preoccupied with the much more pressing throbbing elsewhere.

She looked up at him through her lashes, meeting his eyes. "You're not forgiven," she said, her voice quiet.

"Give me the chance to earn it?" he asked, and kissed the corner of her mouth. She shivered, and he groaned, loving that he'd elicited that response from her.

"May...maybe," she whispered, her mouth moving against his.

"That's all I ask." He planted a quick, hard kiss on her lips and pulled away, smiling when she leaned forward, her mouth chasing his. He kissed her once more, a sweeter, lingering kiss, and then turned and headed back to the backyard.

Operation Second Chance was officially in full effect. He just hoped he knew what he was doing.

Chapter Five

Rain pattered softly and steadily against Charlie's living room window, and she tucked her legs up under herself on the couch, a cup of coffee cradled in her hands. Even though it was almost noon, the sky was dark with purple and gray clouds. Lightning flickered across the sky, lighting up the underbellies of the clouds, and thunder rumbled in the distance as cooler air rolled in, breaking the stifling heat of the past week. She took a sip of her coffee and watched the raindrops race each other down the window pane, loving the cozy feel of being curled up inside during the storm.

Given the weather, Charlie assumed Adam and his crew weren't going to show today. There wasn't much they'd be able to do in the pouring rain. She couldn't figure out if she was disappointed or relieved that she wouldn't be seeing him today.

God, Adam.

That kiss.

She'd lain awake last night, unable to sleep because of that kiss. She'd stared blankly at her computer screen for over an hour, unable to concentrate on work because of that kiss. She couldn't remember the last time she'd been kissed like that. Hell, maybe she'd never been kissed quite like that. He'd been hungry for her, like he hadn't been able to get close enough. Her entire body had roared to life the second his lips had grazed hers, fire curling through her veins and a warm throb settling between her thighs. She'd wanted more, hadn't wanted it to be over when he'd pulled away.

Over and over again, she'd replayed it, savoring every second of the memory. His mouth on hers, his tongue stroking into her mouth. The rasp of his beard against her skin. Those big hands on her, pulling her against him.

If he could disrupt her world like that with only a kiss, letting anything else happen between them was probably a huge, gigantic, elephant-sized mistake.

The simple truth was that she *liked* him. She didn't want to like him, didn't want to want him the way she did, but there it was, all the same. Adam—with his good looks, sense of humor, smartassed charm and ability to shut her brain down with just a kiss—scared her. Big time. Because liking led to loving, and loving led to losing, and she couldn't do that again. She wouldn't.

Her doorbell rang, a dull, buzzing sound. It was halfway broken, and she made a mental note to put it on her ever-growing list of things she needed to fix. Things she had neither the expertise nor the money to tackle right now.

Setting her coffee down on the table beside the couch, she shuffled through the hallway and opened the door.

Adam stood on the front porch, his gray T-shirt speckled with rain, an iPad clutched in one hand. "Oh, good. You're home." He smiled, his entire face lighting up, and her stomach flipped over on itself in response. "I wanted to show you the plans for your deck." He hefted the iPad in his hand, his long, thick fingers curled over the edge. Her eyes, no longer under her control, trailed from his hand and up his arm, skimming over his biceps and broad shoulders. From there, they journeyed down his chest and over his flat, hard stomach. "Uh, Charlie? You okay? Is this a bad time?" he asked, and her eyes flew back up to his. He smirked at her, one eyebrow cocked.

"No, sorry. Just thinking about...baseball. You know. Come in. You want some coffee?"

"Yeah, sure." He followed her into the house, closing the door behind him.

She poured him a cup and found him in the living room, sitting in her discarded seat on the couch. After setting his mug beside her own, she sank down onto the couch beside him as he flipped the cover off the iPad. He tapped on a file, and something in Charlie's chest softened at what he'd named it.

"Charlie's apology deck?" she asked, laying a hand on his forearm.

He stilled when she touched him. After a second, he shrugged and met her eyes. "Yeah. I wanna make it up to you. What I did. I figured maybe this could be a way."

She opened her mouth, but no sound came out. Probably because she had no freaking clue what to say.

Goddamn him for being so likable. For making her like him.

Adam studied her for a moment before scooting a little closer on the couch. "Let me show you." He held the iPad out to her, waving it back and forth slightly when she didn't take it right away. She looked up from the tablet to Adam, his blue eyes slamming into her and stealing her breath. Slowly, awareness of what it meant snapping through her, she reached out and took the tablet, accepting it from him.

He leaned toward her, bringing the scent of rain, clean laundry, and warm skin with him, and his arm brushed hers as he tapped the iPad. Three-dimensional plans filled the screen. "I thought it'd be cool to do two levels. So right off your kitchen, there's an area with space for a grill and a patio set. Then a step goes down to ground level with a separate seating area. I'll do a pergola above this area so you can have some shade. You could also attach a hammock to the posts if you wanted. Or put outdoor furniture under it. I'll use cedar for the decking and trim it out in tigerwood, so the fascia, rails, and banisters will be darker than the rest of it, giving it a modern feel."

She rubbed her fingertips against her palm, curling her hand away from the iPad and the beautiful rendering on the screen. "You designed all of this?"

He nodded, smiling with one corner of his mouth. "Yeah. For you."

She swallowed around the lump pressing against her throat. For several seconds, she stared at the plans, not trusting herself to speak. An ache took root in her chest, but it was a good ache.

Finally, Adam spoke. "It's okay if you don't like it, Charlie."

She looked up and met his eyes. "No, I do. I really, really do."

He frowned. "Then what's wrong?"

"I just... You designed this. For me." She rubbed her hand over her chest, right where that ache was.

"Yeah. I did." His gorgeous blue eyes held hers, and he moved a bit closer. "I did it for you." So, so gently it almost killed her, he tucked a strand of hair behind her ear, his thumb lingering on her cheekbone. "Fuck, I really want to kiss you again."

The air snapped and crackled between them, and she set the iPad aside. "I want that, too." She barely got the last word out before his mouth was on hers, kissing her softly and slowly, his hands cupping her face. She melted into him almost instantly, returning the kiss. With a low growl, he pulled her into his lap, settling her so she was straddling him. Her heart beat furiously in her chest as Adam's big hands slid up her back and tangled in her hair. He deepened the kiss, claiming her mouth, his tongue sliding against hers, and she moved her hips against him, unable to help herself. He groaned, and the kiss became more urgent, lips and tongues melding together hungrily.

As thunder rumbled around them, she eased back a bit and pulled her T-shirt over her head. "This doesn't mean I like you, or that we're dating, or anything like that." She lost her train of thought when Adam unhooked her bra and tugged it down off her shoulders, his palms rough against her tight nipples. He buried his face in her neck, his tongue flicking over her skin as he cupped her breasts, his thumbs tracing over her nipples in a circle. They tightened to the point of aching, and she moved her hips again, unable to hold still under the onslaught of sensation. She shuddered as the heat of his mouth on her bare skin rippled through her.

"I think you like me at least a little bit," he said, his voice a little rough.

She shook her head, struggling to keep the tiniest bit of distance between them. "No. I don't," she lied.

She felt him smile against her skin, and he tipped her back slightly, his mouth scorching a path from her neck and down her collarbone, his beard prickling against the skin of her breast. Oh, Jesus, that felt good. The softness of his mouth surrounded by the rough scrape of his beard set every one of her nerve endings on edge, fear and lust seesawing through her, almost making her dizzy.

His mouth closed over her nipple, his tongue swirling over it before he sucked it gently. "So what does this mean, Charlie?" he asked, his mouth brushing her breast.

"It means that I want to fuck you, Adam. Badly."

He made that ridiculously hot growling sound again and tugged his own shirt over his head. Charlie fell against him before his shirt even hit the floor, wanting to feel that hard chest against hers. She kissed a path up his neck, savoring his clean, masculine scent and then trailed her hands down his sides, tracing the contours of the ridged muscles there. She smiled as she felt goose bumps rise up on his skin at her touch.

He cupped her ass and lifted her, laying her out on the couch, kneeling above her. His hands shook a little as he undid his belt and popped open the button above his fly. She began to wiggle her yoga pants down over her hips, but then slowed when she remembered. Shit.

"Um..." She trailed off, her fingers still hooked in her pants.

Adam's gorgeously sculpted chest heaved as he took a breath and shoved a hand through his hair, leaving it adorably disheveled. "You want to slow down?"

She shook her head, her cheeks heating. "No, I just...should warn you."

His brow creased. "Warn me? About what?"

"It's been a long time for me, and I haven't, um...landscaped in a while." She bit her lip as she studied him, waiting for his reaction.

Relief filled his face, and he smiled, his eyes crinkling. Then he took one of her hands and guided it to his cock, hard and thick beneath his jeans. "Jesus, Charlie. Does it feel like I care?"

She shrugged. "Some guys do."

"Some guys are assholes."

God, did she ever know that fact firsthand. The thought was almost sobering enough to make her reconsider what they were about to do, but then he slipped his fingers into the waistband of her yoga pants and started working them down, and all she could focus on was the here and now and how good he felt. How good he was making her feel.

He peeled her pants off. "How long is a while?"

She trembled as his fingers skimmed along her hips, the outsides of her thighs, the backs of her knees. "Almost a year. I haven't..." She swallowed and licked her lips, her pulse racing. "You're the first. Since the breakup."

His eyes darkened and rain splashed harder against the windows, matching the rhythmic thrumming of her pulse through her veins. He hooked his thumbs into her panties and pulled them down, the cotton scraping delicately over her sensitized skin. "I don't know what to say." He tossed her panties aside. "I'm pretty fucking lucky, I think."

It was Charlie's turn not to know what to say, so she stroked him through his jeans and his eyes flickered closed for a second. He rocked his hips against her hand, pressing into her touch. Quickly, he rose from the couch and shucked his jeans and then his boxers, revealing the most gorgeous cock she'd ever seen, long and thick, with the slightest curve to it. She whimpered and rubbed her thighs together, already anticipating how good he'd feel inside her. Adam reached into his jeans pocket and fished out a condom.

She propped herself up on her elbows, one eyebrow arched. "Pretty sure of yourself there, Hennessy," she said, tipping her head at the condom in his hand.

"Call it wishful thinking," he said, setting the condom on the coffee table and easing himself down on top of her. They sighed in unison at the sensation of being skin to skin. He brushed a lock of hair out of her eyes and swept his thumb over her cheekbone. "God, Charlie," he whispered before capturing her mouth in a hot, hungry kiss. His cock rubbed against her thigh and she moaned into his mouth, scraping her nails lightly down his strong back.

He slipped a hand down between their bodies, the room lighting up with a flicker of lightning as he ran a finger along her lips, teasing them apart. His mouth still on hers, he slowly, slowly slipped a finger inside her, his thumb brushing against her clit. She bucked up into his touch, her muscles clenching around his finger, hot pleasure streaking through her. They'd barely started, and she was already on the brink of orgasm.

"God, you're so wet," he whispered, kissing along her jaw as he slowly moved his finger in and out of her, stretching her. His thumb circled her clit with slow, firm strokes, and a delicious pressure coiled low in her stomach.

"Eleven months, Adam. Eleven long months."

"And here I thought this"—he slipped a second finger into her and she moaned, louder than she'd intended—"was for me." His thumb feathered over her clit and he curled his fingers inside her. The pressure that had been building inside her broke free, that sharp need melting into hot, heavy throbs as she came on his hand, moaning out his name, arching up into him.

After several seconds, when she could breathe again, she smiled lazily up at him. "*That* was for you. Because of you."

He smiled, a slow, lopsided smile. "You turn the prettiest shade of pink when you come. It makes your freckles look like they're glowing." His fingers were still inside her, and she clenched around him at his words, fresh arousal washing over her like a wave.

"You like my freckles?"

Thunder rumbled around them, overpowering the sound of the rain against the windows for a moment. Somewhere in the back of her mind, she thought maybe she should feel embarrassed at how quickly she'd come. But she didn't feel embarrassed with Adam. She couldn't, not when he was looking at her with an almost reverential focus.

"Yes. Very much." He trailed his mouth down her neck and across her collarbone. "I wanna kiss every single one." His beard scratched against her skin, and she arched up into him.

She didn't want him to be sweet, to make it seem like she could be someone to him. She just wanted to *feel*, wanted the temporary oblivion of his body inside hers. "Fuck me, Adam."

His eyes darkened at her words and he slipped his fingers out of her, reaching above her for the condom on the table as his mouth slammed into hers, claiming her with a hot, deep kiss. She hooked her legs around his hips and rocked up into him, and he let out a loud groan when his cock slid against her slick pussy.

"Fuck, Charlie," he said, rolling his hips and sliding his cock against her again. She jerked up at the sound of something smashing to the ground and shattering, almost crashing her head into Adam's.

"I broke your lamp trying to grab the condom. Sorry," he said as he sat up for a second, tearing the packet open and rolling on the condom. He eased himself back down on top of her and lined up the head of his thick cock at her soaking-wet entrance.

She met his eyes and reached up and cradled his face, loving the way his short beard bristled against her palms. "Make it up to me."

"Gladly." With one arm braced on the arm of the couch above her head, he gripped her hip and slid inside her in one stroke. "Fucking Christ," he said, and she wrapped her legs around his hips, urging him deeper. Wanting more. He pushed in another inch and closed his eyes, sweat dotting his hairline.

She brushed a lock of hair off his forehead. "Adam? You okay?"

He pulled out of her and thrust back in with a wonderfully hard, deep stroke. "I'm a hell of a lot better than okay." He stroked in and out of her again, and she moaned softly, loving the way he filled her, the way the curve of his cock hit just the right spot inside her. "You feel so damn good, Charlie."

Her teeth scraped against his earlobe and she clenched around him. "So do you. God, you're in so deep."

He made that growling sound again and began to fuck her in earnest, pumping his hips as he thrust in and out of her, and gloriously hot pressure tightened the muscles in her core. The couch bumped against the table, sending the rest of the contents tumbling to the floor, and she didn't care. All she cared about was Adam's body inside hers, making her feel so fucking good it almost hurt.

He thrust in harder, kissing her roughly, and her toes curled so hard her foot started to cramp. He broke the kiss and his tongue traced the shell of her ear. "I want to feel you come, Charlie."

The fact that he wanted her pleasure, wanted to feel it, seared through her like the lightning flashing outside, and something in her chest softened. He gripped her hip and adjusted the angle, going deeper. The shaft of his cock rubbed against her clit, and she lost it, pulled under by the weight of the pleasure crashing over her. Heat flushed her body and she throbbed and pulsed around him, flooding his cock.

"Fuck! God, Adam...fuck, yes, shit, I can't... Holy fuck," she stuttered out, pretty sure her heart was doing its best to slam its way free of her ribs.

He pulled her even closer, her hair tangled around his hand, and with a low groan, buried himself inside her, so deep she could feel each pulse of his orgasm as he came. The rain streaked against the windows, thunder rumbling around them as she caught her breath.

"Please tell me we can do that again," she said, running her fingers through his hair.

He laughed quietly. "I thought you didn't like me." He trailed his fingers over her shoulder, staring at her skin, at the freckles there, a half-smile on his face. The freckles. God. As though she was enough for him, just the way she was.

She screwed her mouth to the side, trying to hide her smile and ignoring the small, niggling fear that she could get in too deep with him.

He kissed her, slow and sweet and lingering. Lifting his head, he brushed his nose against hers. "Charlie likes Adam," he said in a teasing singsong voice. "Charlie likes Adam."

She scrunched her nose up. "Does not." But he moved inside her, still mostly hard, and she clenched around him.

He wiggled his eyebrows. "Does too."

She laughed, pulling him down for another kiss.

Chapter Six

Adam lay sprawled on his stomach on Charlie's bed, his face buried between her thighs as he swirled his tongue over her clit. Her hands tightened in his hair, and he knew she was getting close. They'd only been sleeping together for a week, but he was already learning her cues, her likes and dislikes.

"Oh God, yes. Right there. Don't stop," she said, panting, her thighs shaking under his hands.

He moaned and moved his tongue against her in the same steady rhythm. Fuck, it was so unbelievably hot when she came, that gorgeous flush sweeping across her skin, her entire body shaking as his name fell from her lips. She got wetter under his mouth and his dick twitched against the mattress, despite the fact that less than fifteen minutes ago Charlie had gotten him off with probably the best blow job of his life. He'd finished up work for the day and jumped into her shower, washing away the sweat and the sawdust clinging to him. She'd joined him in what was becoming their daily routine, although the blow job was a new—and highly welcome—addition.

He couldn't get enough of her. And yeah, it was the sex, which was mind-blowingly great, but it was her. Charlie. She was smart, and fun, and sarcastic and just...everything, really. She was still pretending that it was only sex between them, but he knew that what was happening between them was a hell of a lot more than just sex. And he was willing to wait for her to figure that out on her own.

And until she did, he was happy to fuck her brains out on a daily basis. More than daily, at the rate they were going.

And if she didn't figure it out? This was all going to blow up in his face and would probably be painful and messy. But it was a chance he was willing to take. He'd survived loss before, and if he needed to, he could do it again. If anyone was worth the risk, it was Charlie.

"Oh God, Adam! Yes!" Her nails raked over his scalp and he sucked her clit into his mouth. She bucked against him, hot and wet under his mouth as she came. He nipped at the insides of her thighs, and then trailed his mouth up her belly and over her hips, kissing a path up her body before lying down beside her and pulling her into his arms. She nestled her head against his chest, her fingers teasing through his chest hair.

She sat up suddenly, pulling away. "I almost forgot," she said, turning and pulling open the drawer of her nightstand. "I got you something." The drawer slammed shut and she thrust an envelope in his face.

He took it, peered inside, and then smiled. "Red Sox tickets? You didn't have to do that."

She shrugged and snuggled back down into him. "I wanted to. As a thank you. And I have a connection, so it really wasn't a big deal. Take your friend. Asshat neighbor guy."

He wanted to go with her, not Jared, but he decided not to push it. So instead, he laid the envelope on the bed and kissed the top of her head, wrapping his arms around her. "Thanks, Charlie."

"You're welcome." Her fingers once again moved back and forth over his chest. "So, I've been wanting to ask you. What's the deal with the cupcake?"

He smiled and pressed another kiss into her hair. "I lost a bet."

She looked up at him, one eyebrow raised and an adorable smirk on her flushed face. "Wow. That's commitment."

"Hey, I'm a man of my word."

She studied him and a heavy silence stretched between them, and for a second, he thought she might challenge him. Instead, she moved her hand from his chest to his shoulder, where the word "loyalty" was inked on his skin. With a small, contemplative sigh, she traced her fingers over the word.

"You could get it lasered off," she whispered, and he captured her hand in his, weaving their fingers together.

"Nah. It's grown on me. Besides, you can't just erase mistakes."

"No. I guess you can't."

"As long as you learn from them, you're doing something right. That's what I've tried to teach my younger cousins, anyway."

"Are you close with them?"

"Yeah, a couple of them. Our dads are brothers, or I guess were. Sage's dad, my Uncle Jake, died a while back now. He's a mechanic in Atlanta."

"Who else are you close with?"

"Chris. He's a landscaper in North Carolina." He paused and smiled, wanting her to meet them, these men in his family who meant so much to him. "Truth be told, I think they only put up with me because I help them whenever they need a big project done around the house."

She laughed softly and traced her thumb over the back of his knuckles, her skin pale against his tanned and scarred hand. "So, another question..."

"Shoot."

"What happened? With your divorce, I mean. Is it okay to ask about that?"

"Yeah, it's okay." He paused before continuing, trying to figure out how to explain something he was still trying to understand. "There's no one reason, really. Ultimately, we grew apart and wanted different things. It wasn't anyone's fault. It just..." He shrugged, and she nestled tighter against him. "It ran its course, I guess. To be honest, I still don't fully understand how it happened." He tipped her chin up and kissed her nose. "But I don't regret it. Not anymore. It was hard, but I've made peace with it."

A hint of fear flashed in her eyes, the same fear he'd seen the day they'd first kissed, the first time they'd had sex.

"How?" she whispered, her fingers tracing the wings of the dragon on his chest.

He thought about it for a minute. "Time, I guess. And knowing that it was for the best. I think we're both happier now. We did some crazy shit trying to fix it toward the end, because neither of us wanted to face the truth that it was over."

"What kind of crazy shit?"

"Well, she kept dropping hints about how hot guys with waxed chests are. Finally, she came out and admitted it'd really turn her on if I did it. So I did."

Charlie laughed. "Dude. You waxed your chest for her? Wow."

He laughed too, warmth spreading through him. "I know, right? Hurt like a motherfucker, and was itchy as hell when it grew back in. Guys on my crew probably thought I had fleas."

She ran her fingers through his chest hair. "I like that you're furry. It's manly. It suits you."

"Good, because I'm not doing that again."

"Okay, so you ripped hair out of your body. What other crazy shit did you try?"

He smiled and pulled her closer, a little surprised at how easy it was to share all of this with her. "Ah. Well. There was the grapefruit incident."

She pressed her lips together, hiding a smile. "Tell me."

"You ever heard of a grapefruit blow job?"

"Uh, no. I definitely have not."

"Okay, so the idea is that you cut the ends off a grapefruit so that you've got a ring. I think she read about it in fuckin' *Cosmo* or some shit. So anyway, you got the ring, and then you...you know. You put the ring at, the, uh, the bottom, and move it with your hand while..." He could feel his face getting warmer as he spoke.

She laughed. "I think I get the picture. So what happened?"

"It was really messy, and some of the juice from the grapefruit...it got in there. Like"—he pointed down toward his waist—"*in there.*"

Charlie laughed so hard the bed started to shake.

"I'm glad my pain amuses you," he said, tickling her ribs.

She squealed and then squirmed against him. "So you don't want me to go downstairs and get an orange?" she asked, propping herself up on one elbow. Her eyes sparkled down at him, all fear gone, and he smiled. "Or maybe a banana? You could bend over, and—"

He pulled her down and cut her off with a hard kiss. "We both know you don't have any fresh fruit in this house, smartass."

She laughed against his mouth and melted back into him, climbing on top of him. He wove his fingers into her hair, and the kiss changed into something sweeter and deeper.

"I have a favor to ask you," she said, and kissed just below his ear. "And it's totally cool if you say no, because it's not like we're, you know, dating or anything."

"If it's working on some of the other repairs around your house, I've already got it penciled in." He and his crew were almost finished with the deck, but no way did that mean he planned to stop seeing Charlie every day.

Her teeth scraped over his earlobe, and his hands tightened in her hair as blood surged to his dick. She sat up, her breasts bouncing, her skin glowing in the late afternoon sunlight bathing her bedroom. He trailed his fingers down her shoulders, tracing the freckles there, wanting to memorize them.

"Ha, no, it's not that, but thank you." She paused, and something sad crept into her eyes. "I...I have a wedding to go to this weekend, my cousin's, and I don't want to go by myself." The words tumbled out of her in a rush, like she was ripping off a verbal Band-Aid.

"And you want me to go with you?"

She nodded, worrying her bottom lip between her teeth.

He made a face, wrinkling his nose. "I don't know. Sounds kind of...datey."

He'd meant to tease her, but all the warmth drained out of him when her chest hitched and she blinked rapidly as though fighting back tears. "Yeah, you're right. It's stupid. Forget I asked."

"Hey, hey," he said, and pulled her down to his chest, smoothing his hands up and down her back. "I was kidding. Of course I'll go with you."

"Thanks," she mumbled into his chest. For several moments, he just held her, stroking a hand up and down her back, waiting and hoping she'd open up to him.

Finally, his patience was rewarded.

"About a year ago, I was engaged," she said, her voice a little hoarse.

"Shit, baby. I'm sorry. What happened?"

She took a shuddering breath and nuzzled into him. "He broke up with me the day before the wedding. He told me he'd fallen in love with someone else. Someone more together, more stable. Less bossy and crass, who actually knew how to cook and all kinds of shit. It was awful. He'd been cheating on me for months, and then I had to tell my entire family that the wedding was off. It was humiliating." She sniffled. "I hate weddings."

As her words sank in, everything started to make a lot more sense. Why she'd been so hurt when he'd stood her up for their date. Why she insisted they were only casual. Why she was so guarded. She'd been hurt and rejected in the past and was only protecting herself.

"I also feel like I should warn you that my parents will be there."

He shrugged. "Okay."

She pushed up onto one elbow. "Okay? That doesn't freak you out?"

"Not at all."

She eyed him skeptically, and God, all he wanted to do was make her smile. "Really?"

"I'd love to meet the people responsible for this," he said, stroking a hand down her spine. She fought it for a second, but a smile spread across her face, and something in his chest cracked open.

She kissed him, filling up that crack with everything warm and good.

"Your parents seem nice. And normal," Adam said, looking mouthwateringly hot in his navy-blue suit, his hair styled with a bit of gel. He sipped his champagne, the glass small and delicate in his big hand. Charlie took a swig of her own champagne, both impressed that her parents had behaved and surprised at how well the introduction had gone. Easy. Simple. She'd known she wouldn't be able to get away with bringing someone and not introducing him, but Adam had been great with her parents. And her parents hadn't said anything weird or embarrassing, thankfully.

"They are. And don't sound so surprised." She smacked him on the arm, loving the feel of hard muscle beneath the fabric of his suit.

About two hundred guests mingled in the outdoor ballroom set up on the lawn of the Hyatt Regency Boston Harbor, waiting for the bride and groom to return from pictures. The sun was just starting to dip low, still at least an hour away from setting. Pink and orange light reflected off the few clouds scattered in the sky, sparkling against the water. A handful of sailboats floated by, the sound of flapping sails mixing with the laughter and clinking glasses of the reception around them.

Charlie's phone buzzed from her clutch, and she fished it out. She had two text messages, one from her boss at the *Globe*, and the other from her mother.

From her boss: *We want you to follow the Sox on their road trip, starting Monday. In-depth report on post-season chances.*

From her mother: *Your carpenter is very cute. Just saying.*

And then another from her mother: *I'd let him sand my deck anytime.*

And then another: *I think I've had too much champagne. But seriously. Really cute. Way cuter than Jeff.*

And there it was. At least her mother had kept it in check in front of Adam.

Adam peered over her shoulder, and she quickly shut the screen off. "Everything okay?" he asked, a cocky smirk on his face, and she knew he'd seen the message.

"Yeah. Actually, better than okay. I get to go on the road with the Sox starting on Monday. My boss wants me to write an in-depth profile on their push for the pennant."

His face lit up and he pulled her in for a hug. "Baby, that's amazing. I'm so proud of you." He spoke the words into her hair, and she could almost feel herself splitting in half, so intense was the internal tug-of-war going on. Despite all the walls she'd put up, she'd caught feelings for him. Big time. And damn if she knew what to do about it. Part of her wanted to run, throwing her shields back up as fast as she could. Part of her wanted to let go and take a chance, to let him in.

Both options were at least a little scary. After the way Jeff had shattered and humiliated her, she wasn't sure she was ready—or would ever be ready—to let someone in like that. Because if she did, and she got hurt again, she wasn't sure how she'd survive it.

The bride and groom made their entrance, going straight into their first dance. Adele's "Make You Feel My Love" played through the speakers and floated on the warm early evening air. Something in Charlie's chest tightened as she watched her cousin Caroline dance with her husband, Bruno, gazing at each other with eyes so full of love and happiness it almost hurt to watch. Like staring at the sun, too bright and intense and overwhelming.

She'd thought she'd had that with Jeff, but she'd been so, so wrong, and she still wondered how she hadn't seen the signs before it had all blown up in her face. Maybe she'd been so desperate not to be alone, to belong to someone, that she'd been willing to overlook the warning signs. But it didn't matter now; the damage was done. All she could do was try not to get hurt again. And that meant keeping her heart to herself.

Adam slipped a hand around her waist and kissed her hair. "You look so damn beautiful, Charlie," he whispered in her ear. "I can't stop looking at you."

She smoothed her hands down the front of her black cocktail dress, his words coiling up her insides into confusing knots. Those words, given so freely, spoken so honestly, God, they felt good.

Too good. "You shouldn't say things like that to me," she whispered back.

"Why not?"

"Because you're making me like you too much."

Instead of putting some distance between them, her words only made him smile, his fingers curling into her waist. "Good. My evil plan is working."

She fought the urge to stamp her foot. "No. No evil plans. I'm not your girlfriend, Adam."

The smile stayed in place. "I know."

"This is just casual. Just sex," she said, not sure if she was reminding him or herself.

"Yep. Totally casual. Speaking of sex, you wanna crash at my place tonight? I don't live far from here." He wiggled his eyebrows, and she found herself smiling despite the fear sucking all the air out of her lungs. "I'll curl your toes and make you an omelet in the morning. Can't beat that."

God, why did he have to be so fucking charming? So damn cute? The upcoming road trip was a good thing. It would let her get some distance, and with it, hopefully some clarity.

"Okay, fine." She nodded at him, both loving and hating the way her breath caught when she looked at him. Maybe it had been a mistake to bring him to the wedding. She hadn't wanted to miss it, but she hadn't wanted to go by herself, either, and deal with everyone's semi-disguised "poor Charlie, she was practically jilted" stares. But being here with him...it felt real. Like he was more than the hot carpenter she was banging.

Because he is, whispered a small voice from somewhere deep inside her, and she took a long sip of her champagne, trying to drown that voice. Her stomach churned uncomfortably at the thought, at the truth of it.

"It was the omelet that sealed the deal, wasn't it?"

She laughed despite her weird mood. "Yeah, Hennessy. Definitely the omelet."

She was pushing him away. Adam could feel it. All night, there'd been something off with them, their usual easy banter strained, a slight hesitation in the way she touched him. At first, he'd chalked it up to how much she hated weddings, but as the evening wore on, he had a feeling it was more than that.

All through dinner and the seemingly endless toasts, he'd tried teasing her, tried kissing her, tried making her laugh, and while she'd played along, there'd been something about the light in her eyes that had him on edge.

And the more she pushed him away—with her reminder they were only casual, with the small ways she kept herself closed off—the more desperate he became, a hot pressure clawing at the inside of his chest. He wanted to drag her into the center of the room and kiss her senseless in front of everyone. Wanted her to admit she liked him, because he sure as fuck liked her.

He got that she was scared. Shit, he was scared too. They'd both been hurt, had been through some hard stuff, but he also knew he didn't want to live the rest of his life not taking a chance on something great because he was scared. He'd come to that realization, being with her. He just didn't know how to get her there, too.

He leaned over and draped an arm across the back of her chair. "Dance with me." A statement, not a question, because he knew if he asked, she might turn him down. A flicker of hesitation crossed her face for a second before she bit her lip and nodded, offering him her hand. He led her onto the dance floor, weaving between swaying couples before turning and pulling her into his arms. Spandau Ballet's "True" wafted through the evening air, and he tucked her against him, wanting her as close as possible. She laid her head against his chest, and as he stroked a hand up and down her back, he could've sworn he felt her tremble.

Slipping his hand under her chin, he tilted her face up. "Are you okay?" He couldn't help but wonder if she was thinking about the asshole who'd broken her heart. Was she thinking about the wedding that never happened? Would she tell him if she was?

She blinked rapidly, her eyes shining in the dim light from the paper lanterns strung across the tent's ceiling. "Yeah. I'm fine."

A lie. He could feel it in the tension of her spine, could see it in the set of her mouth. So he did the only thing he could think of. He pulled her tight against him and closed his mouth over hers, kissing her slow and deep, needing to show her how he felt. He couldn't tell her. She'd run. That much he knew.

He broke the kiss and brushed his lips against the outside of her ear, reverting to sex, knowing she'd respond. "You turn me on so fuckin' much, you know that? I can't wait to get you home later."

She looked up at him, her lids hooded and her eyes glazed, no longer sad or panicked. She pressed her hips against him, and his dick twitched in his pants, the flow of blood taking his erection from halfway to completely hard. "What will you do to me when we're alone?" she asked, her fingers threading into his hair.

"Anything you want. I'm yours."

Her breath caught at his words and she spun away, grabbing his hand and leading him through the crowd and inside the hotel. After glancing down the hallway, she pulled him into the family bathroom and flipped the lock behind them, backing him up against the door, something desperate shining in her eyes.

"I want you, right now." She skated a hand over the bulge in his pants, and his eyes shut for a second, heat snapping down his spine.

"I don't have a condom," he said, trying to keep up with her and the sudden turn of events.

"I don't care. I need this, Adam." Her words seared through him, and he cupped her face, kissing her hard and urgent, their tongues tangling together, something desperate spreading between them. She pushed his suit jacket off his shoulders, and he flung it to the floor.

"You are so gorgeous," he said, his lips scraping against hers as he spoke.

She shook her head. "Don't." The single syllable came out on a choked whisper, and her fingers went to his belt buckle, opening it and undoing his fly. She slipped a hand into his pants and stroked his cock, his balls tightening.

"This is fuckin' crazy," he said, and kissed her again, giving in to the need surging through him. The need to be inside her, connect with her. He cupped her ass and lifted her up, backing her against the wall. Her legs came around his waist, her skirt riding up.

"I need you, Adam, and I can't... I want you inside me. Now."

He groaned and pushed her thong to the side, sliding the head of his cock against her, slicking her wetness over himself. He pressed his forehead against hers as he slid slowly inside her. Fuck, she was so wet and hot around his bare cock that he had to remind himself to breathe. He rolled his hips, inching in even deeper, and she cried out, her head falling to the side.

"Charlie, look at me," he said as he pulled almost all the way out before thrusting back in. "Sweetheart, *look at me.*"

She dragged her eyes to his and he stroked in and out of her again, fucking her as deep as possible, burying himself inside her and still not feeling like it was close enough. He held her eyes as he moved his hips, rocking in and out of her. She clenched around him, still maintaining eye contact, her eyes bright and intense as he moved inside her, stretching and filling her.

"Oh, God, Adam," she said, her voice high and breathy.

Still cupping her ass, he adjusted the angle so he rubbed against her clit with each firm, hard thrust into her. The slap of skin on skin echoed off the bathroom tile, punctuated with soft moans and heavy breaths.

"Fuck, I'm gonna come. Can I come inside you?" He panted out the question, his heart throbbing in time with the orgasm building at the base of his spine.

"Yes." She moaned as she started to come, and he pumped into her harder and faster, riding her release to find his own.

He came hard, his fingers digging into her ass as he groaned out her name, nuzzling his face in her neck. For several moments, neither of them spoke, the air thick with the scent of sex, chests rising and falling.

Lifting his head, he kissed her, gentle and soft, still buried deep inside her, not wanting to leave her body. The fantastic sex had switched off his brain, and the words fell out of his mouth. "God, Charlie, I like you so fuckin' much. You're amazing."

She stiffened against him and ducked her head away, and he knew he'd messed up with his honesty. "Put me down." Her voice was quiet, echoing off the bathroom tiles.

Reluctantly, he slid out of her and set her gently on her feet. She adjusted her underwear and her dress, tugging it down over her hips. She hiccupped, and that was when he realized she was crying.

"Charlie, I—"

She cut him off with her gaze, tears streaking down her cheeks. "I'm sorry, Adam. I can't do this. I have to go." She spun and unlocked the door, moving to yank it open.

Hastily, he tucked himself back in his pants and wrapped his fingers around her arm, tugging her back toward him. "No fuckin' way. You don't get to say that after what just happened and then just fuckin' leave. We're not done. We can't be done, just because I said I like you. God, Charlie."

"I don't know why you're so upset. It's just sex." She pulled her arm out of his grip and crossed her arms over her chest, closing herself off from him, despite the fact that not even sixty seconds ago, he'd been bare inside her.

He shook his head, and the truth burst free. "Not for me it isn't. Not anymore."

"No! You don't get to do that. You knew what this was." She blinked rapidly, but it didn't stop the tears from falling.

"What are you so afraid of?" He took a step closer and could feel the heat radiating off her small body as she stared at him with those sad brown eyes. He concentrated on breathing, holding himself together even as his own fear ripped him apart piece by piece. "Charlie, say something. Please."

"I can't do this."

His hands curled into fists at his sides, and he was completely at a loss as to what to say or do. He waited a second too long to speak, and she spun and pulled the door open, disappearing back into the wedding. He stood, rooted to the spot, trying to figure out what the hell had just happened.

By the time he emerged from the bathroom, she was gone. And that crack in Adam's chest, the one Charlie had wormed her way into, split right open. Ripped him in fucking two. He slammed his fist into the wall and left, heading out into the cool evening air as pain churned through him.

Chapter Seven

Charlie hadn't slept well in almost a week, and not just because she was on the road covering one of the biggest stories of her career. The Sox were a game ahead of the Jays, and if they kept up their winning streak, they'd clinch the pennant. And her lack of sleep wasn't because she'd heard from her agent that several publishers were interested in her book proposal. Or because of the shitty hotel mattresses she'd endured in first Oakland, and then San Diego.

No, her sleeplessness was all because of Adam and what she'd done to him. Every time she closed her eyes, all she could see was the hurt etched onto his handsome face as she'd pushed him away.

Goddammit, she missed him. He'd made her like him, maybe even more than like him, and she'd walked away, running scared and trying to save herself future heartbreak. Instead, she'd only induced heartbreak in the present, dumbass that she was. She'd seen his blue eyes darken with pain, his jaw tight, when she'd told him they were done. She'd seen the way he'd curled his hands away from her, hurt practically radiating off him.

She rolled over in her hotel bed, staring at the shadowed popcorn ceiling in the dark, the quiet hum of Toronto traffic buzzing through the window. She'd pushed him away because she'd been scared she was getting in too deep, too fast with a guy who seemed too good to be true.

The simple truth was that Jeff hadn't been half the man Adam was, and he'd found her lacking. She'd been so scared Adam would eventually feel the same way.

She blinked, and two fat tears rolled down over her temples and into her hair. With a frustrated grunt, she rubbed her palms over her eyes, trying to stem the flow of tears making their nightly appearance.

God, she'd blown it, hadn't she? Adam was hot as hell, funny, hardworking, and sweet in a rough-around-the-edges kind of way. He was... Fuck, he was amazing. She'd had a chance at something great and she'd let that fucker Jeff ruin it, just like he'd ruined so much else in her life. Adam had never made her feel like she was less than. Like she didn't deserve happiness. Adam had only ever made her feel good. He'd only ever taken her exactly as she was, never expecting her to be something she wasn't.

Because, as hard as it was for her to believe, she'd been enough. She'd shown him exactly who she was, and he'd wanted her, not for who she could be, but for who she was.

All the days she'd been gone, he hadn't called or texted. Hadn't reached out at all, and she knew it was because she'd hurt him. Sitting up in the dark, she grabbed her phone from the table beside the bed. In some distant part of her brain, she registered that it was late, after one in the morning, and that he was probably sleeping, but she scrolled to his name anyway. She touched the little blue phone icon, a million horrible thoughts streaming through her. What if he didn't want to talk to her? What if he was with another woman? What if he told her to go fuck herself?

It started to ring, and she pushed them all away. At least then she'd know. She felt brave until she heard his voice, deep and rusty with sleep. He didn't say hello. Just her name.

"Charlie."

Those two syllables slammed into her and she clammed up. Everything stopped. Her heart. Her brain. Her lungs. She was a statue made of fear and guilt and confusing uncertainty.

"Hi," she managed to whisper, curling her hand around her phone. A muscle in her pinky finger cramped in protest, but she needed to hang on to the phone or she'd fall apart.

"Hi." It was all he said, and after a few seconds of silence, he let out a sigh. "Are you okay?"

She blinked, tears stinging her eyes as her throat thickened. "Not really."

"Me neither."

His words cut through her, and she couldn't remember why she'd called. She kicked her legs free of the blankets tangled around her, suddenly too hot. Her heart thumped in her chest and the hand holding the phone started to shake.

Oh, God. She was freezing up and chickening out.

Still scared.

"Are you gonna say anything?" he asked, and she could hear the edge of frustration in his voice. She opened her mouth, but all that came out was a choked little sob. She wanted to say so much, but what if she got it wrong?

"I don't want to play this game with you," he said. "I can't." He waited another second, and more tears slipped down her cheeks. "Goodbye, Charlie." He disconnected the call, and Charlie marveled at how silence could be so heavy and so empty at the same time.

She rolled to her side and sobbed into her pillow, aching over what she'd ruined.

Sweat rolled down Adam's back as he moved his sander over the antique door he was refinishing for a client. He'd finished up with Charlie's deck a few days ago and had thrown himself into another project, not wanting to think about her. Not wanting to think about how much he missed her or how pissed he was at her for not even giving what they had a chance.

He switched the sander off and grabbed a sanding block, working it over the delicate edges of the door. Moving. He had to keep moving. It was when he held still that the wound she'd left started to hurt.

He'd laid it all out that night at the wedding. He'd been honest with her, and she'd run. From him. From them. And then when she'd called the other night, God, his entire body had jolted to life. He'd hoped, but she hadn't said a damn thing. Hadn't said she was sorry. That she missed him. That she couldn't stop thinking about him. That she wanted a second chance. She hadn't said a fucking word, and he'd had to hang up.

He glanced around his workshop, at the tools and shelves lined with hardware and stains and rags. A helplessness he hadn't felt since the divorce washed over him. Just like with Melissa, he couldn't fix this. He couldn't make Charlie feel something she didn't, no matter how badly he wanted her to.

His phone buzzed from his back pocket and he yanked it free, squinting at the screen.

Charlie.

Again.

This marked the third time she'd called since their conversation—if you could call it that—the other night. And as he'd done the previous two times, he declined the call. But he didn't jam the phone back into his pocket. No, idiot that he was, he stared at the screen, waiting to see if the voicemail icon would pop up. Still hoping.

It didn't, and he blocked her number.

Charlie knocked on the door and fought the urge to hold her breath. It swung open and Jared's eyebrows shot up in surprise as he stared at her.

"You have the other Red Sox ticket, right?" she said by way of greeting. There was no time to be polite. A woman on a mission, she crossed her arms, her heart pounding furiously, so hard it might actually break free of her body.

"Uh, what?" Jared stared at her, his mouth open.

"I gave Adam tickets for today's game. Did he give you the other one?"

Jared frowned. "Why?"

"I need it."

"Why?"

Charlie ground her teeth together, calling on every ounce of patience she had. She needed his help, and if she ripped his head off, he wouldn't give it to her. "Because Adam's not talking to me, and I need to find him. I know he's going to the game. I need to be there." Shit, what if he'd given the tickets away?

"Oh."

Charlie's shoulders slumped, her mouth dry. "I'll get you tickets to another game. Please."

The morning after she'd called Adam, she'd known she needed to find a way to make it right between them. To tell him she was sorry. To try to explain. But he wasn't taking her calls, and she didn't want to just send an email.

She wasn't going to let fear dictate her life. Not anymore. She had to take this chance. It was the conclusion she'd come to after a week of sleepless, miserable nights. Adam had shown her what she could have, if only she'd let go of that fear. Leap and hope a net would appear.

Jared disappeared into the house and came back with the ticket in his hand, and relief flickered through her chest. "I'm supposed to meet him there," he said. He held it out to her, but then pulled it back when she reached for it. "He misses you. You hurt him, and that means he cares about you. It's been a while since he cared about someone, and if you can make him happy, then I want you to go and fix whatever it is that happened between you guys."

She nodded and took the ticket, slipping it into her purse, her heart leaping up into her throat at Jared's admission that Adam missed her. "Thanks, Jared."

He smiled and shook his head. "He asks, you threatened to beat me up."

She returned the smile. "Deal."

The red plastic of Adam's seat was warm against his back, and he took a sip of his beer. Checking his watch, he took another sip before extending his arm over the back of the empty seat beside him. He glanced around the stadium, taking in the billboards, the vendors walking up and down the aisles, the affectionately named Green Monster. The scents of beer and popcorn and grass filled the warm afternoon air, and the crowd stretched out before him, a buzzing sea of red and white. It had been a while since he'd been to a game, and his chest clenched when he thought of who'd given him the tickets.

And then, as though he'd somehow conjured her, she was there, scooting her way down the row of seats toward him. He watched her, not sure what to think. Or say. Or do. So he just watched her, heat kicking low in his gut, and she sat down in the seat beside him without a word. She held a bag of popcorn in her hands and, without looking at him, tilted it toward him.

His cheek twitched, the seedling of a smile, and he took a small handful of popcorn and settled back in his seat. "Where's Jared?"

Charlie tossed a piece of popcorn high in the air and caught it in her mouth. "I made him give me his ticket." She caught another piece of popcorn in her mouth, and his cheek twitched again. It wasn't fair how damn cute she was.

"Why?"

She set the bag of popcorn down between her feet and turned to face him, sliding her sunglasses off her face. "Because I miss you and I'm sorry."

The words he wanted to hear wrapped themselves around him, and for the first time since the wedding, he felt like he could breathe. Relief and hope tangled together, and that smile finally surfaced. He could feel it taking over his whole damn face. "I miss you, too. A lot."

"I got scared, Adam, and I ran. I shouldn't have done that. It wasn't fair to you, or to..." She paused and licked her lips, swallowing thickly. He noticed her hands were shaking, and he dropped the popcorn and laced his fingers through hers. Her shoulders relaxed a little. "It wasn't fair to us." She glanced down at their hands and then back up at him, her eyes softer than he'd ever seen them. "I'm so sorry for what happened at the wedding. Because the truth is..." She looked up at him, tears clinging to her lashes, and God, he wanted to kiss her. "I really like you, Adam."

Heat radiated through his chest, a feeling he didn't quite have a name for. Happiness and forgiveness and hope and all kinds of fantastic shit, all mixed together. He shrugged. "People do stupid shit when they're scared. Like not showing up for dates."

Her mouth twitched with a smile. "Like ditching their date at a wedding."

Although what she'd done at the wedding had hurt, he got it. Got it and forgave her, because more than anything, he wanted a chance to find out what they could be. "Ah, so it *was* a date."

She laughed and a tear slipped down over her cheek. "Yeah, it was. Adam, God." She shook her head and met his gaze. "I'm sorry. I'm sorry for acting like what we had wasn't something. Because it was. It was more than something. And I know I don't deserve one, but I want a second chance." She took a deep breath. "I want to date you."

He leaned forward and closed his mouth over hers in a tender kiss, swallowing her tears, her smile, her fears, all of it. He'd take it all on for her. For a shot at a future. For the chance to be happy again. It was all he wanted.

He broke the kiss and winked at her. "Get ready, Charlie Grant, because I'm gonna date the shit out of you." He slung an arm over her shoulders and tucked her close as the Red Sox took the field.

"Bring it on, Hennessy," she said as they eased back in their seats. "I'm ready."

ABOUT THE AUTHOR

Tara Wyatt is a contemporary romance and romantic suspense author who got her start making up stories about Hanson and the Backstreet Boys. Known for her humor and steamy love scenes, Tara's writing has won several awards, including the Unpublished Winter Rose, the Linda Howard Award of Excellence, and the Heart of the West. A librarian by day and romance writer by night, Tara lives in Hamilton, Ontario with her dog and husband. Visit her online at www.tara-wyatt.com, or find her on Twitter @taradwyatt.

Also by Tara:

Necessary Risk (Bodyguard #1)

Primal Instinct (Bodyguard #2) (sneak peek in the back of this book!)

Chain Reaction (Bodyguard #3) – Coming February 28, 2017

When Snowflakes Fall—Coming October 4, 2016

Like Fresh Fallen Snow—Coming October 4, 2016

Visit www.tara-wyatt.com/books.html for more information.

Keep reading for an excerpt from Semi-Scripted by Amanda Heger, available November 8, 2016.

Semi-Scripted - DAY ONE

From a distance, Marisol could only make out a shaggy gorilla, giant yellow bird, and diapered adult baby. But by the time she reached the game show studio, the line of would-be contestants snaked from the door, down the sidewalk, and out onto the parking lot. In front of her, a man in a purple unicorn suit swished his tail against her kneecaps. Behind her, a group of middle-aged women in florescent pink and green shirts clumped together, fanning themselves with handwritten signs and checking their bright green lipstick in a compact passed from person to person.

"I promise it is not too revealing." Marisol looked toward the white-blue California sky as she held the phone to her ear.

"Just promise you won't have a wardrobe malfunction onstage." Even from across the Pacific, her mother's voice carried more than a hint of desperation. And two hints of anxiety. Marisol still couldn't understand why this—a few hours on the set of her favorite game show—seemed to worry her mother more than anything else.

"I promise. I am being very responsible." And she was. She'd traded in her long-held plan of wearing a red and green bikini with a string of multicolored Christmas lights for a costume. Instead, she'd opted for a boring black t-shirt, snooze-worthy black jeans, and a pair of insomnia-curing cat ears. She'd even left the tail behind in her hotel room.

"I know you are, Mari. I'm so proud of you."

Marisol felt a million things about this trip, but not one of them was pride.

"I have to go now. They're here." She closed the tiny flip phone—a pay-as-you-go she'd bought when she'd stepped off the plane at LAX only a handful of hours before—and jammed it into her bag.

An army of women with clipboards marched through the crowd. The *Who's Got the Coconut?* staff. Their tennis shoes clomped against the blacktop of the parking lot, and a murmur trickled through the crowd behind them. Each wore a stark white t-shirt with a drawing of a coconut across the front. Smiling from the center of each coconut—and directly between each woman's breasts—was the host of *Who's Got the Coconut*, Sammy Samuelson.

One of the women pushed her way along the edge of the crowd, her gaze shifting steadily between the clipboard and the salivating game show hopefuls. Marisol pulled her sign from between her knees, ignoring the fact that she smacked the unicorn's ass on the way up.

BIRTHDAY QUEEN. She'd written the words in the same bubble letters she'd drawn for years, ever since she was thirteen and watching reruns of the show in her doctor's office.

"Hello? *Hola.* Today is my birthday." She flipped her hair over one shoulder and put on her brightest smile.

The woman remained expressionless and marched on, stopping in the sparse shade of a palm tree at the edge of the lot.

"Is this your first time?" the purple unicorn asked. His horn was covered in silver glitter that rained down on the pavement in front of them.

"Yes. I should have gotten here earlier."

"Naw. If you don't have a ticket, it doesn't matter when you show up. They pick from the crowd at random to fill the extra seats. All those suckers been here for three hours already, but they probably won't get in." More glitter showered them both as he shook out his mane. "I keep telling Ted that—he's the one up there in the diaper—but he never listens."

"How many times have you been here?" she asked.

"Every Monday and Wednesday for the last year." His grin was wide and proud, and the perfect circles of purple blush on his cheeks crinkled with the movement.

Marisol imagined the prizes he must have stored somewhere in the back room of his house. A treadmill with a dozen settings no one could figure out, three sets of golf clubs, fourteen washer and dryer combos.

"Even got in once," he said. "About three months ago."

"Once?"

He nodded. "Maybe today will make two, huh?"

The *Who's Got the Coconut* woman made her way toward them again, eyes narrowed as she stared down at her clipboard. Marisol exhaled. This was it. The show's website said they tried to let in contestants who were celebrating special occasions. A birthday *had* to qualify. Marisol crossed her fingers and prayed this woman with the sweaty face and magical clipboard would let her in. Then she would have one big, mind-bending adventure as a contestant before she had to buckle down and focus on why she was in California in the first place.

"You. Unicorn. You're in." The woman blew her bangs from her forehead and took the mythical creature by the elbow.

"Excuse me," Marisol called after her. "Excuse me, today is my birthday."

"Sorry. The unicorn was my last spot. Try a more unique costume next time."

The last of her hope circled the smoggy Los Angeles drain as the crowd began to dissipate. Scowls marked the faces of fuzzy dragons, and the man dressed as a baby pulled a flask from his diaper. For a moment, Marisol considered asking him for a swig to wash away her sorrows.

Instead, she followed the crowd down a wide alley and then along a fenced-in parking lot. Mercedes after shiny Mercedes filled the spots, and she tried to imagine which television star belonged to which vehicle.

That one is Sammy Samuelson's. No that one? Maybe that one with the funny—

"Watch it!"

Her right foot slipped out from under her. Then her left. Her butt smacked the pavement, and everything became a mess of feathers and expletives—some Spanish, some English. When they stopped, she lay on the ground beside a man dressed as a peacock.

A very large, very angry peacock.

"I said watch it." He sneered at her through the cutout below his beak. "Dumb bitches never look where they're going."

Marisol stood and dusted off her pants. "Excuse me?" This was too much. Being turned away from the show. Falling on her butt in front of all of these people. Then being verbally assaulted by a man dressed as a peacock. *On her birthday.* "It was an accident."

A small crowd had gathered around them, a mix of pedestrians and game show rejects staring at the tiny Latina and the fallen bird—who was still rolling on his back, unable to stand because of the weight of his tail feather display.

"Can somebody give me a hand?" He looked at the crowd.

She waited, arms crossed against her chest. No way she was going to help. In fact, she quite enjoyed watching him roll and grunt on the ground, the beak flopping over his face each time he moved.

"*Buenas dias.*" She stepped around him in long, quick strides, determined to make it back to the hotel without another man-bird related incident.

Footsteps scrambled up beside her, and Marisol whipped around. "You are a grown man in a leotard. Leave me alone."

"I am?" An unfamiliar face—human, definitely not animal—looked back at her. "I knew I was a little color-blind, but—"

"Sorry." She shook her head. "I thought you were someone else."

"Happy birthday, by the way." His dark eyes were a bit sleepy and framed by dark glasses. He had a bit of stubble along his jaw. Like he'd crawled out of bed ten minutes ago, with no time for coffee or shaving.

"How did you know?"

"I assume you're the queen?" He held up her hand-painted Birthday Queen sign in one hand and her cat ears in the other. "And this is your crown? Personally, I would have gone with jewels, but to each their own."

"Oh." She took her props and stuffed them into a nearby garbage can. Her mother had been right. Trying to cram a visit to *Who's Got the Coconut* into the first day of her trip was an irresponsible thing to do. She needed to be settled into her hotel room and practicing for tomorrow's interviews. With a twenty thousand dollar grant on the line, Marisol knew she had to be at the top of her nursing game. And her volunteer coordinator game. And her don't-let-my-family-down game.

"Wait. How about a birthday present?" With three long steps, the guy was beside her. He held out a green wrist band. "A free ticket to see *So Late It's Early.*"

"So late what?" Maybe it was a new game show. Maybe she'd walk out of the studio with a new car. Or a boat.

"*So Late It's Early.*" He pointed at his gray t-shirt, where a cartoon sun poked over a jagged horizon. "A talk show."

"No prizes?"

"Sorry, no prizes. But the warm-up comedian sometimes gives out candy." He slipped the band onto her wrist before she could say yes or no. "Make a right here and someone will scan your band at the holding area," the guy said.

The mid-afternoon sun reflected off the pavement, and sweat beaded along her hairline. The conference hotel was at least an hour-long bus ride from the studio. Plus, she still had to unpack, iron the wrinkles from her suit, and try to get some sleep before her interview tomorrow. The voice of panic settled into the back of her mind, filling it with words like responsibility. Restraint. Face of the organization. Bankruptcy. Sitting in the studio audience of a television show she'd never even heard of would be an epically stupid decision.

"This way? Through those gates?" she asked.

"Yep. Enjoy the show. And happy birthday."

With every step Marisol took, she intended to veer away from the studio and toward the bus stop. But she walked on, winding her way through the velvet ropes and picturing a set full of overstuffed furniture. There'd be air conditioning and candy. And maybe an up close and personal experience with a celebrity. On the plane, she'd spent two hours watching Delta Airlines' *Patriot Ninja Fighter* special. In her dream world, she'd end up sitting primly on a couch, surrounded by shirtless game show ninjas as they fed her birthday cake.

She stared at the line of people on the other side of the gate. This was not her dream world.

A man and woman in beige shorts stared into space while the teenagers beside them stared at the phones in their hands. Twin girls who looked about Marisol's age hooked their arms around an elderly woman. The woman's walker was covered in streamers, and a balloon floated from a string attached to one of the handles. *Birthday Girl!* it read.

"Wrist band?" a brunette with too much eyeliner asked.

"Oh. Sorry. I think I have made a wrong turn."

"*So Late*? This is the right line." The girl scanned her wrist band. "They'll send someone to get you in a few minutes."

Marisol barely heard her. Her mind was occupied not with the old woman or the surly teenagers, but with the group of people at the very front of the line. Their obnoxious pink and green t-shirts hurt her eyes, and she would have recognized them even if there wasn't a grown man in a diaper and bonnet standing directly behind them.

"I am in the wrong place."

The elderly woman in front of her turned, her walker clomping with every tiny movement. "They always let in the freaks that didn't get into the game show next door. Back when Jimmy was here you had to be classy to get into the studio. None of this—" she waved her hand at the over-excited teenagers and the teetering baby "—disgustingness."

"Now, Gran. We talked about this." The girls turned their grandmother forward, the walker making everything happen in slow motion. "Sorry," one of them mouthed.

"Welcome to the *So Late It's Early Show*. My name is Evan," a voice boomed from the front of the line. Marisol stood on tiptoe and craned her neck. It was him. Wristband Guy. Standing on a chair and holding a megaphone to his lips. "We're trying to fill the audience, so stick with us for a few more minutes and then we'll let everyone into the studio. In the meantime, I'll be around with some sticky notes and a bin for all your cell phones. They are not allowed in the studio. Thanks for your patience."

Three minutes later, Marisol's mind was still spinning as he stood in front of her.

"Hi, Betty." He waved to the elderly woman. "I guess you left all your electronic devices at home today."

"Sure did," the woman answered.

"Hey, the birthday girls found each other." He leaned in closer to Marisol. "It's not really her birthday, but she thinks it is. Phone?"

She stared at the sticky note and pen in his hand. "I am not going to stay."

"Why not?"

Because she'd never seen this show? Because she had other things to do? Because what kind of television show couldn't even fill its studio audience without pilfering from the game show next door?

"Look Gran!" One of the twins pointed over the other's shoulder. "There they are."

Marisol turned in the direction of the woman's wide-eyed excitement. A long white van pulled into the nearest fire lane. A giant bald eagle in a ninja mask graced the side, flapping its wings around the gargantuan letters. *PATRIOT NINJA FIGHTER.* The door slid open, and two brawny, muscle-bound ninja hopefuls walked straight into the studio.

"They are the guests?" she asked.

Wristband Guy nodded.

When was she ever going to get another chance to see the inside of a television studio? And an hour or two of fun before she had to buckle down wouldn't hurt anything, right?

Marisol dropped her cell phone into the container. "Happy birthday to me."

When the congratulatory *You've Been Selected for an Internship at the* So Late It's Early Show email showed up in his inbox a few months ago, Evan had been granted the prestigious title of script intern. For the first two weeks, he put in a few hours at the copy machine and a few more hours running scripts all over the studio, getting lost among the maze of nondescript rooms and closets. Every time he dropped a thick stack of papers in the writers' room, a buzz ran through him.

If he played his cards right, one day that could be him. After all, *So Late It's Early* was slated to be a pioneer in the late-night arena. No real competition. A witty host with a cult-like following. A slew of brilliant writers, poached from some of the best network comedy had to offer. Rumor was that James had never been asked to audition for the show. His legion of unrelenting fans had uncovered the location of the auditions—a comedy club down a back alley in Santa Monica—and begged James to show up uninvited.

Apparently it had worked.

Kind of. Until the ratings hit.

The show began to drown. They were probably still number one in the eighteen to twenty-five stoner demographic. But the critics hit hard and fast, and each article was like a wave of icy saltwater filling the show's collective lungs.

James January: The Biggest Flop Since Donald Trump's Comb Over.

So Late It's Early? More Like So Late It's Over.

And Evan's personal favorite, *Patty Duke Spanks James January Every Night: Affiliates Choose Reruns Over So Late It's Early.*

The other interns started jumping ship. Then the writers. A mess of production assistants. A month into his internship and the show was being renewed on a week-to-week basis. Which was why today's celebrity guests were a couple of "ninjas" with IQ scores lower than their body fat percentages. It was also why Evan's duties had expanded to luring audience members into the studio, scouring the Internet for old videos of celebrity guests, and setting out food in the green room.

And today, he found himself dropping off a tray of protein shakes for tonight's esteemed guests, Tim and Tony. They'd requested three flavors: chocolate, banana, and chocolate banana. In frosted glasses with green twisty straws.

"Do you guys need anything else?" he asked.

"When do we go on?" one of them grunted.

"After the monologue and the main comedy piece. It's like..." He glanced at the monitor, which gave a live feed of the show. Currently, James was mid-monologue, and the guys' glazed stares said they weren't following. "Don't worry about it. Someone will come get you when it's time." He unmuted the volume on the television.

"Did you hear about the truck that overturned in South Dakota this afternoon?" Onscreen, James leaned in to address the camera directly. "Hold on. Do people really live in South

Dakota? Where is that anyway? Shite. Can I say that one? Probably not." He shoved his bony middle finger up at the camera. "Anyway, truck overturns in South Dakota and spills five hundred pounds of McDonald's french fries all over the highway. Cops arrested the driver for driving under the influence. Said he'd been dipping into the *Special Sauce*."

Evan groaned.

"I don't get it," one of the Patriot Ninja Fighter guys said, producing a white powder from a bag and dumping it into a bottle of water. "Protein powder. Don't worry."

The door swung open, and Julia bolted in with her usual air of crisis and caffeine. She'd been promoted three times in the last two weeks, from writer to head writer to producer. Evan wasn't sure if she was a genius or on the verge of a nervous breakdown. Maybe both.

"We need to replace the *Facts of Life* parody." Her short brown hair stood up in fourteen different directions, and the circles under her eyes said she hadn't slept in days. "Couldn't get it past the network with James dropping the F-bomb every ten seconds."

"What do you need?" Evan asked.

"Another audience piece. Did Betty make it in today?"

"Yep." The snarky old woman was there every day, with her crinkled Birthday Girl balloon tied to her walker.

"Good. Grab her and one more. *Not* the giant baby this time. Please."

"Got it."

"I mean it, Evan. Not the baby."

"Don't worry," Evan told her. "I don't think that guy has washed his diaper in a month. Not going near him." But as he jogged out of the green room, he knew exactly where he was going. To the girl who'd cussed out the peacock on the front lawn. She was one of the only people in the audience not wearing a costume. And it was her birthday.

And she was hot.

He wound through the audience, stepping over outstretched legs and ignoring the smell of people who'd spent hours waiting—in hot costumes—in the late afternoon sun. Onstage, James threw the show to a commercial break. On a well-run, highly rated talk show, it would have been impossible to find the girl among the tightly packed house. But *So Late* was only seventy percent full, and half the audience looked like rejects from a furry convention.

The girl sat in the second row, eyes narrowed on the set. "They were coming to this show, yes? They must have been coming to this show," she said to the man beside her.

"Who?" Evan asked.

She jolted, sitting up tall with a light crease between her brows. "The ninjas. Are they next?"

"No. You are."

"What?"

"We need an audience member to play a game, and you're our lucky contestant. But we have to hurry. The show's going to start back up in a few minutes."

Her face fell into a frown.

She was going to say no. Maybe the guy beside her would do it. Or worst case scenario, one of those over-excited choir parents near the back. Their shirts would make for eye-gouging TV, but it had to be a better option than Ted the Man Baby.

"What do I need to do?" she asked.

"I don't know. It's, uh, kind of last minute." Everything they did was last minute. "But you'll get to go backstage. That's where the ninjas are."

She sprang from her seat as the lights dimmed. From across the room, he waved to Betty and the twins. By now, they knew their cue to shuffle their grandma backstage. The old woman had been a participant in every audience game the show had done in the last month. At first, she'd seemed reluctant and even a bit disgusted by James's onscreen persona. But with time and charm, the host wore her down. Now, Betty never missed a chance to flirt with James onstage.

Evan led the peacock fighter backstage and left her a few feet outside the green room. "I have to go help the other contestant. She's, uh, not exactly a spring chicken. Someone will be by to tell you what to do. Her name is Julia. She's about this tall." He held a hand to shoulder height. "Short brown hair. Kind of flops in her eyes all the time. Got it?"

No response.

He knew this must seem insane and confusing to anyone stepping onto their first television set, but it would take more time than he had to sort it all out. "So you're good?" he asked.

"*Gracias a dios,*" she whispered.

Evan followed her gaze through the open door of the green room, where Tim and Tony were engaged in some sort of one-handed push-up competition. "Okay, good luck then."

Several minutes later, he found himself in a darkened hall, standing in front of one of the backstage monitors. There were a hundred things left to do before the taping was done, but he couldn't resist a quick peek at the screens. The girl stood on James's left side and Betty—with her birthday balloon—stood on the right. Both dressed as Uncle Sam.

Uncle Sam from the early 1970s.

Onscreen, James put on his pipe-and-smoking-jacket accent. "Betty, I swear you're getting younger every day."

"It's my birthday, you know." She slowly lifted one hand from the walker and straightened her long white beard.

"You don't say." James looked directly at the camera, sharing the secret of Betty's daily birthdays with the home audience.

At this point, Evan suspected the home audience equaled the three people watching the show live and the other two recording it on their DVRs.

"And I understand we have another birthday girl in the studio. What's your name and how old are you today?" James asked.

The girl grinned and bounced on her toes. She was gorgeous, even in those ridiculous red and white striped bell-bottoms. "Marisol. I'm twenty-three."

"She's practically a baby," Betty said. The thin skin on her cheeks pinked and her blue eyes narrowed.

"Now, Betty. You're still my number one girl. Don't worry." James patted her arm. "Here's what we're going to do. Our guests tonight are from the not-quite-a-hit television show *Patriot Ninja Fighter*."

Marisol squealed. The studio audience laughed.

Maybe for the first time all night. A burst of self-congratulatory hot air filled Evan's chest.

"I take it you're a fan?" James asked.

She nodded.

"Well, you're in luck." Even the host couldn't keep a straight face in the midst of her excitement. "Because they're going to help us play a game we call Uncle Sam. That's it?" he asked to someone offscreen. "We couldn't come up with a better title? Fine then. Welcome Tim and Tony."

The muscle men strutted onstage, and the shorter of the two stood next to Marisol. She wasted no time in running her fingers up his arm. A ripple of laughter ran through the audience, growing louder and louder as she hammed it up. First, the petite Uncle Sam squeezed the guy's right bicep. Then the left, letting her mouth fall wide open.

"All right, all right," James said. "Any more of that and I'm going to have to charge you."

The audience rippled again. Their laughter echoed from the studio half a second before Evan heard it through the monitors.

"So what we're going to do is..." James's voice rolled on, explaining the rules.

Marisol and Betty would run to the other side of the stage, down a glass of "whiskey"—which was actually iced tea—run back, and concoct a replica of the Statue of Liberty out of all the grape-flavored bubblegum they could cram in their mouths. All in under three minutes. At the end, the wannabe ninjas would pick a winning sculpture.

Evan sighed. He'd seen this idea when he'd cleaned up the writers' room that morning. Someone—he suspected Julia—had crossed it off a list of ideas and scrawled a giant NO across the top.

On the monitor, Betty slammed her walker against the faux-hardwood, like a horse pawing at the ground before a race. But Marisol's smile slid from her face as she looked back and forth between James and the woman.

"I know what you're thinking," James said. "How unfair it is to put you up against someone like Betty, with all her age and experience and grit." He lowered his voice to a stage whisper. "She's got a liver like Fort Knox, and she won't hesitate to knock you down with her walker."

More laughter. Not the fake ha-ha-ha's the warm-up comedian forced out of the audience with threats and promises of candy. Real laughter.

Betty took off, not bothering to wait for a start.

"Well, go on." James pushed Marisol forward. "Someone in the audience has gotta stopwatch, right?"

Evan chuckled as Marisol jogged toward the end of the stage. A muzak version of *American Pie* played over the PA system while she ran.

"Bet-ty. Bet-ty. Bet-ty." The woman slammed her walker against the stage as the crowd roared their usual chant. Not only did Betty appear in every conceivable audience game, but she won them all too. Who was going to take on an eighty-something woman who genuinely believed every day was her birthday?

"Mar-i-sol. Mar-i-sol. Mar-i-sol." A few voices rang out in the crowd.

That split-second decision to offer her tickets was paying off in spades. Super funny, really attractive spades.

"Evan?" A buzz of static followed the voice in his earpiece. "Someone puked in the holding area. Clean it up before we let the audience out."

Keep reading for an excerpt from The Innocent and the Outlaw by Harper St. George, available now!

The Innocent and the Outlaw - Chapter One

Emmaline Drake knew trouble when it walked through the door. Five years of serving drinks had taught her that only three kinds of strangers ever entered Jake's Saloon in the tiny backwater town of Whiskey Hollow. The first two were drifters and loners who sought the saloon as a refuge from a world that didn't accept them. They kept to themselves and rarely caused trouble. A drink, a meal and conversation with a pretty girl were enough to send them on their way. But then there were men like the three who stood just inside the saloon's swinging, slatted doors. These men were the third type and just looking at them caused a knot of dread to churn tight in her stomach.

These men were outlaws.

If there was anything Emmaline knew, it was how to spot an outlaw. Thanks to her stepfather's profession, she'd had years of experience identifying the variations in that type of man. As a rule they were notoriously badly dressed, though the clothing of this particular group belied that rule. Even with their dusters covered with a layer of dust, the fine cloth and texture of their breeches and coats were apparent and their boots were obviously high quality. But it wasn't the clothing that made the outlaw. It was the eyes. Outlaws had the eyes of predators—full of violence and aggression.

Violence crackled like energy in the eyes of these men.

They paused to boldly survey the room and all conversation died. A quiet wave sucked out the sound as it moved throughout the handful of tables, silencing the patrons and leaving tension in its wake. Even Lucy, Jake's wife, who'd been pounding away on the woefully out of tune piano in the corner, faltered and let her fingers fall still. No one overtly acknowledged the newcomers, unless you counted the sideways glances from behind hunched shoulders as the men in the room took note of them without shifting their positions. The customers were like dogs, bristling at potential intruders.

After taking note of every occupant in the room, they did another pass, no doubt noting the bare wood floors and rough edges of the place. Jake hadn't spent much money on making the place appealing. There was no need when the nearest competition was more than a two days' ride away.

Emmaline stood at the bar, her hands clenched on the scarred and polished wood. She swallowed as she watched them through the narrow, cracked mirror that hung behind it. It was framed in an elaborate plaster that had been gilded at one time, but most of it had long since chipped away, leaving it a mere ghost of its former self. She had thought many times that that was probably an apt description of the town itself. Once it had been a thriving mining community, but when the creek had been picked clean of gold, everyone had moved on.

Gesturing to Jake for three whiskeys, she turned to set eyes on the strangers. They were taller than the mirror had suggested and meaner looking. The quality of their clothing struck her again. Their breeches weren't patched with the leather that sometimes adorned the thighs of the men who spent most of their time in the saddle. They were tailored, not the simple clothing of ranchers and cowhands. Even their coats were a thick wool that would have made her envious if she hadn't been so busy trying not to be afraid. They were no ordinary outlaws. These weren't the same type of men she'd known in her stepfather's gang. These men exuded power along with danger, a dark intent that said it was no accident that they had found their way to the saloon on that particular night. They were on the hunt and every man in this room had something to hide. It was a combination that could turn deadly with only the slightest provocation.

Each of them was over six feet tall, but the one on the right towered over the others by a few inches. He wasn't the least bit gaunt as often happened with tall men, as if they couldn't possibly eat enough food to support such a build. His powerful frame matched his height and his black eyes blazed with fury as he boldly looked over everyone in the room, sizing each of them up for the threat they might present and then discarding them one by one. It was hard to imagine the man who could pose a threat to him. An angry red scar ripped down his cheek and contributed to his fierce appearance, but he would've had no problems carrying out the look without it.

The middle one, a Spaniard, with his thick black hair and furrowed brow, appeared just as fierce as his partner, but more measured and calm. Less brute power, despite his broad shoulders and thick chest. His vivid green eyes were alight with intelligence and intensity, and he exuded an autocratic air that left her willing to bet anything that he was the leader.

But it was the one on the left who drew her attention and held it. With his physique, he could've been a match for the leader, except that his hair was lighter, that indefinable shade that hovered between rich brown and golden blond. His features were more refined, too, though undeniably masculine, a square chin with the hint of an indentation and a full, sculpted bottom lip. He seemed almost lazily indifferent, except that his eyes carried a calculating intensity that held her momentarily rooted to the floor when he happened to glance her way. A bolt of awareness shot directly to her belly as their eyes met, sending her pulse soaring and making her look away quickly as if she'd been caught doing something sinful.

The giant of a man moved to a table near the door and the other two followed suit, moving with caution, clearly suspicious of everyone else. The dark blond one on the left moved with surprising grace for a man of his strength, like he knew the full power of his body and knew how to control it. Somehow, observing that made her more aware of her own body and exactly how much of her breasts were on display. The realization made her blush.

"Em?" Jake's voice penetrated the strange fog that had come over her.

"Yeah?"

Eyebrows raised, he nodded to the three drinks on the tray beside her.

Always sensible and rarely flustered, she shook off the inexplicable fog that had come over her and grabbed the discolored tin tray with both hands.

"Be careful." Because she knew him well, she could easily discern the grimace lurking behind the caterpillar moustache that obliterated any hint of a mouth. But it was the nervous gesture of his hand running through his graying hair that ratcheted her anxiety up a level. He was always calm, even on that night two years ago when that bank robber had come in and everyone had recognized him from the flyer hanging beside the door. Jake had merely grabbed the short-barreled shotgun he kept behind the bar and offered the man a chance to leave. He had taken it.

Unable to stifle the impulse in time, she turned her head to look at the billboard postings. There were five posters there, but none of the drawings resembled the strangers. Of course, two of them were drawings of men with kerchiefs covering the lower halves of their faces, so there was always the possibility.

"Do you know them?" she whispered and turned her attention back to Jake.

He shook his head, but his eyes shifted to their table again. "No, but I have my suspicions. Go on now. We'll talk later."

How was she supposed to remain composed when he went and said something like that? Now that the men had settled themselves at a table, the conversations resumed and the tension in the room decreased notably. Lucy even resumed her piano playing, but at a more sedate pace. Her own anxiety should have begun to abate, but it hadn't, her stomach refused to stop its churning and she couldn't shake the feeling that something was terribly wrong. That something dangerous and profound was about to happen and she was powerless to stop it, like being stuck on a runaway train that was about to run out of track and she could only hold on and watch as it flew over the edge of a cliff.

With Jake's warning spinning around in her mind, Emmaline tightened her grip on the tray and slowly made her way to the table. She'd long ago become accustomed to the revealing nature of her outfit, but as she approached, she longed for the modest dresses she wore everyday on the farm. The costume she wore at the saloon had been one of her mother's gowns from her days in the brothel in Helena. Emmaline and her sisters had modified it by shortening the deep red silk to knee-length and adding two layers of black lace taken from another gown. The bodice had already been obscenely low, so they had only had to add the matching black lace there. It revealed a large amount of her cleavage with its nonexistent sleeves, mere scraps of fabric that dropped low off her shoulders to hang down her upper arms. Her legs at least were covered in sensible black, woolen stockings. She'd started out with her mother's silk ones, but they had worn out years ago. She'd always disliked the costume, but never more so than now as she walked toward a table full of outlaws.

She shivered as she approached the doorway. Though the days were getting warmer, winter had refused to relinquish its grip on the nights. The other customers were drinking and keeping warm at tables near the cast-iron stove that sat further inside, but not the strangers. Apparently they preferred to keep their distance, as if she needed any further proof of their dubious intentions.

As she advanced, the pretty one with light hair—*is that how she was referring to him?*—turned the full force of his gaze on her. It licked its way up her legs and over her hips, settling on her breasts for a moment before finally making its way to her face. He'd sat back in his chair, one leg stretched out before him, almost lazy in his regard of her. She had worked at the saloon for almost five years, so she was used to the looks men gave her. She even encouraged them in the hopes that those passing through would leave a little extra on the table for her—the locals had nothing extra to leave. But with him...the look was different. It wasn't merely taking in what the dress put on display. His eyes demanded her attention, demanded her response, demanded much more than she was willing to give, while his lips promised more than she could risk imagining. One corner of his mouth turned upward, a suggestive smile that had her blushing again. Holy hell, what was happening to her? Men didn't affect her this way. She didn't allow it, because she knew they couldn't be trusted.

Tearing her gaze away from him, she focused her attention safely on the scarred, wooden tabletop as she sat the tray down and offered her customary greeting. "Welcome, gentlemen. Jake sends his regards."

"Jake?" The pretty one spoke, his voice a deep rumble that warmed her deep down in ways she refused to acknowledge.

"The owner." Without looking up, she gestured over her shoulder toward the bar where Jake stood watching...she hoped. Then she carefully sat a tumbler with a finger of whiskey in front of each man. On the rare occasions Jake thought it necessary, he'd preemptively send over a free drink to welcome a new customer. If the man felt indebted or grateful to the proprietor, he'd be less likely to leave a mess behind. Sometimes it worked, sometimes it didn't.

The giant picked his up and tossed it back before she'd even finished.

"Rotgut." The hard voice matched its owner.

Glancing up, she met his disapproving look with a challenge in hers. "We don't serve rotgut, sir." She actually didn't know if that was true or not. Men complained that other saloons cut their whiskey, but nobody had ever complained about Jake's. She wouldn't put it past him, though. With the amount of business they'd had lately, it was barely worth her time to make the trip into town for work.

"My friend has expensive tastes." The pretty one pulled a wallet out of a pocket hidden inside his coat. It was a smooth, chocolate-colored leather with no creases, almost brand new, she'd guess. When he opened it to extract a note, she could see many others nestled inside. The confident way he carried himself, along with his clothing, had left little doubt in her mind as to his wealth, but this only confirmed that she was right to be suspicious. What were they doing in Whiskey Hollow? Bringing trouble, she was certain of it. "A bottle of your finest Kentucky bourbon." His gaze licked over her and one corner of his mouth tipped up as he extended a ten-dollar note to her.

"We only have rye. Overholt?" The question forced her to look at him. She was struck anew by the strong, masculine beauty of his features. High wide cheekbones, strong granite jaw covered with a dusting of honeyed stubble, perfectly formed lips. This one was trouble in more ways than one.

He merely gave a single nod, indicating the substitution would be fine, and lifted an eyebrow when she hadn't taken the money.

Remembering herself, she grabbed the note, deliberately making sure to not touch him, and gave a small smile to the other two. They did not return her smile. "I'll be right back."

Emmaline managed to keep her steps even and measured all the way back to the bar. But when she placed the tray down, her gaze speared Jake where he stood. "They want a bottle of rye. Come to the back and help me get one."

He looked like he wanted to argue—she knew he kept a few bottles under the bar—but she needed to know what he knew of them. Some instinct warned her that their presence had something to do with her stepfather's absence. He and her older stepbrother, Pete, were over a week late coming home from their latest job, which wasn't entirely uncommon, but no one had heard from them. A hollow feeling in the pit of her stomach said that the job had gone terribly wrong. As much as she disagreed with their lifestyle, it turned her stomach to think of what would happen to her and her younger sisters without them.

"Who are they?" she asked the moment Jake stepped through the door to the tiny storeroom filled with crates of bottled beer and barrels of moonshine. "Does their presence have anything to do with Ship?" Though he was her stepfather, everyone called him Ship, even her younger sisters who were his blood.

"Calm down, Em." He placed a hand on her shoulder. "I don't know anything for sure and getting upset won't help anything. You've heard of the Reyes Brothers? That could be them. That one in the middle, the one that looks like a Spaniard, I think he's their leader."

The Reyes Brothers. A chill prickled her scalp and cold ribbons of fear trailed down her spine. Ship had talked about them the last time he'd been home. Though she hadn't gotten the impression the two had crossed paths, he'd described the successes of the gang with the glee and admiration only someone hoping to rise to those levels could summon. They moved cattle across the border. Lots of cattle. Which was only illegal depending on which side of the border they were on. But to hear Ship tell it, they'd made a fortune guarding mining and land claims and even that wasn't technically illegal, unless it involved killing. She couldn't remember anything else he'd said. The only detail she'd taken to heart from that conversation was that no one crossed them and lived to tell about it.

Had Ship done something stupid like try to steal from them? Had he taken Pete with him?

"That doesn't make sense. They work down near the border. Las Cruces, or was it Santa Fe? Damn, I can't remember. Why would they be here?"

Jake shrugged. "My buddy down off Green River swears he saw the Spaniard there last month buying supplies. He'd know because he spent some time near the border just last year. Says he was in a saloon down in Perez and in walked the Spaniard with a giant, I suppose that one he brought with him tonight. Both better dressed than normal outlaws. He walked in and called out to a fella playing faro. The man charged him with his gun drawn so they shot him. The Spaniard left and the giant followed him out. No one said a word and the poor son of a bitch was carted out the back and his winnings divided amongst those at the table." He ran a hand over the back of his neck and glanced at the closed door leading to the bar. "Seems like if they were in Green River last month they could be here now. It's not that far away."

"Is this the same buddy you have to carry out every time he comes in because he drinks an entire jar of moonshine?" When he gave an irritated sigh, confirming her words, she continued, "That man could be anybody."

"Sure it could, but how often do you see men dressed like that step foot in here?"

Not many passed through here if they could help it, not since all the mines had been bought out and the creek picked clean of gold, and certainly none dressed like those men. They were here for a reason. "Do you think they're looking for Ship? Is he hiding?"

"I don't know, Em. I wish I could say. I haven't heard a word from him. Just go back out there and act as if nothing's wrong. You don't know anything."

Grabbing a bottle of Old Overholt—how anyone could drink it, she didn't know—she gave Jake a quick nod and headed back out. A small part of her had hoped they'd left, but there they sat, deep in discussion about something. Perhaps their next murder.

Jake followed her out and placed three fresh tumblers on her tray. He gave her a nod of encouragement and then she was off to the lion's den. She kept her gaze down the entire walk over, unwilling to lock eyes with the pretty one again. If she could just get through this, then she could prove to the knot in her belly that nothing was wrong, that nothing had happened to Ship and Pete.

Without a word, she sat the tray down on the table and unloaded the bottle and three fresh tumblers, before retrieving the tray and turning to go. It was easy, simple. There was absolutely no reason to believe that these men meant her any harm. The pretty one had actually smiled at her earlier. And she knew that smile. He wanted to do something, but it didn't involve hurting her. Quite the opposite, in fact. Everything was fine.

But then the Spaniard reached out and put a hand on her arm, his long, tapered fingers curling gently around her wrist. "A moment, please." His voice was soft and quiet, commanding respect from the confidence and intensity of the tone rather than the volume. Though his grip was gentle, she could feel the strength he held in check.

She followed the length of his arm up to his face, afraid to hear his next words. But he held silent, waiting for her to meet his gaze. When she did, she was startled to realize his eyes were the exact odd shade of greenish-gold as the pretty one's. They were striking against his darker complexion. Could the two be related?

"Yes?"

"Tell us what you know of Ship Campbell."

Keep reading for an excerpt of Primal Instinct by Tara Wyatt, available now!

Primal Instinct - Chapter One

Taylor Ross needed it to happen tonight.

If she closed her eyes, she could even pretend to feel it, almost taste it, the way she used to. And then the dry spell would end, and things would go back to normal. Tonight. What she needed shimmered around her, in front of her, and if she reached out her fingers, if she touched the gauzy inspiration floating in the air, she might finally be able to write music again.

She drummed her fingers against the table, the red tablecloth absorbing the restless rhythm she tapped out. She blew out a breath and reached for her Jack and Coke, staring at the blinking light on her phone that lay on the table in front of her. She took a sip of her drink and then ran her finger across the screen, frowning at the numerous text messages, e-mails, and Google Alerts all begging for her attention. She took another sip and pushed her phone away, then flipped several pages of the notebook that lay open on the table in front of her, scowling at the scribbled and hastily scratched out chord progressions and lyrics.

She didn't want to think about any of it—breaking up with Zack, getting booted off a plane and the subsequent viral video of her in-air meltdown, or her inability to write. If her life was a sentence, the past few months had been a semicolon. An interruption, a pause. The past and the future linked by a tiny, little wink in time. She was tired of standing still, so for tonight, all she wanted was to catch a buzz so that she could numb the pain, the doubt, and the loneliness that were always simmering just below the surface.

She rested her chin in her hand as she scanned the dim interior of the Rainbow, a favorite LA hangout for rockers, groupies, some locals, and the occasional tourist. Red vinyl booths lined the walls, which were covered with rock paraphernalia. Autographed pictures, gold records, vinyl albums, all encased in glass and staring down at her. She knew, if she wandered over the garishly carpeted floor to a corner near a window, she'd find a picture of herself and two assholes, all glaring moodily at the camera. She remembered autographing that picture. Hell, she remembered posing for that picture, full of the kind of cocky swagger only a twenty-two-year-old with a hit record can pull off.

How had ten years gone by so damn fast?

She glared up at the plants lining the ceiling, a row of lights shining from underneath them. Frustration rolled through her as her eyes landed once again on her phone. She was gripped by a sudden urge to hurl it across the room, but she forced herself to pick up her drink and drain it instead. She certainly wouldn't be the first musician to throw a tantrum at the Rainbow, but it wouldn't accomplish anything.

She shook her head and forced herself to focus on the blank page. Her brain scrambled for an idea, a melody, a lyric, a hook, *anything*, but the harder she tried to pull a song out of her brain, the more she felt like she was spinning her wheels in mud. Sweating and working and stressing and getting nowhere fast. The album was already six months overdue, and she needed something to show the label within the next week, otherwise they'd dump her, and she'd be out on her ass. And then what? If she wasn't a musician, a performer, then who was she? It was how she'd defined herself for over ten years now, and if she lost that part of herself, she didn't know how she'd stay whole.

It wasn't lost on her that her fame had dwindled to the point where she was able to sit in a bar, alone, without anyone even noticing her presence. But it wasn't the loss of fame that bothered her. It was the loss of the music. The fame was simply a perk that came with making something that people connected with, of performing on a stage, guitar in hand, feeding on the crowd's energy.

She sifted through the scraps of ideas littered throughout the notebook. She'd hoped maybe coming to the Rainbow where so many greats had hung out would inspire her. As if sitting in a sticky vinyl booth would somehow miraculously move her to finally write a new song. Lips pursed together, she shook her head again. She had nothing. Her brain spun emptily, filled with nothing but frustration and disappointment and fear.

Shoving the notebook aside, she scrolled through a series of texts from Jeremy Nichols, her manager, and then opened her phone's web browser and navigated to a video of her disgrace at thirty thousand feet.

Like pressing on a bruise, she pressed Play. She'd already watched it several times; she couldn't seem to stop watching it, and she couldn't stop herself from cringing every time she did. She'd been trying to make herself numb so that she wouldn't *hurt* so much. And God, she hurt. Several months ago, she'd started casually dating bodyguard Zack De Luca, and much to her surprise, she'd fallen fast and hard for him. For the first time in years, she'd wanted something more than casual. But Zack hadn't, and even though he hadn't meant to, he'd broken her heart.

So, to numb the pain of walking away from Zack, she'd joined the mile-high club with a cute guy she'd met earlier in the airport lounge. They'd flirted, had coffee, and gone their separate ways. When she'd boarded the plane and found her first-class seat, she'd been pleasantly surprised to discover that cute coffee guy was right across the aisle from her. The flirting had resumed, and she'd moved over to the empty seat beside him. One thing had led to another, and after about forty-five minutes, they'd wound up in the bathroom together. As soon as they'd emerged, they'd been confronted by the flight attendant, who knew exactly what they'd done, and threatened to have them arrested when the plane landed. When Taylor had started to apologize, the woman had turned on her, calling her a dirty slut. Livid and with no patience for bullshit double standards, Taylor had had a few choice words for the woman. The air marshal had come over to see what the commotion was about, and the flight attendant had called Taylor a white trash whore. So she'd slapped the flight attendant across the face, and the confrontation had devolved into flailing limbs and hair pulling. The air marshal had had to separate them, and she'd accidentally caught him in the throat with her elbow.

Not her finest moment.

She'd been escorted off the plane, and the video of the whole thing had gone viral almost immediately.

She shook her head and closed the video. Her pulse throbbed ominously in her temples, warning her of an oncoming headache. Everything was falling apart, and hell if she knew how to fix it.

A gawky guy with a slim build approached her table, and as his eyes met Taylor's through his thick horn-rimmed glasses, a chill crept over her skin. His dark brown hair was long on top and shaved close on the sides, his plain white T-shirt and jeans boring but clean. A surge of something weird, something cold, pushed up through her chest, and she forced herself to take a breath. He was probably just a fan looking for a picture. She should be grateful she still had fans. And yet something about this guy set her on edge.

"Hi, um, Taylor? Taylor Ross?" His voice was higher than she'd expected.

"Yeah, hi," she said, wanting to get this interaction over with.

"Can I, um, get a picture?" His eyes darted around the bar, oddly bright, and the hairs on the back of her neck prickled. He pushed his glasses back up his nose and made an awkward, fluttering gesture with his hand before shoving it in his pocket. She glanced around, trying to figure out what he was looking at.

She plastered a smile on her face that she hoped didn't look as fake as it felt. "Sure." Pressing her palms against the table, she stood from her booth.

He slipped his arm around her, and another chill shivered down her spine, making her shrink away from him a little. Raising his phone in front of them, he took the picture. Relieved, she started to move away from him, but his arm tightened around her. He smiled shyly.

"One more." She held still for the picture and didn't smile this time. As soon as he'd clicked the button, she pulled away. He let her this time, his fingers trailing over her waist and leaving her feeling as though she'd been slimed. "You shouldn't be here by yourself. I can keep you company."

"No thanks." She turned away and moved to slip back into the booth when he tapped her on her shoulder. She spun, ready to tell him to fuck off, but froze at the look on his face, his eyes blazing, his lips curled into a thin sneer.

When he spoke, his voice was quiet and determined. "But I want to. You have to let me."

Anger melted her fear, and she scoffed out an impatient laugh. "I don't have to let you do sh—" But the rest of her words died as he grabbed her, curling a surprisingly strong hand around her arm, and her heart leaped into her throat. There was a time when she hadn't gone anywhere without security, but that level of fame was long behind her.

"Get off me," she growled through clenched teeth, jerking away from him. His fingers dug in harder, and she raised her knee, ready to hit him in his tiny balls.

"What's going on here?" At the sound of the deep voice, the creep released her.

"Nothing." The creep stuffed his phone back into his pocket and stalked away toward the exit, disappearing quickly into the crowd. Taylor let out the breath she'd been holding, her shoulders slumping slightly. Her skin itched, a physical remnant of the anxiety.

"Are you okay?" The man's voice was deliciously warm and rumbly, washing over her and chasing away the chill the creep had left behind.

"Yeah, I...thanks." Taking another deep breath, she ran her hands through her hair and turned to face her rescuer. For the second time in as many minutes, her heart was in her throat, but for an entirely different reason now.

Taken individually, the man's features were all so pretty. The intensely green eyes with the long lashes. The perfectly formed nose. The high, sculpted cheekbones. The lush, tempting mouth. The thick, short, light brown hair. And yet together, all prettiness disappeared, coalescing into the most handsome male face she'd ever seen. Her eyes scraped down his body, and she took in the way his black Led Zeppelin T-shirt was stretched tight over strong, broad shoulders and hugged his thick, muscular biceps. His right arm was covered in a sleeve tattoo, consisting entirely of intricate, detailed feathers overlapping each other, muscles rippling beneath the ink. The T-shirt fell straight down over his flat stomach and narrow waist, leading to well-built legs clad in denim.

He looked...sturdy. Like he'd been made to lean on.

She couldn't remember ever having that initial impression of a guy before. Hot, yes. Sexy, sure. But sturdy? That was a new one.

"I...need another drink." Taking a deep breath and trying to get her heart to slow down, she grabbed her purse and jacket out of the booth and made her way toward the bar at the back of the room. Her rescuer followed a few feet behind.

"Jack and Coke, please." She tipped her head at the bartender and could feel the gorgeous guy's eyes on her, leaving her skin tingling with excitement.

"You sure you're all right?" He turned sideways to face her, leaning one arm on the bar. Never had a man looked so good in an old T-shirt and jeans. Never. And never had a man been so immediately appealing. It was the model-worthy face paired with that deep, rumbly voice; the strong, muscular body with the relaxed, confident posture; the alertness in his gaze with his slow, easy smile.

"I'm fine. Really, he should be thanking you. It's because of you that his balls are still intact."

He chuckled, the sound low and warm. "Trust me, there isn't a doubt in my mind that you can take care of yourself."

She arched an eyebrow, twirling a finger around the rim of her fresh Jack and Coke. "So why'd you come over?"

"I was worried about the guy's balls." He winked, and she found herself smiling as her heart flickered in her chest.

The man scrubbed a hand over his hair and smiled, flashing a row of straight, white teeth, and the skin around his light emerald eyes crinkled in a way that had her stomach doing a slow turn. The bartender pointed at him, and he nodded.

She sat down on the barstool, crossed her legs, and ran her hands through her hair again. "I'm Taylor."

He nodded and picked up the bottle of beer the bartender had set down in front of him. "I know." He took a swig of the beer, and she watched his Adam's apple bob as he swallowed. A faint layer of stubble covered his jaw, and she found herself wondering what that stubble would feel like beneath her fingertips or against her neck, rasping over her skin. "I'm Colt."

Her heart gave a little kick against her ribs. "Thanks again for stepping in." She signaled to the bartender and pointed at Colt's beer. "You can go ahead and put that on my tab."

He smiled at her again, a cocky half grin that sent heat chasing over her skin. "You don't have to do that. That asshole crossed a line with you, and I just wanted to make sure you were okay."

She shook her head, returning the smile. "I'm trying to say thank you."

"Well, in that case, you're welcome." He leaned in closer. Jesus, he smelled good. Like warm leather and something else both mouthwatering and masculine. She bit her lip and looked down into her drink.

"Anyway. Thank you for the drink. I should let you get back to whatever you were working on," he said, tipping his head at her notebook.

It was her turn to lean in, and she smiled sweetly, looking up at him through her lashes. "Nah. You vanquished a creepy nerd for me. Have a seat."

He touched his thumb to his lips as his eyes traveled up and down her body and a slow smile turned up the corners of his mouth, his eyes crinkling once again. "Yeah. Okay."

He sat down on the bar stool next to her, pulling in close, his broad body angled toward her, but instead of feeling crowded, she felt sheltered. Her eyes slammed into his, and heat flared through her.

Oh, holy hell, but this man is trouble.

"So you didn't know that guy?" The way his low voice rumbled over the words sent a warm shiver down her spine and curled her toes.

She shook her head. "No. Just a fan, I guess."

"Lucky you."

She chuckled down into her drink and then met his eyes again.

Lucky her, indeed.

Colt Priestley took a long pull on his beer, his eyes once more roving over Taylor's long, lean body. She was so tall, almost as tall as him, and as he was six-two, that didn't happen very often. His eyes kept sliding down to her long, slim legs, wrapped in black denim. For now. Soon, they'd be wrapped around him, if he got his way. And when it came to women, Colt almost always got his way.

Huey Lewis began thumping through the bar's speakers, and Taylor made a face, scrunching her cute little nose. "I thought this was a rock bar."

"Hey, don't rag on Huey Lewis. He had some great hits." Colt smiled and bopped his head with cheesy, put-on enthusiasm in time to the music. She touched her fingers to her mouth and stifled a laugh before her eyes found his, and suddenly, her hand was on his chest. Hopefully she couldn't feel his heart pounding harder than a damn kick drum.

"I would've thought with this"—her fingers traced over the Led Zeppelin logo on his T-shirt—"and this"—the fingers of her opposite hand trailed up his right forearm and over his tattoo—"you'd have better taste than Huey Lewis."

He tried to think of something sexy, something flirty to say back, but his eyes were glued to her mouth, and goose bumps were trailing up his arm where she touched him. He cleared his throat and flashed her a smile.

She bit her lip and looked up at him, amusement flashing in her huge, blue eyes. "Did you know that Huey Lewis and the News were originally called Huey Lewis and the American Express? They had to change it when the credit card company threatened to sue them."

"Now who's hip to be square?" He shot her a teasing smile.

She flung her head back and laughed, a throaty, husky sound that sent blood flowing straight to his already heavy cock.

"Touché," she said, taking another sip of her drink.

God, he couldn't take his eyes off of her. The bar could've been on fire and he wouldn't have noticed. He wanted to fist his hands in all that blond hair and pull her close, taste her mouth, feel her skin against his and lose himself in her. But just for tonight.

It was all he could offer. All he had any right to want.

He watched her as she took another sip of her drink, trying to memorize the exact way her hair was falling over her shoulders, the precise shade of blue in her wide, bright eyes, the sound of her laugh.

"So why feathers?" Her fingers still trailed over his arm, sending little sparks of lust shooting through him.

Fuck. Nope. Not talking about that. Not with her, not tonight. He'd come here not to think about all of that shit. He'd come here to find a woman, or get drunk, or to start a fight. Colt knew that as long as he kept the demons fed, he wouldn't have to feel anything he didn't want to feel.

And there was a lot he didn't want to feel.

"You like it?" he asked, dodging the question. If she noticed, she didn't seem to mind.

"Mmm. I do." Her voice was beautiful, rich and sultry with a slight rasp to it, and he couldn't help wondering what she'd sound like moaning out his name. He was already imagining the feel of her fingers digging into his shoulders, her heels pressed into his ass as he sank himself deep inside her.

He forced himself to take a breath and a swallow of beer.

"You have any?" he asked, relieved she hadn't pressed him about the meaning behind his own ink.

She slipped out of her leather jacket, rolled up the sleeve of her denim shirt, and flipped her arm over. A swirled line of black stars decorated the inside of her right wrist. "And," she said and swept her hair up, showing him the Egyptian ankh on the back of her neck, just below her hairline. "I have a couple of others." She let her hair drop back around her shoulders, the blond waves fanning out around her.

His eyebrows rose. "Oh yeah? Where?"

She took one of his hands in hers and pressed it against her rib cage. Instinctively, his fingers flexed into her, and her eyes fluttered closed for a second. "Here." She felt warm and soft through the fabric of her shirt as he moved his hand down her side toward her hip in gentle strokes, still not quite able to believe that this wasn't a fantasy.

"Where else?" His eyes held hers. She slipped off the stool and stood between his legs, erasing all distance between them. He slid his hand up and around to her shoulder blade.

"Here." Her warm breath tickled his ear, and he clenched his jaw against the need to bury his face in her neck, right here at the bar. "What about you? Any others?"

With his free hand, he took one of hers, placing it over his heart. "Here."

Her long fingers curled into the cotton of his shirt, and heat crackled in the air around them. His stomach flipped, and if he was reading her right—and he would've bet a bottle of fifty-year-old scotch he was—she wanted him as much as he wanted her.

Damn, but he needed this. Needed the release. Needed the temporary oblivion of hot sex with a gorgeous woman. He didn't want to think. Not tonight. Hell, not most nights.

Time to test the waters.

He slid a hand up to her face and grazed his lips against hers, a tease of a kiss. She held stone still, her eyes fixed on his mouth, her lips slightly parted. All of the noise around him seemed to drop away, and in that moment, Taylor was all that existed for him. Well, her and the erection doing its damndest to bust free of his jeans.

He closed his mouth over hers and felt the vibration of her sigh against his lips. He fought back a groan when she slid her tongue against his, and heat exploded over his skin as he tasted her, drinking in the soft warmth of her mouth.

He couldn't remember the last time he'd been so aroused from just a kiss. His chest tightened, and as he deepened the kiss, he pressed down the cold, hard knot of fear eating at him. Already, he knew sticking to his one-night rule would suck big-time. She felt so good, so perfect, so fucking *right* kissing him, as her fingernails scraped lightly down his back.

She opened her mouth to him a little more, which he immediately took full advantage of, greedily claiming everything she offered him. He caressed her mouth with his tongue, and she moaned softly, her hips nestling snugly against his. He wove his fingers into her hair and crushed his mouth against hers as arousal and lust and need all sang through his veins. Lips and tongues melded together with increasing urgency, and the kiss seared through him. She rocked against him and bit gently at his lower lip.

Fuck, this was going to be good.

"Get a room, why don't ya?" The bartender chirped at them, and Taylor broke the kiss, pressing her forehead against his. For a second, he just stood there, trying to breathe.

She was pretty much a total stranger, and yet the intensity of that kiss had been off the charts. Hot, and bruising and so, so promising.

He swallowed, trying to find his voice. "Come home with me."

She nodded against his forehead, and his dick rejoiced.

From his little table in the corner, Ronnie adjusted his glasses as he watched Taylor walk out of the bar, her fingers laced with those of the brute who'd intruded on them earlier. He finished the rest of his Coke and slammed the empty glass down. Possessive anger coupled with an almost blinding jealousy churned through him. It'd been hard to watch that interaction, and now she was leaving with him? He'd been much happier watching her while she'd been alone, even if she'd looked sad.

He knew he shouldn't have gone over and talked to her, but he couldn't help himself. He'd been warned, but no one knew what they were talking about. They didn't see. They couldn't see. He loved her, and she loved him. Soon, everyone would know, and everyone who'd called him crazy and obsessed and delusional would fucking see.

Ever since he'd first heard her sing, he'd known he was listening to the future mother of his children.

He dropped a five on the table and pushed his way out of the bar, getting in his car just in time to follow Taylor. He had to. He couldn't let her go off alone with that brute, unprotected. And if she was going to betray him, he needed to know. He needed to see.

Because Taylor was his. Every part of her. Her gorgeous blond hair, those huge, blue eyes, the long, lean body. The incredible voice. The skilled hands. Her mind. Her soul. Her body.

She belonged to him.

Made in the USA
Charleston, SC
11 August 2016